HISTORIC STRANGE EVENTS
BY
S. BARING GOULD

PREFACE.

A reader of history in its various epochs in different countries, comes upon eccentric individuals and extraordinary events, lightly passed over, may be, as not materially affecting the continuity of history, as not producing any seriously disturbing effect on its course. Such persons, such events have always awakened interest in myself, and when I have come on them, it has been my pleasure to obtain such details concerning them as were available, and which would be out of place in a general history as encumbering it with matter that is unimportant, or of insufficient importance to occupy much space. Two of the narratives contained in this work have appeared already in the "Cornhill Magazine," but I have considerably[Pg viii] enlarged them by the addition of fresh material; some of the others came out in the "Gentleman's Magazine," and one in "Belgravia." With only two of them—"Peter Nielsen" and "A Wax and Honey-Moon"— are the authorities somewhat gone beyond and the facts slightly dressed to assume the shape of stories.

S. BARING GOULD.

LEW TRENCHARD, N. DEVON,
July, 1889.

HISTORIC ODDITIES.

The Disappearance of Bathurst.

The mystery of the disappearance of Benjamin Bathurst on November 25, 1809, is one which can never with certainty be cleared up. At the time public opinion in England was convinced that he had been secretly murdered by order of Napoleon, and the "Times" in a leader on January 23, 1810, so decisively asserted this, that the "Moniteur" of January 29 ensuing, in sharp and indignant terms repudiated the charge. Nevertheless, not in England only, but in Germany, was the impression so strong that Napoleon had ordered the murder, if murder had been committed, that the Emperor saw fit, in the spring of the same year, solemnly to assure the wife of the vanished man, on his word of honour, that he knew nothing about the disappearance of her husband. Thirty years later Varnhagen von Ense, a well-known German author, reproduced the story and reiterated the accusation against Napoleon, or at all events against the French. Later still, the "Spectator," in an article in 1862, gave a brief sketch of the[Pg 2] disappearance of Bathurst, and again repeated the charge against French police agents or soldiers of having made away with the Englishman. At that time a skeleton was said to have been discovered in the citadel of Magdeburg with the hands bound, in an upright position, and the writer of the article sought to identify the skeleton with the lost man.[1]

We shall see whether other discoveries do not upset this identification, and afford us another solution of the problem—What became of Benjamin Bathurst?

Benjamin Bathurst was the third son of Dr. Henry Bathurst, Bishop of Norwich, Canon of Christchurch, and the Prebendary of Durham, by Grace, daughter of Charles Coote, Dean of Kilfenora, and sister of Lord Castlecoote. His eldest brother, Henry, was Archdeacon of Norwich; his next, Sir James, K.C.B., was in the army and was aide-de-camp to Lord Wellington in the Peninsula.

Benjamin, the third son of the bishop, was born March 14, 1784,[2] and had been secretary of the Legation at Leghorn. In May, 1805, he married Phillida, daughter of Sir John Call, Bart., of Whiteford, in Cornwall, and sister of Sir William Pratt Call, the second baronet. Benjamin is a Christian name that occurs repeatedly in the Bathurst family after[Pg 3] the founder of it, Sir Benjamin, Governor of the East India Company and of the Royal African Company. He died in 1703. The grandfather of the subject of our memoir was a Benjamin, brother of Allen, who was created Baron in 1711, and Earl in 1772.

Benjamin had three children: a son who died, some years after his father's disappearance, in consequence of a fall from a horse at a race in Rome; a daughter, who was drowned in the Tiber; and another who married the Earl of Castlestuart in 1830, and after his death married Signor Pistocchi.

In 1809, early in the year, Benjamin was sent to Vienna by his kinsman, Earl Bathurst, who was in the ministry of Lord Castlereagh, and, in October, Secretary of State for the Foreign Department. He was sent on a secret embassy from the English Government to the Court of the Emperor Francis. The time was one of great and critical importance to Austria. Since the Peace of Pressburg she had been quiet; the Cabinet of Vienna had adhered with cautious prudence to a system of neutrality, but she only waited her time, and in 1808 the government issued a decree by which a militia, raised by a conscription, under the name of the "Landwehr," was instituted, and this speedily reached the number of 300,000 men. Napoleon, who was harassed by the insurrection in the Peninsula, demanded angrily an explanation, which was evaded. To overawe Austria, he met the Emperor Alexander of Russia at Erfurth, and the latter when sounded by Austria refused to have any part in the confederation against Napoleon. England, in the meantime, was urging Austria to[Pg 4] cast down the gauntlet. In pledge of amity, the port of Trieste was thrown open to the English and Spanish flags. In December, a declaration of the King of England openly alluded to the hostile preparations of Austria, but the Cabinet at Vienna were as yet undecided as to the course they would finally adopt. The extreme peril which the monarchy had undergone already in the wars with Napoleon made them hesitate. England was about to send fifty thousand men to the Peninsula, and desired the diversion of a war in the heart of Germany. Prussia resolved to remain neutral. Napoleon rapidly returned from Spain, and orders were despatched to Davoust to concentrate his immense corps at Bamberg; Massena was to repair to Strasburg, and press on to Ulm; Oudenot to move on Augsburg, and Bernadotte, at the head of the Saxons, was to menace Bohemia. It was at this juncture that Benjamin Bathurst hurried as Ambassador Extraordinary to Vienna, to assure the Cabinet there of the intentions of England to send a powerful contingent into Spain, and to do all in his power to urge Austria to declare war. Encouraged by England, the Cabinet of Vienna took the initiative, and on April 8 the Austrian troops crossed the frontier at once on the Inn, in Bohemia, in Tyrol, and in Italy.

The irritation and exasperation of Napoleon were great; and Bathurst, who remained with the Court, laboured under the impression that the Emperor of the French bore him especial enmity, on account of his exertions to provoke the Austrian Ministry to declaration of war. Whether this opinion of his were[Pg 5] well founded, or whether he had been warned that Napoleon would take the opportunity, if given him, of revenging himself, we do not know; but what is certain is, that Bathurst was prepossessed with the conviction that Napoleon regarded him with implacable hostility and would leave no stone unturned to compass his destruction.

On July 6 came the battle of Wagram, then the humiliating armistice of Znaim, which was agreed to by the Emperor Francis at Komorn in spite of the urgency of Metternich and Lord Walpole, who sought to persuade him to reject the proposals. This armistice was the preliminary to a peace which was concluded at Schönbrun in October. With this, Bathurst's office at Vienna came to an end, and he set out on his way home.

Now it was that he repeatedly spoke of the danger that menaced him, and of his fears lest Napoleon should arrest him on his journey to England. He hesitated for some time which road to take, and concluding that if he went by Trieste and Malta he might run the worst risks, he resolved to make his way to London by Berlin and the north of Germany. He took with him his private secretary and a valet; and, to evade observation, assumed the name of Koch, and pretended that he was a travelling merchant. His secretary was instructed to act as courier, and he passed under the name of Fisher. Benjamin Bathurst carried pistols about his person, and there were firearms in the back of the carriage.

On November 25, 1809, about midday, he arrived at Perleberg, with post-horses, on the route from Berlin to Hamburg, halted at the post-house for[Pg 6] refreshments, and ordered fresh horses to be harnessed to the carriage for the journey to Lenzen, which was the next station.

Bathurst had come along the highway from Berlin to Schwerin, in Brandenburg, as far as the little town of Perleberg, which lies on the Stepnitz, that flows after a few miles into the Elbe at Wittenberge. He might have gone on to Ludwigslust, and thence to Hamburg, but this was a considerable détour, and he was anxious to be home. He had now before him a road that led along the Elbe close to the frontier of Saxony. The Elbe was about four miles distant. At Magdeburg were French troops. If he were in danger anywhere, it would be during the next few hours—that is, till he reached Dömitz. About a hundred paces from the post-house was an inn, the White Swan, the host of which was named Leger. By the side of the inn was the Parchimer gate of the town, furnished with a tower, and the road to Hamburg led through this gate, outside of which was a sort of suburb consisting of poor cottagers' and artisans' houses.

Benjamin Bathurst went to the Swan and ordered an early dinner; the horses were not to be put in till he had dined. He wore a pair of grey trousers, a grey frogged short coat, and over it a handsome sable greatcoat lined with violet velvet. On his head was a fur cap to match. In his scarf was a diamond pin of some value.

As soon as he had finished his meal, Bathurst inquired who was in command of the soldiers quartered in the town, and where he lodged. He was told that[Pg 7] a squadron of the Brandenburg cuirassiers was there under Captain Klitzing, who was residing in a house behind the Town Hall. Mr. Bathurst then crossed the market place and called on the officer, who was at the time indisposed with a swollen neck. To Captain Klitzing he said that he was a traveller on his way to Hamburg, that he had strong and well-grounded suspicions that his person was endangered, and he requested that he might be given a guard in the inn, where he was staying. A lady who was present noticed that he seemed profoundly agitated, that he trembled as though ague-stricken, and was unable to raise a cup of tea that was offered him to his lips without spilling it.

The captain laughed at his fears, but consented to let him have a couple of soldiers, and gave the requisite orders for their despatch; then Mr. Bathurst rose, resumed his sable overcoat, and, to account for his nervous difficulty in getting into his furs again, explained that he was much shaken by something that had alarmed him.

Not long after the arrival of Mr. Bathurst at the Swan, two Jewish merchants arrived from Lenzen with post-horses, and left before nightfall.

On Mr. Bathurst's return to the inn, he countermanded the horses; he said he would not start till night. He considered that it would be safer for him to spin along the dangerous portion of the route by night when Napoleon's spies would be less likely to be on the alert. He remained in the inn writing and burning papers. At seven o'clock he dismissed the soldiers on guard, and ordered the horses to be ready[Pg 8] by nine. He stood outside the inn watching his portmanteau, which had been taken within, being replaced on the carriage, stepped round to the heads of the horses—*and was never seen again.*

It must be remembered that this was at the end of November. Darkness had closed in before 5 P.M., as the sun set at four. An oil lantern hung across the street, emitting a feeble light; the ostler had a horn lantern, wherewith he and the postillion adjusted the harness of the horses. The landlord was in the doorway talking to the secretary, who, as courier, was paying the account. No one particularly observed the movements of Mr. Bathurst at the moment. He had gone to the horses' heads, where the ostler's lantern had fallen on him. The horses were in, the postillion ready, the valet stood by the carriage door, the landlord had his cap in hand ready to wish the gentleman a "lucky journey;" the secretary was impatient, as the wind was cold. They waited; they sent up to the room which Mr. Bathurst had engaged; they called. All in vain. Suddenly, inexplicably, without a word, a cry, an alarm of any sort, he was gone—spirited away, and what really became of him will never be known with certainty.

Whilst the whole house was in amazement and perplexity the Jewish merchants ordered their carriage to be got ready, and departed.

Some little time elapsed before it was realised that the case was serious. Then it occurred to the secretary that Mr. Bathurst might have gone again to the captain in command to solicit guards to attend his carriage. He at once sent to the captain, but Mr.[Pg 9]Bathurst was not with him. The moment, however, that Klitzing heard that the traveller had disappeared, he remembered the alarm expressed by the gentleman, and acted with great promptitude. He sent soldiers to seize the carriage and all the effects of the missing man. He went, in spite of his swollen neck, immediately to the Swan, ordered a chaise, and required the secretary to enter it; he placed a cuirassier and the valet on the box, and, stepping into the carriage, ordered it to be driven to the Golden Crown, an inn at the further end of the town, where he installed the companions of Bathurst, and placed a soldier in guard over them. A guard was also placed over the Swan, and next morning every possible search was made for the lost man. The river was dragged, outhouses, woods, marshes, ditches were examined, but not a trace of him could be found. That day was Sunday. Klitzing remained at Perleberg only till noon, to wait some discovery, and then, without delay, hurried to Kyritz, where was his commandant, Colonel Bismark, to lay the case before him, and solicit leave to hasten direct to Berlin, there to receive further instructions what was to be done.

He was back on Monday with full authority to investigate the matter.

Before he left he had gone over the effects of Mr. Bathurst, and had learned that the fur coat belonging to him was missing; he communicated this fact to the civil magistrate of the district, and whilst he was away search was instituted for this. It was the sable coat lined with violet velvet already mentioned, and this, along with another belonging to the [Pg 10]secretary, Fisher was under the impression had been left in the post-house.

The amazing part of the matter is that the city authorities—and, indeed, on his return, Captain Klitzing—for a while confined themselves to a search for the fur coat, and valuable time was lost by this means. Moreover, the city authorities, the police, and the military were all independent, and all jealous of each other. The military commander, Klitzing, and the burgomaster were in open quarrel, and sent up to headquarters charges against each other for interference in the matter beyond their rights. The head of the police was inert, a man afterwards dismissed for allowing defalcation in the monies entrusted to him. There was no system in the investigation, and the proper clues were not followed.

On December 16th, two poor women went out of Perleberg to a little fir wood in the direction of Quitzow, to pick up broken sticks for fuel. There they found, a few paces from a path leading through the wood, spread out on the grass, a pair of trousers turned inside out. On turning them back they observed that they were stained on the outside, as if the man who had worn them had lain on the earth. In the pocket was a paper with writing on it; this, as well as the trousers, was sodden with water. Two bullet holes were in the trousers, but no traces of blood about them, which could hardly have been the case had the bullets struck a man wearing the trousers. The women took what they had found to the burgomaster. The trousers were certainly those of the missing man. The paper in the pocket was a half-finished letter[Pg 11] from Mr. Bathurst to his wife, scratched in pencil, stating that he was afraid he would never reach England, and that his ruin would be the work of Count d'Entraigues, and he requested her not to marry again in the event of his not returning.

The English Government offered £1,000 reward, and his family another £1,000; Prince Frederick of Prussia, who took a lively interest in the matter, offered in addition 100 Friedrichs d'or for the discovery of the body, or for information which might lead to the solution of the mystery, but no information to be depended upon ever transpired. Various rumours circulated; and Mrs. Thistlethwaite, the sister of Benjamin Bathurst, in her Memoirs of Dr. Henry Bathurst, Bishop of Norwich, published by Bentley in 1853, gives them. He was said to have been lost at sea. Another report was that he was murdered by his valet, who took an open boat on the Elbe, and escaped. Another report again was that he had been lost in a vessel which was crossing to Sweden and which foundered about this time. These reports are all totally void of truth. Mrs. Thistlethwaite declares that Count d'Entraigues, who was afterwards so cruelly murdered along with his wife by their Italian servant, was heard to say that he could prove that Mr. Bathurst was murdered in the fortress of Magdeburg. In a letter to his wife, dated October 14, 1809, Benjamin Bathurst said that he trusted to reach home by way of Colberg and Sweden. D'Entraigues had been a French spy in London; and Mrs. Thistlethwaite says that he himself told Mrs. Bathurst that her husband had been carried off by *douaniers-montés* from [Pg 12]Perleberg to Magdeburg, and murdered there. This it is hard to believe.

Thomas Richard Underwood, in a letter from Paris, November 24, 1816, says he was a prisoner of war in Paris in 1809, and that both the English and French there believed that the crime of his abduction and murder had been committed by the French Government.

The "European Magazine" for January, 1810, says that he was apparently carried off by a party of French troops stationed at Lenzen, but this was not the case. No French troops were on that side of the Elbe. It further says, "The French Executive, with a view to ascertain by his papers the nature of the relations subsisting between this country and the Austrian Government, has added to the catalogue of its crimes by the seizure, or probably the murder, of this gentleman."

If there had been French troops seen we should have known of it; but none were. Every effort was made by the civil and military authorities to trace Bathurst. Bloodhounds were employed to track the lost man, in vain. Every well was explored, the bed of the Stepnitz thoroughly searched. Every suspicious house in Perleberg was examined from attic to cellar, the gardens were turned up, the swamps sounded, but every effort to trace and discover him was in vain.

On January 23, 1810, in a Hamburg paper, appeared a paragraph, which for the first time informed the people of Perleberg who the merchant Koch really was who had so mysteriously vanished. The[Pg 13] paragraph was in the form of a letter, dated from

London, January 6, 1810—that is, six weeks after the disappearance. It ran thus: "Sir Bathurst, Ambassador Extraordinary of England to the Court of Austria, concerning whom a German newspaper, under date of December 10, stated that he had committed suicide in a fit of insanity, is well in mind and body. His friends have received a letter from him dated December 13, which, therefore, must have been written after the date of his supposed death."

Who inserted this, and for what purpose? It was absolutely untrue. Was it designed to cause the authorities to relax their efforts to probe the mystery, and perhaps to abandon them altogether?

The Jewish merchants were examined, but were at once discharged; they were persons well-to-do, and generally respected.

Was it possible that Mr. Bathurst had committed suicide? This was the view taken of his disappearance in France, where, in the "Moniteur" of December 12, 1809, a letter from the correspondent in Berlin stated: "Sir Bathurst on his way from Berlin showed signs of insanity, and destroyed himself in the neighbourhood of Perleberg." On January 23, 1810, as already said, the "Times" took the matter up, and not obscurely charged the Emperor Napoleon with having made away with Mr. Bathurst, who was peculiarly obnoxious to him.

In the mean time, the fur coat had been found, hidden in the cellar of a family named Schmidt, behind some firewood. Frau Schmidt declared that it had been left at the post house, where she had found[Pg 14] it; and had conveyed it away, and given it to her son Augustus, a fellow of notoriously bad character. Now, it is remarkable that one witness declared that she had seen the stranger who had disappeared go out of the square down the narrow lane in which the Schmidts lived, and where eventually the fur coat was found. When questioned, Augustus Schmidt said that "his mother had told him the stranger had two pistols, and had sent her to buy him some powder. He supposed therefore that the gentleman had shot himself." Unfortunately the conflict of authorities acted prejudicially at this point, and the questions how the Schmidts came to know anything about the pistols, whether Frau Schmidt really was sent for powder, and whether Bathurst was really seen entering the alley in which they lived, and at what hour, were never properly entered into. Whatever information Klitzing obtained, was forwarded to Berlin, and there his reports remain in the archives. They have not been examined.

Fresh quarrels broke out between Klitzing and the Burgomaster, and Klitzing instead of pursuing the main investigations, set to work to investigate the proceedings of the Burgomaster. So more time was lost.

On Thursday, November 30th, that is to say, five days after the disappearance of Bathurst, Captain Klitzing ordered the town magistrates; 1. To have all ditches and canals round the place examined; 2. To have the neighbourhood of the town explored by foresters with hounds; 3. To let off the river Stepnitz and examine the bed. Then he added, "as I have[Pg 15] ascertained that Augustus Schmidt, who is now under arrest for the theft of the fur coat, was *not at home at the time that the stranger disappeared*, I require that this fact be taken into consideration, and investigated"—and this, as far as we can ascertain, was not done; it was just one of those valuable clues which were left untraced.

The whole neighbourhood was searched, ditches, ponds, the river bed, drains, every cellar, and garden, and nothing found. The search went on to December 6, and proved wholly resultless. It was not till December 16 that the trousers were found. It is almost certain that they were laid in the Quitzow wood after the search had been given over, on December 6th.

As nothing could be proved against the Schmidt family, except that they had taken the fur coat, Frau Schmidt and her son were sentenced to eight weeks' imprisonment.

The matter of the pistols was not properly cleared up. That, again, was a point, and an important point that remained uninvestigated.

The military authorities who examined the goods of Mr. Bathurst declared that nothing was missing except the fur cloak, which was afterwards recovered, and we suppose these pistols were included. If not, one may be sure that some notice would have been taken of the fact that he had gone off with his pistols, and had not returned. This would have lent colour to the opinion that he destroyed himself. Besides no shot was heard. A little way outside the gateway of the town beyond the Swan inn is a bridge over the[Pg 16]small and sluggish stream of the Stepnitz. It was possible he might have shot himself there, and fallen into the water; but this theory will not bear looking closely into. A shot fired there would certainly have been heard at night in the cottages beside the road; the river was searched shortly after without a trace of him having been found, and his trousers with bullet holes made in them after they had been taken off him had been discovered in another direction.

The "Moniteur" of January 29 said: "Among the civilised races, England is the only one that sets an example of having bandits[3] in pay, and inciting to crime. From information we have received from Berlin, we believe that Mr. Bathurst had gone off his head. It is the manner of the British Cabinet to commit diplomatic commissions to persons whom the whole nation knows are half fools. It is only the English diplomatic service which contains crazy people."

This violent language was at the time attributed to Napoleon's dictation, stung with the charge made by the "Times," a charge ranking him with "vulgar murderers," and which attributed to him two other and somewhat similar cases, that of Wagstaff, and that of Sir George Rumbold. It is very certain that the "Moniteur" would not have ventured on such insulting language without his permission.

In April Mrs. Bathurst, along with some relatives,[Pg 17] arrived in Perleberg. The poor lady was in great distress and anxiety to have the intolerable suspense alleviated by a discovery of some sort, and the most liberal offers were made and published to induce a disclosure of the secret. At this time a woman named Hacker, the wife of a peasant who lived in the shoe-market, was lying in the town gaol—the tower already mentioned, adjoining the White Swan. She was imprisoned for various fraudulent acts. She now offered to make a confession, and this was her statement:

"A few weeks before Christmas I was on my way to Perleberg from a place in Holstein, where my husband had found work. In the little town of Seeberg, twelve miles from Hamburg, I met the shoemaker's assistant Goldberger, of Perleberg, whom I knew from having danced with him. He was well-dressed, and had from his fob hanging a hair-chain with gold seals. His knitted silk purse was stuffed with louis d'ors. When I asked him how he came by so much money, he said, 'Oh, I got 500 dollars and the watch as hush-money when the Englishman was murdered.' He told me no more particulars, except that one of the seals was engraved with a name, and he had had that altered in Hamburg."

No credit was given to this story, and no inquiry was instituted into the whereabouts of Goldberger. It was suspected that the woman had concocted it in the hopes of getting Mrs. Bathurst to interest herself in obtaining her release, and of getting some of the money offered to informers.

Mrs. Bathurst did not return immediately to[Pg 18] England; she appealed to Napoleon to grant her information, and he assured her through Cambacières, and on his word of honour, that he knew nothing of the matter beyond what he had seen in the papers.

So the matter rested, an unsolved mystery.

In Prussia, among the great bulk of the educated, in the higher and official classes, the prevailing conviction was that Napoleon had caused the disappearance of Bathurst, not out of personal feeling, but in political interests, for the purpose of getting hold of the dispatches which he was believed to be conveying to England from the Austrian Government. The murder was held to be an accident, or an unavoidable consequence. And in Perleberg itself this was the view taken of the matter as soon as it was known who the stranger was. But then, another opinion prevailed there, that Klitzing had secretly conveyed him over the frontier, so as to save him from the spies, and the pursuit which, as he and Bathurst knew, endangered the safety of the returning envoy.

In Perleberg two opinions were formed, by such as conceived that he had been murdered, as to the manner in which he had been made away with.

Not far from the post-house was at the time a low tavern kept by Hacker, who has been mentioned above; the man combined shoemaking with the sale of brandy. Augustus Schmidt spent a good deal of his time in this house. Now shortly after this affair, Hacker left Perleberg, and set up at Altona, where he showed himself possessed of a great deal of money. He was also said to have disposed of a gold repeater watch to a jeweller in Hamburg. This was never[Pg 19] gone into; and how far it was true, or idle rumour, cannot be said. One view was that Bathurst had been robbed and murdered by Hacker and Schmidt.

The other opinion was this. Opposite the post-house was a house occupied at the time by a fellow who was a paid French spy; a man who was tried for holding secret communication with the enemy of his Fatherland. He was a petty lawyer, who stirred up quarrels among the peasants, and lived by the result. He was a man of the worst possible character, capable of anything. The opinion of one section of the people of Perleberg was, that Bathurst, before entering the carriage, had gone across the square, and had entered into conversation with this man, who had persuaded him to enter his door, where he had strangled him, and buried him in his cellar. The widow of this man on her death-bed appeared anxious to confess something, but died before she could speak.

In 1852 a discovery was made at Perleberg which may or may not give the requisite solution.

We may state before mentioning this that Captain Klitzing never believed that Bathurst had been spirited away by French agents. He maintained that he had been murdered for his money.

On April 15, 1852, a house on the Hamburg road that belonged to the mason Kiesewetter was being pulled down, when a human skeleton was discovered under the stone threshold of the stable. The skeleton lay stretched out, face upwards, on the black peat earth, covered with mortar and stone chips, the head embedded in walling-stones and mortar. In the back[Pg 20] of the skull was a fracture, as if a blow of a heavy instrument had fallen on it. All the upper teeth were perfect, but one of the molars in the lower jaw was absent, and there were indications of its having been removed by a dentist. The house where these human remains were found had been purchased in 1834 by the mason Kiesewetter from Christian Mertens, who had inherited it from his father, which latter had bought it in 1803 of a shoemaker. *Mertens, the father, had been a serving man in the White Swan at the time of the disappearance of Mr. Bathurst.*

Inquiry was made into what was known of old Mertens. Everyone spoke highly of him as a saving, steady man, God-fearing; who had scraped together during his service in the Swan sufficient money to dower his two daughters with respectively £150 and £120. After a long illness he had died, generally respected.

Information of the discovery was forwarded to the Bathurst family, and on August 23, Mrs. Thistlethwaite, sister of Benjamin, came to Perleberg, bringing with her a portrait of her brother, but she was quite unable to say that the skull that was shown her belonged to the missing man, whom she had not seen for forty-three years. And—no wonder! When Goethe was shown the skull of his intimate friend Schiller he could hardly trace any likeness to the head he remembered so well. Mrs. Thistlethwaite left, believing that the discovery had no connection with the mystery of her brother's disappearance, so ineradicably fixed in the convictions of the family was the belief that he had been carried away by French agents.

[Pg 21]

However, let us consider this discovery a little closer, and perhaps we shall be led to another conclusion.

In the first place, the skeleton was that of a man who had been murdered by a blow on the back of his head, which had fractured the skull. It had been stripped before being buried, for not a trace of clothing could be found.

Secondly, the house of the Mertens family lay on the Hamburg road, on the way to Lenzen, outside the Parchimer Gate, only three hundred paces from the White Swan. In fact, it was separated from the White Swan only by the old town-gate and prison tower, and a small patch of garden ground.

At the time of the disappearance of Mr. Bathurst it was inhabited by Christian Mertens, who was servant at the White Swan. No examination was made at the time of the loss of Bathurst into the whereabouts of Mertens, nor was his cottage searched. It was assumed that he was at the inn waiting for his "vale," like the ostler and the *Kellner*. It is quite possible that he may have been standing near the horses' heads, and that he may have gone on with Mr. Bathurst a few steps to show him the direction he was to go; or, with the pretence that he had important information to give him, he may have allured him into his cottage, and there murdered him, or, again, he may have drawn him on to where by pre-arrangement Goldberger was lying in wait with a hammer or hatchet to strike him down from behind. Considering how uneasy Mr. Bathurst was about the road, and how preoccupied with the idea that French spies and[Pg 22] secret agents were on the look-out for him, he might easily have been induced by a servant of the inn where he was staying to go a few steps through the gate, beyond earshot of the post-boy and landlord and ostler, to hear something which the boots pretended was of importance to him. Goldberger or another may have lain in wait in the blackness of the shadow of the gateway but a short distance from the lights about the carriage, and by one stroke have silenced him. It is possible that Augustus Schmidt may have been mixed up in the matter, and that the sable coat was taken off Mr. Bathurst when dead.

Again, Mertens was able on the marriage of his two daughters to give one 150*l*. and the other 120*l*. This would mean that Mertens had saved as boots of the Swan at the least 300*l*., for he would not give every penny to his children. Surely this was a considerable sum for a boots in a little inn to amass from his wage and from "vales."

Mrs. Thistlethwaite asserts in her Memoirs of Bishop Bathurst that shortly after the disappearance of her brother the ostler—can she mean Mertens?—also disappeared, ran away. But we do not know of any corroborating evidence.

Lastly, the discovery of the trousers in the wood near Quitzow points to the traveller having been murdered in Perleberg; the murderers, whoever they were, finding that an investigation of houses, barns, gardens and stables was being made, took the garments of the unfortunate man, discharged a couple of shots through them to make believe he had been fired at by several persons lying in wait for him, and[Pg 23] then exposed them in a place away from the road along which Mr. Bathurst was going. The man who carried these garments was afraid of being observed, and he probably did not go through the town with them, but made a circuit to the wood, and for the same reason did not take them very far. The road to Lenzen ran S.W. and that to Quitzow N.W. He placed the trousers near the latter, but did not venture to cross the highway. He could get to the wood over the fields unperceived.

Supposing that this is the solution of the mystery, one thing remains to be accounted for—the paragraph in the Hamburg paper dated from London, announcing that Mr. Bathurst was alive and had been heard of since the disappearance.

This, certainly, seems to have been inserted with a design to divert or allay suspicion, and it was generally held to have been sent from London by a French agent, on instruction from Paris. But it is possible that the London correspondent may have heard a coffee-house rumour that Bathurst was still alive, and at once reported it to the paper. Its falsehood was palpable, and would be demonstrated at once by the family of the lost man to the authorities at Perleberg. It could not answer the purpose of arresting inquiry and staying investigation.

It remains only to inquire whether it was probable that Napoleon had any hand in the matter.

What could induce him to lay hands on an envoy? He could not expect to find on the person of Mr. Bathurst any important dispatches, for the war was over, peace with Austria was concluded. He was[Pg 24] doubtless angry at Austria having declared war, and angry at England having instigated her to do so, but Mr. Bathurst was very small game indeed on which to wreak his anger; moreover, the peace that had been concluded with Austria gave great advantages to France. He can have had no personal dislike to Bathurst, for he never saw him. When Napoleon entered Vienna, Bathurst was with the Emperor Francis in Hungary, at Komorn.

And yet, he may have suspected that Austria was insincere, and was anxious to renew the conflict, if she could obtain assurance of assistance from England. He may have thought that by securing the papers carried to England by Bathurst, he would get at the real intentions of Austria, and so might be prepared for consequences. We cannot say. The discovery of the body in Mertens' house, under the threshold—supposing it to be that of Bathurst, does not by any means prove that the murder was a mere murder for the purpose of robbery.

If Napoleon had given instructions for the capture of Bathurst, and the taking from him of his papers, it does not follow that he ordered his murder, on the contrary, he would have given instructions that he should be robbed—as if by highwaymen—and let go with his life. The murder was against his wishes, if he did give orders for him to be robbed.

The Bathurst family never doubted that Benjamin had been murdered by the agents of Napoleon. It is certain that he was well aware that his safety was menaced, and menaced at Perleberg. That was why he at once on reaching the place asked for the[Pg 25]protection of a guard. He had received warning from some one, and such warning shows that an attempt to rob him of his papers was in contemplation.

That caution to be on his guard must have been given him, before he left Vienna. He probably received another before he reached Perleberg, for he appeared before the Commandant in a state of great alarm and agitation. That this was mere spiritual presage of evil is hardly credible. We cannot doubt—and his letter to his wife leads to this conviction—that he had been warned that spies in the pay of the French Government were on the look-out for him. Who the agents were that were employed to get hold of his papers, supposing that the French Government did attempt to waylay him, can never be determined, whether Mertens or Augustus Schmidt.

In 1815 Earl Bathurst was Secretary of State for War and the Colonial Department. May we not suspect that there was some mingling of personal exultation along with political satisfaction, in being able to send to St. Helena the man who had not only been the scourge of Europe, and the terror of kings, but who, as he supposed—quite erroneously we believe—had inflicted on his own family an agony of suspense and doubt that was never to be wholly removed?

FOOTNOTES:

[1] The discovery of a skeleton as described was denied afterwards by the Magdeburg papers. It was a newspaper sensational paragraph, and unfounded.

[2] Register of Baptisms, Christchurch, Oxford, 1784, March 14, Benjamin, s. of Henry Bathurst, Canon, and Grace his wife, born, and bap. April 19.

[3] When, in 1815, Napoleon was at St. Helena, on his first introduction to Sir Hudson Lowe, he addressed the governor with the insulting words, "Monsieur, vous avez commandé des brigands." He alluded to the Corsican rangers in the British service, which Lowe had commanded.

[Pg 26]
The Duchess of Kingston.

Elizabeth Chudleigh, Countess of Bristol and Duchess of Kingston, who was tried for bigamy in Westminster Hall by the Peers in 1776, was, it can hardly be doubted, the original from whom Thackeray drew his detailed portrait of Beatrix Esmond, both as young Trix and as the old Baroness Bernstein; nor can one doubt that what he knew of his prototype was taken from that scandalous little book, "An Authentic Detail of Particulars relative to the late Duchess of Kingston," published by G. Kearsley in 1788. Thackeray not only reproduced some of the incidents of her life, but more especially caught the features of her character.

Poor Trix! Who does not remember her coming down the great staircase at Walcote, candle in hand, in her red stockings and with a new cherry ribbon round her neck, her eyes like blue stars, her brown hair curling about her head, and not feel a lingering liking for the little coquette, trying to catch my Lord Mohun, and the Duke of Hamilton, and many another, and missing all? and for the naughty old baroness, with her scandalous stories, her tainted past, her love of cards, her complete unscrupulousness, and yet with one soft corner in the withered heart for the young Virginians?

The famous, or infamous, Duchess has had hard[Pg 27] measure dealt out to her, which she in part deserved; but some of the stories told of her are certainly not true, and one circumstance in her life, if true, goes far to palliate her naughtiness. Unfortunately, almost all we know of her is taken from unfriendly sources. The only really impartial source of information is the "Trial," published by order of the Peers, but that covers only one portion of her life, and one set of incidents.

Elizabeth Chudleigh was the daughter of Colonel Thomas Chudleigh, of Chelsea, and his wife Henrietta, who was his first cousin, the fourth daughter of Hugh Chudleigh, of Chalmington, in Dorset. Thomas was the only brother of Sir George Chudleigh, fourth baronet of Asheton, in Devon. As Sir George left only daughters, Thomas, the brother of Elizabeth, whose baptism in 1718 is recorded in the Chelsea registers, succeeded as fifth baronet in 1738. Unfortunately the Chelsea registers do not give the baptism of Elizabeth, and we are not able to state her precise age, about which there is some difference. Her father had a post in Chelsea College, but apparently she was not born there. There can, however, be little doubt that she saw the light for the first time in 1726, and not in 1720, as is generally asserted.

Her family was one of great antiquity in the county of Devon, and was connected by marriage with the first families of the west of England. The old seat, Asheton, lies in a pleasant coombe under the ridge of Haldon; some remains of the old mansion, and venerable trees of the park, linger on; and in the picturesque parish church, perched on a rock in the[Pg 28] valley, are many family monuments and heraldic blazonings of the Chudleigh lions, gules on an ermine field. Elizabeth lost her father very early, and the widow was left on a poor pension to support and advance the prospects of her two children. Though narrowed in fortune, Mrs. Chudleigh had good connections, and she availed herself of these to push her way in the world. At the age of sixteen—that is, in 1743—Elizabeth was given the appointment of maid of honour to the Princess of Wales, through the favour of Mr. Pulteney, afterwards Earl of Bath, who had met her one day while out shooting. The old beau was taken with the vivacity, intelligence and beauty of the girl. She was then not only remarkable for her beauty, delicacy of complexion, and sparkling eyes, but also for the brilliancy of her wit and the liveliness of her humour. Even her rival, the Marquise de la Touche, of whom more hereafter, bears testimony to her charms. Pulteney, himself a witty, pungent, and convivial man, was delighted with the cleverness of the lovely girl, and amused himself with drawing it out. In after years, when she was asked the secret of her sparkling repartee, she replied, "I always aim to be short, clear, and surprising."

The Princess of Wales, Augusta, daughter of Frederick of Saxe-Gotha, who with the Prince, Frederick Lewis, had their court at Leicester House, became greatly attached to her young maid of honour. The beautiful Miss Chudleigh was speedily surrounded by admirers, among whom was James, sixth Duke of Hamilton, born in 1724, and therefore two years her senior.

[Pg 29]

According to the "Authentic Detail," the Duke obtained from her a solemn engagement that, on his return from a tour on the Continent which he was about to take, she would become his wife. Then he departed, having arranged for a mutual correspondence.

In the summer of 1744 she went on a visit to Lainston, near Winchester, to her maternal aunt, Anne Hanmer, who was then living at the house of Mr. Merrill, the son of another aunt, Susanna, who was dead.

To understand the relationship of the parties, a look will suffice at the following pedigree.[4]

Mrs. Hanmer, a widow, kept house for her nephew, who was squire. At the Winchester races, to which she went with a party, Elizabeth met Lieutenant Hervey, second son of the late John, Lord Hervey, and grandson of the Earl of Bristol. Lieutenant[Pg 30] Hervey, who was in the "Cornwall," then lying at Portsmouth, a vessel in Sir John Danver's squadron, was born in 1724, and was therefore two years the senior of Elizabeth; indeed, at the time he was only just twenty. He was fascinated by the beautiful girl, and was invited by Mrs. Hanmer to Lainston. "To this gentleman," says the "Authentic Detail," "Mrs. Hanmer became so exceedingly partial that she favoured his views on her niece, and engaged her efforts to effect, if possible, a matrimonial connexion. There were two difficulties which would have been insurmountable if not opposed by the fertile genius of a female: Miss Chudleigh disliked Captain Hervey, and she was betrothed to the Duke of Hamilton. To render this last nugatory, the letters of his Grace were intercepted by Mrs. Hanmer, and his supposed silence giving offence to her niece, she worked so successfully on her pride as to induce her to abandon all thoughts of the lover, whose passion she had cherished with delight."

Is this story true? It seems incredible that Mrs. Hanmer should have urged her niece to throw over such a splendid prospect of family advancement as that offered by marriage with the Duke of Hamilton, for the sake of an impecunious young sailor who was without the means of supporting his wife, and who, at that time, had not the faintest expectation of succeeding to the Earldom of Bristol.

It is allowable to hope that the story of the engagement to the Duke of Hamilton, broken through the intrigues of the aunt, is true, as it forms some excuse for the after conduct of Elizabeth Chudleigh.

[Pg 31]

It is more probable that the Duke of Hamilton had not said anything to Elizabeth, and did not write to her, at all events not till later. She may have entertained a liking for him, but not receiving any token that the liking was reciprocated, she allowed her aunt to engage and marry her to young Hervey. That the poor girl had no fancy for the young man is abundantly clear. The Attorney General, in the trial, said that Mrs. Hanmer urged on the match "as advantageous to her niece;" but advantageous it certainly was not, and gave no prospect of being.

In August, Augustus John Hervey got leave from his ship and came to Lainston. The house, which had belonged to the Dawleys, had passed into the possession of the Merrills. In the grounds stands the parish church, but as the only house in the parish is the mansion, it came to be regarded very much as the private chapel of the manor house. The living went with Sparsholt. There was no parsonage attached, and though the Dawleys had their children baptized in Lainston, they were registered in the book of Sparsholt. The church is now an ivy-covered ruin, and the mansion is much reduced in size from what it was in the time when it belonged to the Merrills.

"Lainston is a small parish, the value of the living being £15 a year; Mr. Merrill's the only house in it, and the parish church at the end of his garden. On the 4th August, 1744, Mr. Amis, the then rector, was appointed to be at the church, alone, late at night. At eleven o'clock Mr. Hervey and Miss Chudleigh went out, as if to walk in the garden, followed by Mrs. Hanmer, her servant—Anne Craddock, Mr. Merrill,[Pg 32] and Mr. Mountenay, which last carried a taper to read the service by. They found Mr. Amis in the church, according to his appointment, and there the service was celebrated, Mr. Mountenay holding the taper in his hat. The ceremony being performed, Mrs. Hanmer's maid was despatched to see that the coast was clear, and they returned into the house without being observed by any of the servants." This is the account of the wedding given at the trial by the Attorney General, from the evidence of Anne Craddock, then the sole surviving witness.

There was no signing of registers, Mr. Amis was left to make the proper entry in the Sparsholt book—and he forgot to do this. The happiness of the newly-married couple lasted but a few days—two, or at the outside, three; and then Lieutenant Hervey left to rejoin his vessel, and in November sailed for the West Indies. The "Authentic Detail" declares that a violent quarrel broke out immediately on marriage between the young people, and that Elizabeth declared her aversion, and vowed never to associate with him again.

So little was the marriage to her present advantage that Elizabeth was unable to proclaim it, and thereby forfeit her situation as maid of honour to the Princess, with its pay and perquisites. Consequently, by her aunt's advice, she kept it concealed.

"Miss Chudleigh, now Mrs. Hervey,—a maid in appearance, a wife in disguise,—seemed from those who judge from externals only, to be in an enviable situation. Of the higher circles she was the attractive centre, of gayer life the invigorating spirit. Her royal[Pg 33] mistress not only smiled on, but actually approved her. A few friendships she cemented, and conquests she made in such abundance that, like Cæsar in a triumph, she had a train of captives at her heels. Her husband, quieted for a time, grew obstreperous as she became more the object of admiration. He felt his right, and was determined to assert it. She endeavoured by letter to negotiate him into peace, but her efforts succeeded not. He demanded a private interview, and, enforcing his demands by threats of exposure in case of refusal, she complied through compulsion."

The Duke of Hamilton returned from the grand tour, and he at once sought Elizabeth to know why his letters had not been answered. Then the fraud that had been practised on her was discovered, and the Duke laid his coronet at her feet. She was unable to accept the offer, and unable also to explain the reasons of her refusal. Rage at having been duped, disappointment at having lost the strawberry leaves, embittered Elizabeth, and stifled the germs of good principle in her.

This is the generally received story. It is that given by the author, or authoress, of the "Authentic Detail," usually well informed. But, as we have seen, it is hardly possible to suppose that Mrs. Hanmer can have suppressed the Duke's letters. No doubt she was a fool, and a woman, when a fool, is of abnormal folly, yet she never loses sight of her own interest; and it was not Mrs. Hanmer's interest to spoil the chances of her niece with the Duke.

After the Duke of Hamilton had been refused, and[Pg 34] his visits to her house in Conduit Street prohibited, the Duke of Ancaster, Lord Howe, and other nobles made offers, and experienced a fate similar to that of his Grace of Hamilton. This astonished the fashionable world, and Mrs. Chudleigh, her mother, who was a stranger to the private marriage of her daughter, reprehended her folly with warmth.[5] To be freed from her embarrassments, Elizabeth resolved to travel. She embarked for the Continent, and visited Dresden, where she became an attached friend of the Electress of Saxony.

On her return to England she was subjected to annoyance from her husband. She could not forgive him the deception practised on her, though he was probably innocent of connivance in it.

"Captain Hervey, like a perturbed spirit, was eternally crossing the path trodden by his wife. Was she in the rooms at Bath? he was sure to be there. At a rout, ridotto, or ball, there was this fell destroyer of peace, embittering every pleasure and blighting the fruit of happiness by the pestilential malignity of his presence. As a proof of his disposition to annoy, he menaced his wife with an intimation that he would disclose the marriage to the Princess of Wales. In this Miss Chudleigh anticipated him by being the first relater of the circumstance. Her royal mistress heard and pitied her. She continued her patronage to the hour of her death."

In 1749, Elizabeth attended a masquerade ball in the dress, or rather undress, of the character of[Pg 35] Iphigenia. In a letter of Mrs. Montague to her sister, she says, "Miss Chudleigh's dress, or rather undress, was remarkable, she was Iphigenia for the sacrifice, but so naked, the high priest might easily inspect the entrails of the victim. The Maids of Honour (not of maids the strictest) were so offended they would not speak to her." Horace Walpole says, "Miss Chudleigh was Iphigenia, but so naked that you would have

14

taken her for Andromeda." It was of her that the witty remark was then first made that she resembled Eve in that she was "naked and not ashamed." On May 17th Walpole writes: "I told you we were to have another masquerade; there was one by the King's command for Miss Chudleigh, the Maid of Honour, with whom our gracious monarch has a mind to believe himself in love, so much in love, that at one of the booths he gave her a fairing for her watch, which cost him five-and-thirty guineas, actually disbursed out of his privy purse, and not charged on the civil list. I hope some future Holinshed or Speed will acquaint posterity that five-and-thirty guineas were an immense sum in those days."

In December 1750, George II. gave the situation of Housekeeper at Windsor to Mrs. Chudleigh, Elizabeth's mother. Walpole says, "Two days ago, the gallant Orondates (the King) strode up to Miss Chudleigh, and told her he was glad to have the opportunity of obeying her commands, that he appointed her mother Housekeeper at Windsor, and hoped she would not think a kiss too great a reward—against all precedent he kissed her in the circle. He has had a hankering these two years. Her life,[Pg 36]which is now of thirty years' standing, has been a little historic. Why should not experience and a charming face on her side, and near seventy years on his, produce a title?"

In 1760 she gave a soirée on the Prince's birthday, which Horace Walpole describes: "Poor thing," he writes, "I fear she has thrown away above a quarter's salary!"

The Duke of Kingston saw and was captivated by Elizabeth. Evelyn Pierrepoint, Duke of Kingston, Marquis of Dorchester, Earl of Kingston, and Viscount Newark, was born in 1711. Horace Walpole says of him that he was "a very weak man, of the greatest beauty and finest person in England."

He had been to Paris along with Lord Scarborough, taking with him an entire horse as a present to the Duke of Bourbon, and was unable to do this without a special Act of Parliament to authorise him. The Duke of Bourbon, in return for the compliment, placed his palace at Paris, and his château of Chantilly at the disposal of the visitor.

The Duke was handsome, young, wealthy and unmarried. A strong set was made at him by the young ladies of the French court; but of all the women he there met, none attracted his attentions and engaged his heart but the Marquise de la Touche, a lady who had been married for ten years and was the mother of three children. He finally persuaded her to elope with him to England, where, however, he grew cold towards her, and when he fell under the fascinations of Elizabeth Chudleigh he dismissed her. The Marquise returned to France, and was reconciled[Pg 37] to her husband; there in 1786 she published her version of the story, and gave a history of her rival, whom naturally she paints in the blackest colours.

Now follows an incident which is stated in the English accounts of the life of Elizabeth Chudleigh; but of which there is no mention in the trial, and which is of more than doubtful truth.

She had become desperate, resolved at all hazard to break the miserable tie that bound her to Captain Hervey. She made a sudden descent on Lainston—so runs the tale—visited the parsonage, and whilst Mr. Amis was kept in conversation with one of her attendants, she tore out the leaf of the register book that contained the entry of her marriage.

This story cannot possibly be true. As already said, Lainston has no parsonage, and never had. Lainston goes with Sparsholt, half-a-mile off. But Mr. Amis never held Sparsholt, but acted as curate there for a while in 1756 and 1757. Lainston had no original register. What Elizabeth did was probably to convince herself that through inadvertence, her marriage had not been registered in the parish book of Sparsholt.

In 1751 died John, Earl of Bristol, and was succeeded by his grandson, George William, who was unmarried. He was in delicate health; at one time seriously ill, and it was thought he would die. In that case Augustus John, Elizabeth's husband, would succeed to the Earldom of Bristol. She saw now that it was to her interest to establish her marriage. She accordingly took means to do so.

She went at once to Winchester and sent for the[Pg 38] wife of Mr. Amis, who had married her. She told Mrs. Amis that she wanted the register of her marriage to be made out. Mr. Amis then lay on his death-bed, but, nevertheless, she went to the rectory to obtain of him what she desired. What ensued shall be told in the words of Mrs. Amis at the trial.

"I went up to Mr. Amis and told him her request. Then Mr. Merrill and the lady consulted together whom to send for, and they desired me to send for Mr. Spearing, the attorney. I did send for him, and during the time the messenger was gone the lady concealed herself in a closet; she said she did not care that Mr. Spearing should know that she was there. When Mr. Spearing came, Mr. Merrill produced a sheet of stamped paper that he brought to make the register upon. Mr. Spearing said it would not do; it must be a book, and that the lady must be at the making of it. Then I went to the closet and told the lady. Then the lady came to Mr. Spearing, and Mr. Spearing told the lady a sheet of stamped paper would not do, it must be a book. Then the lady desired Mr. Spearing to go and buy one. Mr. Spearing went and bought one, and when brought, the register was made. Then Mr. Amis delivered it to the lady; the lady thanked him, and said it might be an hundred thousand pounds in her way. Before Mr. Merrill and the lady left my house the lady sealed up the register and gave it to me, and desired I would take care of it until Mr. Amis's death, and then deliver it to Mr. Merrill."

The entries made thus were those:

[Pg 39]

"2 August, Mrs. Susanna Merrill, relict of John Merrill, Esq. buried.

4 August, 1744, married the Honourable Augustus Hervey, Esq., in the parish Church of Lainston, to Miss Elizabeth Chudleigh, daughter of Col. Thomas Chudleigh, late of Chelsea College, by me, Thos. Amis."

Unfortunately this register book was taken up to Westminster at the trial of the Duchess and was never returned. Application was made to Elbrow Woodcock, solicitor in the trial, for the return of the book, by the then rector and patron of the living, but in vain; and in December, 1777, a new register book was purchased for the parish.

The Earl recovered, and did not die till some years later, in 1775, when Augustus John did succeed to the earldom.

In 1751, the Prince of Wales died, and this necessitated a rearrangement of the household of the Princess. Elizabeth was reappointed maid of honour to her, still in her maiden name. Soon after—that is, in 1752—the Duke of Hamilton married the beautiful Miss Gunning.

In 1760 the king was dead. "Charles Townshend, receiving an account of the impression the king's death had made," writes Walpole, "was told Miss Chudleigh cried. 'What,' said he, 'oysters?'" "There is no keeping off age," he writes in 1767, "as Miss Chudleigh does, by sticking roses and sweet peas in one's hair."

Before this, in 1765, the Duke of Kingston's affection for her seeming to wane, Elizabeth, who was getting fat as well as old, started for Carlsbad to drink the waters. "She has no more wanted the[Pg 40] Carlsbad waters than you did," wrote Lord Chesterfield. "Is it to show the Duke of Kingston he can not live without her? A dangerous experiment, which may possibly convince him that he can. There is a trick, no doubt, in it, but what, I neither know nor care." "Is the fair, or, at least, the fat Miss Chudleigh with you still? It must be confessed she knows the arts of courts to be so received at Dresden and so connived at in Leicester Fields."

At last the bonds of a marriage in which he was never allowed even to speak with his wife became intolerable to Captain Hervey; and some negotiations were entered into between them, whereby it was agreed that she should institute a suit in the Consistory Court of the Bishop of London for the jactitation of the marriage, and that he should not produce evidence to establish it. The case came on in the Michaelmas term, 1768, and was in form, proceedings to restrain the Hon. Augustus John Hervey from asserting that Elizabeth Chudleigh was his wife, "to the great danger of his soul's health, no small prejudice to the said Hon. Elizabeth Chudleigh, and pernicious example of others."

There was a counter-suit of Captain Hervey against her, in which he asserted that in 1743 or 1744, being then a minor of the age of seventeen or eighteen, he had contracted himself in marriage to Elizabeth Chudleigh, and she to him; and that they had been married in the house of Mr. Merrill, on August 9, 1744, at eleven o'clock at night, by the Rev. Thomas Amis, since deceased, and in the presence of Mrs. Hanmer and Mr. Mountenay, both also deceased.

[Pg 41]

As will be seen, the counter-libel was incorrectly drawn. The marriage had not taken place in the house, but in the church; Mr. Hervey was aged twenty, not seventeen or eighteen; and Anne Craddock, the sole surviving witness of the ceremony, was not mentioned. The register of the marriage was not produced,[6] and no serious attempt was made to establish it. Accordingly, on February 10, 1769, sentence was given, declaring the marriage form gone through in 1744 to have been null and void, and to restrain Mr. Hervey from asserting his claim to be husband to Miss Elizabeth Chudleigh, and condemning him in costs to the sum of one hundred pounds.

As the Attorney-General said at her subsequent trial, "a grosser artifice, I believe, than this suit was never fabricated."

On March 8, 1769, the Duke of Kingston married Elizabeth Chudleigh by special licence from the Archbishop, the minister who performed it being the Rev. Samuel Harper, of the British Museum, and the Church, St. Margaret's, Westminster. The Prince and Princess of Wales wore favours on the occasion.

No attempt was made during the lifetime of the Duke to dispute the legality of the marriage. Neither he nor Elizabeth had the least doubt that the former marriage had been legally dissolved. It was, no doubt, the case that Captain Hervey made no real attempt[Pg 42] to prove his marriage, he was as impatient of the bond as was she. It can hardly be doubted that the sentence of the Ecclesiastical Court was just. Captain Hervey was a minor at the time, and the poor girl had been deluded into marrying him by her wretched aunt. Advantage had been taken of her—a mere girl—by the woman who was her natural guardian in the absence of her mother. Such a marriage would at once be annulled in the Court of the Church of Rome; it would be annulled in a modern English divorce court.

The fortune of the Duke was not entailed; his Grace had, therefore, the option to bequeath it as seemed best to his inclination. His nearest of kin were his nephews, Evelyn and Charles Meadows, sons of Lady Francis Pierrepont; Charles was in 1806 created Earl Manners; he had previously changed his name to Pierrepont, and been created Baron Pierrepont and Viscount Newark in 1796.

The Duke was and remained warmly attached to the Duchess. She made him happy. She had plenty of conversation, had her mind stored with gossip, and though old, oldened gracefully and pleasantly. Her bitter enemy—an old servant and confidant, who furnished

17

the materials for the "Authentic Detail," says, "Contrarily gifted and disposed, they were frequently on discordant terms, but she had a strong hold on his mind."

On September 23, 1773, the Duke died. The Duchess had anticipated his death. He had already made his will, bequeathing to her the entire income of his estates during her life, subject to the proviso[Pg 43] that she remained in a state of widowhood. This did not at all please the Duchess, and directly she saw that her husband was dying she sent for a solicitor, a Mr. Field, to draw up a new will, omitting the obnoxious proviso; she was only by two years on the right side of fifty, and might marry again. When Mr. Field was introduced to the Duke, he saw that the dying man was not in a mental condition capable of executing a will, and he refused to have anything to do with an attempt to extort his signature from him. The Duchess was very angry; but the refusal of Mr. Field was most fortunate for her, as, had the will proposed been executed, it would most indubitably have been set aside.

As soon as the Duke was dead the dowager Duchess determined to enjoy life. She had a pleasure yacht built, placed in command of it an officer who had served in the navy, fitted it up with every luxury, sailed for Italy, and visited Rome, where the Pope and the cardinals received her with great courtesy. Indeed, she was given up one of the palaces of the cardinals for her residence. Whilst she was amusing herself in Italy something happened in England that was destined to materially spoil her happiness. Anne Craddock was still alive, the sole witness of her marriage that survived. She was in bad circumstances, and applied to Mr. Field for pecuniary relief. He refused it, but the Duchess sent to offer her twenty guineas per annum. This Anne Craddock refused, and gave intimation to Mr. Evelyn Meadows that she had information of importance which she could divulge.

[Pg 44]

When Mr. Meadows heard what Anne Craddock had to say, he set the machinery of the law in motion to obtain the prosecution of the Duchess, in the hopes of convicting her of bigamy, and then of upsetting the will of the late Duke in her favour. A bill of indictment for bigamy was preferred against her; the bill was found, Mr. Field had notice of the procedure, and the Duchess was advised to return instantly to England and appear to the indictment, to prevent an outlawry.

At this time—that is, in 1775—the Earl of Bristol died without issue, and Augustus John, her first husband, succeeded to the title.

The anxieties of the Duchess were not confined to the probable issue of the trial. Samuel Foote, the comedian, took a despicable advantage of her situation to attempt to extort money from her. He wrote a farce, entitled "A Trip to Calais," in which he introduced her Grace under the sobriquet of Lady Kitty Crocodile, and stuffed the piece with particulars relative to the private history of the Duchess, which he had obtained from Miss Penrose, a young lady who had been about her person for many years. When the piece was finished, he contrived to have it communicated to her Grace that the Haymarket Theatre would open with the entertainment in which she was held up to ridicule and scorn. She was alarmed, and sent for Foote. He attended with the piece in his pocket. She desired him to read a part of it. He obeyed; and had not read far before she could no longer control herself, but, starting up in a rage, exclaimed, "This is scandalous, Mr. Foote![Pg 45] Why, what a wretch you have made me!" After a few turns round the room, she composed herself to inquire on what terms he would suppress the play. Foote had the effrontery to demand two thousand pounds. She offered him fourteen, then sixteen hundred pounds; but he, grasping at too much, lost all. She consulted the Duke of Newcastle, and the Lord Chamberlain was apprised of the circumstances, and his interference solicited. He sent for the manuscript copy of the "Trip to Calais," perused, and censured it. In the event of its publication she threatened to prosecute Foote for libel. Public opinion ranged itself on the side of the Duchess, and Dr. Schomberg only expressed its opinion when he said that "Foote deserved to be run through the body for such an attempt. It was more ignoble than the conduct of a highwayman."

On April 17, 1776, the trial of the Duchess came on in Westminster Hall, and lasted five days. The principal object argued was the admission, or not, of a sentence of the Spiritual Court, in a suit for jactitation of marriage, in an indictment for polygamy. As the judges decided against the admission of such a sentence in bar to evidence, the fact of the two marriages was most clearly proved, and a conviction of course followed. The Duchess was tried by the Peers, a hundred and nineteen of whom sat and passed judgment upon her, all declaring "Guilty, upon mine honour," except the Duke of Newcastle, who pronounced "Guilty, erroneously; but not intentionally, upon mine honour."

No sooner did the Duchess see that her cause was lost than she determined to escape out of England.[Pg 46] The penalty for bigamy was death, but she could escape this sentence by claiming the benefits of the statute 3 and 4 William and Mary, which left her in a condition to be burnt in the hand, or imprisoned; but she claimed the benefit of the peerage, and the Lord Chief Baron, having conferred with the rest of the judges, delivered their unanimous opinion that she ought "to be immediately discharged." However, her prosecutors prepared a writ "ne exeat regno," to obtain her arrest and the deprivation of her personal property. To escape this she fled to Dover, where her yacht was in waiting, and crossed to Calais, whilst amusing the public and her prosecutors by issuing invitations to a dinner at Kingston House, and causing her carriage to appear in the most fashionable quarters of the town. Mr. Meadows had carried his first point; she could no longer call herself Dowager Duchess of Kingston in England, but she was reinstated in her position of wife to Augustus John Hervey, and was therefore now Countess of Bristol. Mr. Meadows next proceeded to attack the will of the late Duke, but in this attempt he utterly failed. The will was confirmed, and Elizabeth, Countess of Bristol, was acknowledged as lawfully possessed of life interest in the property of the Duke so long as she remained unmarried. Mr. Meadows was completely ruined, and his sole gain was to keep the unhappy woman an exile from England.

Abroad the Countess was still received as Duchess of Kingston. She lived in considerable state, and visited Italy, Russia, and France. Her visit to St.[Pg 47] Petersburg was splendid, and to ensure a favourable reception by the Empress Catharine she sent her a present of some of the valuable paintings by old masters from Kingston House. When in Russia she purchased an estate near the capital, to which she gave the name of Chudleigh, and which cost her 25,000l.[7] The Empress also gave her a property on the Neva. She had a corvette built of mahogany which was to be a present to the Empress, but the vessel stranded on the coast of Ingermanland. Eight of the cannons out of her are now at Chudleigh, almost the only things there that recall the Duchess. She gave magnificent entertainments; at one of these, to which the Empress was invited, a hundred and forty of her own servants attended in the Kingston livery of black turned up with red and silver.

On her return from Russia she bought an estate at Montmartre, which cost her 9,000l., and another that belonged to one of the French royal princes at Saint Assise, which cost her 55,000l. The château was so large that three hundred beds could be made up in it.

She was getting on in years, but did not lose her energy, her vivacity, and her selfishness. Once in Rome, the story goes, she had been invited to visit some tombs that were famous. She replied with a touch of real feeling: "Ce n'est pas la peine de chercher des tombeaux, on en porte assez dans son cœur."

[Pg 48]

The account of her death shall be given in the words of the author of "Authentic Detail."

"She was at dinner, when her servants received intelligence of a sentence respecting the house near Paris having been awarded against her. She flew into a violent passion, and, in the agitation of her mind and body, burst an internal blood-vessel. Even this she appeared to have surmounted, until a few days afterwards, on the morning of the 26th August (1788), when about to rise from her bed, a servant who had long been with her endeavoured at dissuasion. The Duchess addressed her thus: 'I am not very well, but I *will* rise. At your peril disobey me; I will get up and walk about the room. Ring for the secretary to assist me.' She was obeyed, dressed, and the secretary entered the chamber. The Duchess then walked about, complained of thirst, and said, 'I could drink a glass of my fine Madeira and eat a slice of toasted bread; I shall be quite well afterwards; but let it be a large glass of wine.' The attendant reluctantly brought and the Duchess drank the wine. She then said, 'I knew the Madeira would do me good. My heart feels oddly; I will have another glass.' She then walked a little about the room, and afterwards said, 'I will lie on the couch.' She sat on the couch, a female having hold of each hand. In this situation she soon appeared to have fallen into a profound sleep, until the women found her hands colder than ordinary; other domestics were rung for, and the Duchess was found to have expired, as the wearied labourer sinks into the arms of rest."

[Pg 49]

Was it a touch of final malice or of real regret that caused the old lady, by codicil to her will dated May 10, 1787, to leave pearl earrings and necklace to the Marquise de la Touche? Was it a token that she forgave her the cruel book, "Les aventures trop amoureuses; ou, Elizabeth Chudleigh," which she wrote, or caused to be written, for the blackening of her rival, and the whitewashing of herself? Let us hope it was so. The proviso in the Duke's will saved her from herself; but for that she would have married an adventurer who called himself the Chevalier de Wortha, a man who obtained great influence over her, and finally died by his own hand.

Elizabeth Chudleigh's character and career have never been sketched by friends; her enemies, those jealous of her fascinations, angry at her success, discontented with not having been sufficiently considered in her will, have given us their impressions of her, have poured out all the evil they knew and imagined of her. She has been hardly used. The only perfectly reliable authority for her history is the report of her trial, and that covers only one portion of her story. The "Authentic Detail" published by G. Kearsley, London, in 1788, is anonymous. It is fairly reliable, but tinctured by animosity. The book "Les Aventures trop Amoureuses, ou, Elizabeth Chudleigh, ex-duchesse douairière de Kingston, aujourd'hui Comtesse de Bristol, et la Marquise de la Touche. Londres, aux depens des Interessez, 1776," was composed for the justification of Madame de la Touche, and with all the venom of a discomfited and supplanted rival.

[Pg 50]

An utterly worthless book, "Histoire de la vie et des Aventures de la Duchesse de Kingston, a Londres, et se trouve à Paris, Chez Quillot, 1789," is fiction. It pretends to be based on family papers. At the commencement it gives a portion of the diary of Col. Thomas Chudleigh, in which, among other impossibilities, he records his having reduced the rents of his tenants on his estates twenty per cent. because the year was bad. As it happened, Col. Thomas Chudleigh neither possessed an acre of land, nor a tenant.

In 1813 appeared "La Duchesse de Kingston, memoires rédigés par M. de Favolle," in two volumes; this is based solely on the preceding with rich additions from the imagination of the author. Not a statement in it can be trusted.

Some little reliable information may be found in the "Memoires de la Baronne d'Oberkirch," Paris 1853.

FOOTNOTES:

[4] In Col. Vivian's "Visitations of the County of Devon," the pedigree is not so complete. He was unaware who the wife of Thos. Chudleigh was, and he had not seen the will of the duchess.

[5] Mrs. Chudleigh died in 1756, and her will mentions her daughter by her maiden name.

[6] Mr. John Merrill died February 1767, and his burial was entered in it. Mr. Bathurst, who had married his daughter, found the register book in the hall, and handed it over to the rector, Mr. Kinchin. Nevertheless it was not produced at the hearing of the case for jactitation in the Consistory Court.

[7] This place still bears the name. It is on the main road through Livland and Esthonia to St. Petersburg; about twenty miles from Narwa. It also goes by the name of Fockenhof. The present mansion is more modern, and belongs to the family of Von Wilcken.

[Pg 51]

General Mallet.

On the return of Napoleon to Paris from Moscow, he was depressed with news that troubled him more than the loss of his legions. The news that had reached him related to perhaps the most extraordinary conspiracy that was ever devised, and which was within an ace of complete success. It was the news of this conspiracy that induced him to desert the army in the snows of Russia and hasten to Paris. The thoughts of this conspiracy frustrated by an accident, as Alison says, "incessantly occupied his mind during his long and solitary journey."

"Gentlemen," said Napoleon, when the report of the conspiracy was read over to him, "we must no longer disbelieve in miracles."

Claude François Mallet belonged to a noble family in the Franche Comté. He was born on June 28th, 1754, at Dole, and passed his early life in the army, where he commanded one of the first battalions of the Jura at the commencement of the Revolution. In May 1793, he was elevated to the rank of adjutant-General, and in August 1799, made General of Brigade, and commanded a division under Championnet. He was a man of enthusiastically Republican views, and viewed the progress of Napoleon with dissatisfaction mingled with envy. There can be no question as to what his opinions were at first;[Pg 52] whether he changed them afterwards is not so certain. He was a reserved, hard, and bitter man, ambitious and restless. Envy of Napoleon, jealousy of his success seems to have been the ruling motive in his heart that made of him a conspirator, and not genuine disgust at Cæsarism.

Bonaparte knew his political opinions; and though he did not fear the man, he did not trust him. He became implicated in some illegal exactions at Civita Vecchia, in the Roman States, and was in consequence deprived of his command, and sent before a commission of enquiry at Paris, in July 1807; and, in virtue of their sentence, he was confined for a short while, and then again set at liberty and reinstated. In 1808, when the war in the Peninsula broke out, Mallet entered at Dijon into a plot, along with some old anarchists, for the overthrow of the Emperor, among them the ex-General Guillaume, who betrayed the plot, and Mallet was arrested and imprisoned in La Force. Napoleon did not care that conspiracies against himself and his throne should be made public, and consequently he contented himself with the detention of Mallet alone.

In prison, the General did not abandon his schemes, and he had the lack of prudence to commit them to paper. This fell into the hands of the Government. The minister regarded the scheme as chimerical and unimportant. The papers were shown to Napoleon, who apparently regarded the scheme or the man as really dangerous, and ordered him to perpetual detention in prison.

Time passed, and Mallet and his schemes were [Pg 53]forgotten. Who could suppose that a solitary prisoner, without means, without the opportunity of making confederates, could menace the safety of the Empire?

Then came the Russian campaign, in 1812. Mallet saw what Napoleon did not; the inevitable failure that must attend it; and he immediately renewed his attempts to form a plot against the Emperor.

But the prison of La Force was bad headquarters from which to work. He pretended to be ill, and he was removed to a hospital, that of the Doctor Belhomme near the Barrière du Trône. In this house were the two brothers Polignac, a M. de Puyvert, and the Abbé Lafon, who in 1814 wrote and published an account of this conspiracy of Mallet. These men were Royalists, and Mallet was a Republican. It did not matter so long as Napoleon could be overthrown, how divergent their views might be as to what form of Government was to take the place of the Empire.

They came to discussion, and the Royalists supposed that they had succeeded in convincing Mallet. He, on his side, was content to dissemble his real views, and to make use of these men as his agents.

The Polignac brothers were uneasy, they were afraid of the consequences, and they mistrusted the man who tried to draw them into his plot. Perhaps, also, they considered his scheme too daring to succeed. Accordingly they withdrew from the hospital, to be out of his reach. It was not so with the others. The Polignacs had been mixed up in the enterprise of Georges, and had no wish to be again involved.[Pg 54] Whether there were many others in the plot we do not know, Lafon names only four, and it does not seem that M. de Puyvert took a very active part in it.

Mallet's new scheme was identical with the old one that had been taken from him and shown to Napoleon. Napoleon had recognized its daring and ability, and had not despised it. That no further fear of Mallet was entertained is clear, or he would never have been transferred from the prison to a private hospital, where he would be under very little supervision.

In his hospital, Mallet drew up the following report of a Session of the Senate, imagined by himself:

"Sénat Conservateur

"Session of 22 October, 1812.

"The Session was opened at 8 P.M., under the presidency of Senator Sieyes.

"The occasion of this extraordinary Session was the receipt of the news of the death of the Emperor Napoleon, under the walls of Moscow, on the 8th of the month.

"The Senate, after mature consideration of the condition of affairs caused by this event, named a Commission to consider the danger of the situation, and to arrange for the maintenance of Government and order. After having received the report of this Commission, the following orders were passed by the Senate.

"That as the Imperial Government has failed to satisfy the aspirations of the French people, and secure peace, it be decreed annulled forthwith.

"That all such officers military and civil as shall use their authority prejudicially to the re-establishment of the Republic, shall be declared outlawed.

"That a Provisional Government be established, to consist of 13 members:—Moreau, President; Carnot, Vice-President; General Augereau, Bigonet, Destutt-Tracy, Florent Guyot, Frochot; Mathieu Montmorency, General Mallet, Noailles, Truguet; Volney, Garat.

[Pg 55]

"That this Provisional Government be required to watch over the internal and external safety of the State, and to enter into negociations with the military powers for the re-establishment of peace.

"That a constitution shall be drawn up and submitted to the General Assembly of the French realm.

"That the National Guard be reconstituted as formerly.

"That a general Amnesty be proclaimed for all political offences; that all emigrants, exiles, be permitted to return.

"That the freedom of the Press be restored.

"That the command of the army of the Centre, and which consists of 50,000 men, and is stationed near Paris, be given to General Lecombe.

"That General Mallet replaces General Hulin as commandant of Paris, and in the first division. He will have the right to nominate the officers in the general staff that will surround him."

There were many other orders, 19 in all, but these will suffice to indicate the tendency of the document. It was signed by the President and his Secretaries.

President, SIEYES.

Secretaries, LANJUINAIS, et GREGOIRE.

"Approved, and compared with a similar paper in my own hands,

Signed, MALLET,

General of Division, Commandant of the main army of

Paris, and of the forces of the First Division."

This document, which was designed to be shown to the troops, to the officers and officials, was drawn up in a form so close to the genuine form, and the signatures and seals were so accurately imitated, that the document was not likely at the first glance to excite mistrust.

Moreover, Mallet had drawn up an order for the day, and a proclamation, which was printed in many thousand copies.

[Pg 56]

On the 22nd October, 1812, at 10 o'clock at night, after he had been playing cards with great composure in the hospital, Mallet made his escape, along with four others, one was the Abbé Lafon, another a corporal named Rateau, whom he had named as his aide-de-camp. Mallet had just twelve francs in his pocket, and so furnished he embarked on his undertaking to upset the throne of the Emperor. He at once went to a Spanish monk, whose acquaintance he had made in prison; and in his rooms found his general's uniform which had been brought there by a woman the evening before. Uniforms and swords for his confederates were also ready. But it rained that night—it rained in torrents, and the streets of Paris ran with water. It has been remarked that rain in Paris has a very sobering effect on political agitations, and acts even better than bayonets in preventing a disturbance of the public peace.

Mallet and his confederates could not leave their shelter till after midnight, and some of them did not appear at the place of rendezvous till 6 o'clock in the morning. Indisputably this had much to do with the defeat of the plot.

The success of the undertaking depended on darkness, on the sudden bewilderment of minds, and the paralysis of the government through the assassination of some of the ministers. About 2 A.M. Mallet appeared in his general's uniform, attended by some of his confederates also in uniform, at the Popincour barracks, and demanded to see the Commandant Soulier at once, giving his name as Lamothe. Soulier was in bed asleep. He was also unwell. He was[Pg 57] roused from his slumbers, hastily dressed himself, and received a sealed letter, which he broke open, and read:

"To the General of Division, Commandant-in-Chief of the troops under arms in Paris, and the troops of the First Division, Soulier, Commandant of the 10th Cohort."

"General Headquarters,
"Place Vendôme.
"23*rd* Oct., 1812, 10 o'clock a.m.

"M. LE COMMANDANT,—I have given orders to the General Lamothe with a police commissioner to attend at your barracks, and to read before you and your Cohort the decree of the senate consequent on the receipt of the news of the death of the Emperor, and the cessation of the Imperial Government. The said general will communicate to you the Order for the Day, which you will be pleased to further to the General of Brigade. You are required to get the troops under arms with all possible despatch and quietness. By daybreak, the officers who are in barracks will be sent to the Place de Grève, there to await their companies, which will there assemble, after the instructions which General Lamothe will furnish have been carried out."

Then ensued a series of dispositions for the troops, and the whole was signed by Mallet.

When Soulier had read this letter, Mallet, who pretended to be General Lamothe, handed him the document already given, relating to the assembly of the Senate, and its decisions. Then he gave him the Order for the Day, for the 23rd and 24th October.

Colonel Soulier, raised from sleep, out of health, bewildered, did not for a moment mistrust the messenger, or the documents handed to him. He hastened at once to put in execution the orders he had received.

The same proceedings were gone through in the[Pg 58] barracks of Les Minimes, and of Picpus; the decree of the Senate, the Order of the Day, and a Proclamation, were read by torchlight.

Everywhere the same success. The officers had not the smallest doubt as to the authenticity of the papers presented to them. Everywhere also the Proclamation announcing the death of the Emperor, the cessation of the Empire, and the establishment of the Provisional Government was being placarded about.

At 6 A.M., at the head of a troop, Mallet, still acting as General Lamothe, marched before the prison of La Force, and the Governor was ordered to open the gates. The Decree of the Senate and the Order of the Day were read to him, and he was required at once to discharge three state prisoners he held, General Guidal, Lahorie, and a Corsican, Bocchejampe, together with certain officers there confined. He did as required, and Mallet separated his troops into four detachments, keeping one under his own command, and placing the others under the orders of Guidal, Lahorie and Bocchejampe.

Guidal and Lahorie, by his orders, now marched to the Ministry of Police, where they arrested Savary, Duke of Rovigo, Minister of Police. At the same time Boutreux, another confederate, had gone to the prefecture of the Paris police, had arrested the prefect, Pasquier, and sent him to be confined in La Force.

Mallet, now at the head of 150 men, went to the État-Major de-la-place, to go through the same farce with the Commandant-de-place, and get him to subscribe the Order for the Day. Count Hullin refused. Mallet presented a pistol at his head, fired, and[Pg 59] Hullin fell covered with blood to the ground. Mallet left him for dead, but fortunately only his jaw was broken. By means of a forged order addressed to the commandant of one of the regiments of the paid guard of Paris, he occupied the National Bank, in which, at the time, there was a considerable treasure in specie.

The État-Major of Paris was a post of the highest importance, as it was the headquarters of the whole military authority in Paris. Before Mallet approached it, he sent a packet to the Adjutant-General Doucet, of a similar tenor to that given to Soulier and the other colonels, and containing his nomination as general of brigade, and a treasury order for a hundred thousand francs.

Soulier, Colonel of the 10th Cohort, obeying the orders he had received, the authenticity of which he did not for a moment dispute, had in the meantime made himself master of the Hôtel-de-Ville, and had stationed a strong force in the square before the building. Frochot, Prefect of the Seine, was riding into Paris from his country house at half-past eight in the morning, when he was met by his servants, in great excitement, with a note from Mallet, on the outside of which were written the ominous words "Fuit Imperator." Now it so happened that no tidings of the Emperor had been received for twenty-five days, and much uneasiness was felt concerning him. When Frochot therefore received this notice, he believed it, and hurried to the Hôtel-de-Ville. There he received a despatch from Mallet, under the title of Governor of Paris, ordering him to make ready the[Pg 60] principal apartment in the building for the use of the Provisional Government. Not for a moment did Frochot remember that—even if the Emperor were dead, there was the young Napoleon, to whom his allegiance was due; he at once obeyed the orders he had received, and began to make the Hôtel ready for the meeting of the Provisional Government. Afterwards when he was reminded that there was a son to Napoleon, and that his duty was to support him, Frochot answered, "Ah! I forgot that. I was distracted with the news."

By means of the forged orders despatched everywhere, all the barriers of Paris had been seized and were closed, and positive orders were issued that no one was to be allowed to enter or leave Paris.

Mallet now drew up before the État-Major-Général, still accompanied and obeyed by the officer and detachment. Nothing was wanting now but the command of the adjutant-general's office to give to Mallet the entire direction of the military force of Paris, with command of the telegraph, and with it of all France. With that, and with the treasury already seized, he would be master of the situation. In another ten minutes Paris would be in his hand, and with Paris the whole of France.

An accident—an accident only—at that moment saved the throne of Napoleon. Doucet was a little suspicious about the orders—or allowed it afterwards to be supposed that he was. He read them, and stood in perplexity. He would have put what doubts presented themselves aside, had it not been for his aide-de-camp, Laborde. It happened that Laborde[Pg 61] had had charge of Mallet in La Force, and had seen him there quite recently. He came down to enter the room where was Doucet, standing in doubt before Mallet. Mallet's guard was before the door, and would have prevented him from entering; however, he peremptorily called to them to suffer him to pass, and the men, accustomed to obey his voice, allowed him to enter. The moment he saw Mallet in his general's uniform, he recognised him and said, "But—how the devil!— That is my prisoner. How came he to escape?" Doucet still hesitated, and attempted to explain, when Laborde cut his superior officer short with, "There is something wrong here. Arrest the fellow, and I will go at once to the minister of police."

Mallet put his hand in his pocket to draw out the pistol with which he had shot Hullin, when the gesture was observed in a mirror opposite, and before he had time to draw and cock the pistol, Doucet and Laborde were on him, and had disarmed him.

Laborde, with great promptitude, threw open the door, and announced to the soldiers the deceit that had been practised on them, and assured them that the tidings of the death of the Emperor were false.

The arrest of Mallet disconcerted the whole conspiracy. Had Generals Lahorie and Guidal been men of decision and resolution they might still have saved it, but this they were not; though at the head of considerable bodies of men, the moment they saw that their chief had met with a hitch in carrying out his plan, they concluded that all was lost, and made the best of their way from their posts to places of concealment.

[Pg 62]

It was not till 8 o'clock that Saulnier, General Secretary of Police, heard of the arrest and imprisonment of his chief, Savary, Duke of Rovigo. He at once hastened to Cambacérès, the President of the Ministry in the absence of the Emperor, and astonished and alarmed him with the tidings. Then Saulnier hastened to Hullin, whom he found weltering in his blood, and unable to speak.

Baron Pasquier, released from La Force, attempted to return to his prefecture. The soldiers posted before it refused to admit him, and threatened to shoot him, believing that he had escaped from prison, and he was obliged to take refuge in an adjoining house. Laborde, who about noon came there, was arrested by the soldiers, and conducted by them as a prisoner to the État-Major-Général, to deliver him over to General Mallet; and it was with difficulty that they could be persuaded that they had been deceived, and that Mallet was himself, at that moment, in irons.

Savary, released from La Force, had Mallet and the rest of the conspirators brought before him. Soulier also, for having given too ready a credence to the forged orders, was also placed under arrest, to be tried along with the organisers and carriers out of the plot.

Mallet confessed with great composure that he had planned the whole, but he peremptorily refused to say whether he had aiders or sympathisers elsewhere.

Lahorie could not deny that he had taken an active part, but declared that it was against his will, his whole intention being to make a run for the United States, there to spend the rest of his days in tranquillity.[Pg 63] He asserted that he had really believed that the Emperor was dead.

Guidal tried to pass the whole off as a joke; but when he saw that he was being tried for his life, he became greatly and abjectly alarmed.

Next day the generals and those in the army who were under charge were brought before a military commission. Saulnier had an interesting interview with Mallet that day. He passed through the hall where Mallet was dining, when the prisoner complained that he was not allowed the use of a knife. Saulnier at once ordered that he might be permitted one; and this consideration seems to have touched Mallet, for he spoke with more frankness to Saulnier than he did before his judges. When the General Secretary of Police asked him how he could dream of success attending such a mad enterprise, Mallet replied, "I had already three regiments of infantry on my side. Very shortly I would have been surrounded by the thousands who are weary of the Napoleonic yoke, and are longing for a change of order. Now, I was convinced that the moment the news of my success in

Paris reached him, Napoleon would leave his army and fly home, I would have been prepared for him at Mayence, and have had him shot there. If it had not been for the cowardice of Guidal and Lahorie, my plot would have succeeded. I had resolved to collect 50,000 men at Chalons sur Marne to cover Paris. The promise I would have made to send all the conscripts to their homes, the moment the crisis was over, would have rallied all the soldiers to my side."

[Pg 64]

On October 23, the prisoners to the number of twenty-four were tried, and fourteen were condemned to be shot, among these, Mallet, Guidai, Lahorie, and the unfortunate Soulier. Mallet at the trial behaved with great intrepidity. "Who are your accomplices?" asked the President. "The whole of France," answered Mallet, "and if I had succeeded, you yourself at their head. One who openly attacks a government by force, if he fails, expects to die." When he was asked to make his defence, "Monsieur," he said, "a man who has constituted himself defender of the rights of his Fatherland, needs no defence."

Soulier put in as an apology, that the news of the death of the Emperor had produced such a sudorific effect on him, that he had been obliged to change his shirt four times in a quarter of an hour. This was not considered sufficient to establish his attachment to the Imperial government.

In the afternoon of the same day the fourteen were conveyed to the plain of Grenelle to be shot, when pardon was accorded by the Empress Regent to two of the condemned, the Corporal Rateau, and Colonel Rabbe. When the procession passed through the Rue Grenelle, Mallet saw a group of students looking on; "Young men," he called to them, "remember the 23rd October." Arrived on the place of execution, some of the condemned cried out, "Vive l'empereur!" only a few "Vive la République."

Mallet requested that his eyes might not be bandaged, and maintained the utmost coolness. He received permission, at his own desire, to give the requisite orders to the soldiers drawn up to shoot him[Pg 65] and his party. "Peloton! Present!" The soldiers, moved by the tragic catastrophe, obeyed, but not promptly. "That is bad!" called Mallet, "imagine you are before the foe. Once again—Attention!—Present!" This time it was better. "Not so bad this time, but still not well," said the General; "now pay attention, and mind, when I say Fire, that all your guns are discharged as one. It is a good lesson for you to see how brave men die. Now then, again, Attention!" For a quarter of an hour he put the men through their drill, till he observed that his comrades were in the most deplorable condition. Some had fainted, some were in convulsions. Then he gave the command: Fire! the guns rattled and the ten fell to the ground, never to rise again. Mallet alone reeled, for a moment or two maintaining his feet, and then he also fell over, without a sound, and was dead.

"But for the singular accident," says Savary, "which caused the arrest of the Minister of War to fail, Mallet, in a few moments, would have been master of almost everything, and in a country so much influenced by the contagion of example, there is no saying where his success would have stopped. He would have had possession of the treasury, then extremely rich; the post office, the telegraph, and the command of the hundred cohorts of the National Guard. He would soon have learned the alarming situation in Russia; and nothing could have prevented him from making prisoner of the Emperor himself if he returned alone, or from marching to meet him, if he had come at the head of his shattered forces."

[Pg 66]

As Alison says, "When the news reached Napoleon, one only idea took possession of his imagination—that in this crisis the succession of his son was, by common consent, set aside; one only truth was ever present to his mind—that the Imperial Crown rested on himself alone. The fatal truth was brought home to him that the Revolution had destroyed the foundations of hereditary succession; and that the greatest achievements by him who wore the diadem afforded no security that it would descend to his progeny. These reflections, which seem to have burst on Napoleon all at once, when the news of this extraordinary affair reached him in Russia, weighed him down more than all the disasters of the Moscow retreat."

[Pg 67]
Schweinichen's Memoirs.

Memoirs, says Addison, in the Tatler, are so untrustworthy, so stuffed with lies, that, "I do hereby give notice to all booksellers and translators whatsoever, that the word *memoir* is French for a novel; and to require of them, that they sell and translate it accordingly."

There are, however, some memoirs that are trustworthy and dull, and others, again, that are conspicuously trustworthy, and yet are as entertaining as a novel, and to this latter category belong the memoirs of Hans von Schweinichen, the Silesian Knight, Marshal and Chamberlain to the Dukes of Liegnitz and Brieg at the close of the 16th century. Scherr, a well known writer on German Culture, and a scrupulous observer and annotator of all that is ugly and unseemly in the past, says of the diary of Schweinichen: "It carries us into a noble family at the end of the 16th century and reveals boorish meanness, coarseness and lack of culture." That is, in a measure, true, but, as is invariably the case with Scherr, he leaves out of sight all the redeeming elements, and there are many, that this transparently sincere diarist discloses.

The MS. was first discovered and published in 1823, by Büsching; it was republished in 1878 at Breslau by Oesterley. The diary extends to the[Pg 68] year 1602, and Schweinichen begins with an account of his birth in 1552, and his childish years. But we are wrong in saying that he begins with his birth—characteristic of the protestant theological spirit of his times, he begins with a confession of his faith.

As a picture of the manners and customs of the highest classes in the age just after the Reformation it is unrivalled for its minuteness, and for its interest. The writer, who had not an idea that his diary would be printed, wrote for his own amusement, and, without intending it, drew a perfect portraiture of himself, without exaggeration of his virtues and observation of his faults; indeed the virtues we admire in him, he hardly recognised as virtues, and scarcely considered as serious the faults we deplore. In reading his truthful record we are angry with him, and yet, he makes us love and respect him, and acknowledge what sterling goodness, integrity, fidelity and honour were in the man.

Hans was son of George, Knight of Schweinichen and Mertschütz, and was born in the Castle of Gröditzberg belonging to the Dukes of Silesia, of which his father was castellan, and warden of the Ducal Estates thereabouts. The Schweinichens were a very ancient noble Silesian family, and Hans could prove his purity of blood through the sixteen descents, eight paternal and eight maternal.

In 1559, Duke Frederick III. was summoned before the Emperor Ferdinand I. at Breslau, to answer the accusations of extravagance and oppression brought against him by the Silesian Estates, and was deposed, imprisoned, and his son Henry XI.[Pg 69] given the Ducal crown instead. The deposition of the Duke obliged the father of our hero to leave Gröditzberg and retire to his own estates, where Hans was given the village notary as teacher in reading and writing for a couple of years, and was then sent, young noble though he was, to keep the geese for the family. However, as he played tricks with the geese, put spills into their beaks, pegging them open, the flock was then withdrawn from his charge. This reminds us of Grettir the Strong, the Icelandic hero, who also as a boy was sent to drive the family geese to pasture, and who maltreated his charge.

His father sent Hans to be page to the imprisoned Duke Frederick at Liegnitz, where also he was to study with the Duke's younger son, afterwards Frederick IV. Hans tells us he did not get as many whippings as his companion, because he slipped his money-allowance into the tutor's palm, and so his delinquencies were passed over. As page, he had to serve the Duke at table. A certain measure of wine was allowed the imprisoned Duke daily by his son, the reigning Duke; what he did not drink every day, Hans was required to empty into a cask, and when the cask was full, the Duke invited some good topers to him, and they sat and drank the cask out, then rolled over on the floor. All night Hans had to sit or lie on the floor and watch the drunken Duke.

Duke Frederick took a dislike to the chaplain, and scribbled a lampoon on him, which may be thus rendered, without injustice to the original:—

"All the mischief ever done
Twixt the old Duke and his son,
[Pg 70]Comes from that curs't snuffy one
Franconian Parson Cut-and-run."

The Duke ordered Hans to pin this to the pulpit cushion, and he did so. When the pastor ascended the pulpit he saw the paper, and instead of a text read it out. The reigning Duke Henry was very angry, and Hans was made the scape-goat, and sent home in disgrace to his father.

In 1564, Hans attended his father, himself as page, his father as Marshal, when Duke Henry and his Duchess visited Stuttgard and Dresden. Pages were not then allowed to sit astride a horse, they stood in a sort of stirrup slung to the pommel, to which they held. At Dresden old Schweinichen ran a tilt in a tournament with the elector Augustus and unhorsed him, but had sufficient courtesy to at once throw himself off his own horse, as though he also had been cast by the elector. This so gratified the latter, that he sent old Schweinichen a gold chain, and a double florin worth about 4 shillings to the young one.

When Hans was fifteen, he went to the marriage of Duke Wenceslas of Teschen with the daughter of Duke Franz of Saxony, and received from his father a present of a sword, which, he tells us, cost his father a little under a pound. One of the interesting features of this diary is that Hans enters the value of everything. For instance, we are given the price of wheat, barley, rye, oats, meat, &c., in 1562, and we learn from this that all kinds of grain cost one fifth or one sixth of what it costs now, and that meat—mutton, was one eighteenth or one twentieth the present cost. For a thaler, 3 shillings, in 1562 as[Pg 71] much food could be purchased as would now cost from 25 to 30 shillings. Hans tells us what pocket money he received from his parents; he put a value on every present he was given, and tells what everything cost him which he give away.

In the early spring of 1569 Duke Henry XI. went to Lublin in Poland to a diet. King Sigismund was old, and the Duke hoped to get elected to the kingdom of Poland on his death. This was a costly expedition, as the Duke had to make many presents, and to go in great state. Hans went with him, and gives an infinitely droll account of their reception, the miserable housing, his own dress, one leg black, the other yellow, and how many ells of ribbon went to make the bows on his jacket. His father and he, and a nobleman called Zedlitz and his son were put in a garret under the tiles in bitter frost—and "faith," says Hans, "our pigs at home are warmer in their styes."

This expedition which led to no such result as the Duke hoped, exhausted his treasury, and exasperated the Silesian Estates. All the nobles had to stand surety for their Duke, Schweinichen and the rest to the amount of—in modern money £100,000.

When Hans was aged eighteen he was drunk for the first time in his life, so drunk that he lay like a dead man for two days and two nights, and his life was in danger.

Portia characterised the German as a drunkard, she liked him "very vilely in the morning, when he is sober; and most vilely in the afternoon, when he is drunk. Set a deep glass of Rhenish wine on the contrary casket: for, if the devil be within, and that[Pg 72]temptation without, I know he will choose it. I will do anything, Nerissa, ere I will be married to a sponge."

How true this characterisation was of the old German noble, Schweinichen's memoirs show; it is a record of drunken bouts at small intervals. There was no escape, he who would live at court must drink and get drunken.

At the age of nineteen old Schweinichen made his son keep the accounts at home, and look after the mill; he had the charge of the fish-ponds, and attended to the thrashing of the corn, and the feeding of the horses and cattle.

Once Hans was invited to a wedding, and met at it four sisters from Glogau, two were widows and two unmarried. Their maiden name was Von Schaben. Hans, aged twenty, danced with the youngest a good deal, and before leaving invited the four sisters to pay his father and him a visit. A friend of his called Eicholz galloped ahead to forewarn old Schweinichen. Some hours later up drove Hans in a waggon with the four sisters; but he did not dare to bring them in till he had seen his father, so he went into the house, and was at once saluted with a burst of laughter, and the shout, "Here comes the bridegroom," and Eicholz sang at the top of his voice an improvised verse:

"Rosie von Schaben
Hans er will haben."

"Where are the ladies?" asked the old knight.

"In the waggon outside," answered Hans.

"Send for the fiddlers, bring them in. We will eat, drink, dance and be merry," said the old man.

But Hans was offended at being boisterously saluted[Pg 73] as bridegroom, and he now kept Rosie at a distance. Somewhat later, the Duke tried to get him to marry a charming young heiress called Hese von Promnitz, and very amusing is Hans' account of how he kept himself clear of engagement. When he first met her at court she was aged fourteen, and was passionately fond of sugar. Hans says he spent as much as £3 in our modern money on sweets for her, but he would make no proposal, because, as he concluded, she was too young to be able "to cook a bowl of soup." Two years passed, and then an old fellow called Geisler, "looking more like a Jew than a gentleman," who offered Hese a box of sweets every day, proposed for her. Hese would not answer till she knew the intentions of Hans, and she frankly asked him whether he meant to propose for her hand or not. "My heart's best love, Hese," answered Schweinichen, "at the right time, and when God wills I shall marry, but I do not think I can do that for three years. So follow your own desires, take the old Jew, or wait, as you like."

Hese said she would wait any number of years for Hans. This made Hans the colder. The Duke determined that the matter should be settled one way or other at once, so he sent a crown of gold roses to Hans, and said it was to be Hese's bridal wreath, if he desired that she should wear it for him, he was to lay hold of it; Hans thereupon put his hands behind his back. Then he went to his Schweinichen coat-of-arms and painted under it the motto, "I bide my time, when the old man dies, I'll get the prize." This Geisler read, and—says Hans, didn't like.

[Pg 74]

Hans was now installed as gentleman-in-waiting to the Duke, and was henceforth always about his person. He got for his service free bed and board, a gala coat that cost in our modern money about £36, and an every day livery costing £18. His father made him a small allowance, but pay in addition to liveries and keep he got none. The Duke's great amusement consisted in mumming. For a whole year he rambled about every evening in masquerade, dropping in on the burghers unexpectedly. Some were, we are told, pleased to see and entertain him, others objected to these impromptu visits. The special costume in which the Duke delighted to run about the town making these visits was that of a Nun. Hans admits that this was very distasteful to him, but he could not help himself, he was obliged to accommodate himself to the whims of his master. He made an effort to free himself from the service of the Duke, so as to go out of the country to some other court—he felt intuitively that this association would be fatal to his best interests, but the Duke at once took him by his better side, pleaded with him to remain and be faithful to him, his proper master and sovereign, and Hans with misgivings at heart consented.

There was at Court an old lady, Frau von Kittlitz, who acted as stewardess, and exercised great influence over the Duke, whom she had known from a boy. The Duchess resented her managing ways, and interference, and was jealous of her influence. One day in 1575 she refused to come down from her room and dine with the Duke unless the old Kittlitz were sent to sit at the table below the dais. This led to[Pg 75]words and hot blood on both sides. The Duchess used a gross expression in reference to the stewardess, and the Duke who had already some wine under his belt, struck the Duchess in the face, saying, "I'll teach you not to call people names they do not deserve." Hans, who was present, threw himself between the angry couple; the Duke stormed and struck about. Hans entreated the Duchess to retire, and then he stood in her door and prevented the Duke following, though he shouted, "She is my wife, I can serve her as I like. Who are you to poke yourself in between married folk?"

As soon as the Duchess had locked herself in, Hans escaped and fled; but an hour after the Duke sent for him, and stormed at him again for his meddlesomeness. Hans entreated the Duke to be quiet and get reconciled to the Duchess, but he would not hear of it, and dismissed Schweinichen. A quarter of an hour later another messenger came from his master, and Hans returned to him, to find him in a better mood. "Hans," said his Highness, "try if you can't get my wife to come round and come down to table—all fun is at an end with this."

Hans went up and was admitted. The Duchess, in a towering rage, had already written a letter to her brother the Margrave of Anspach, telling him how her husband had struck her in the face and given her a black eye, and she had already dispatched a messenger with the letter. After much arguing, Hans wrung from her her consent to come down, on two conditions, one that the Duke should visit her at once and beg her pardon, the other that the old[Pg 76] Kittlitz should sit at the table with the pages. The Duke was now in a yielding mood and ate his leek humbly. The Duchess consented to tell the Court that she had got her black eye from striking her face against a lamp, and the Duke ordered ten trumpeters and a kettledrum to make all the noise they could to celebrate the reconciliation.

The Duchess in an aside to Schweinichen admitted that she had been rash and unjust, and regretted having sent off that letter. An unlucky letter—says our author—for it cost the duchy untold gold and years of trouble.

The Duke had made several visits to Poland, chasing that Jack o' lantern—the Polish crown, and it had cost him so much money that he had quarrelled with his Estates, bullied and oppressed his subjects to extort money, and at last the Estates appealed to the Emperor against him, as they had against his father; and the Emperor summoned him to Prague. The Duke had great difficulty in scraping together money enough to convey him so far; and on reaching Prague, he begged permission of the Kaiser to be allowed to visit the Electors and the Free Cities, and see whether he could not obtain from them some relief from his embarrassments, and money wherewith to pacify the angry Estates of the Silesian Duchy. The consent required was given, and then the Duke with his faithful Schweinichen, and several other retainers, started on a grand begging and borrowing round of the Empire. Hans was constituted treasurer, and he had in his purse about £400. The Duke took with him five squires, two pages, three serving men, a[Pg 77] cook, and several kitchen boys, one carriage drawn by six horses, another by four. And not only was this train to make the round of the Empire, but also to visit Italy—and all on £400.

The first visit was paid, three days' journey from Prague, at Theusing to a half-sister of the Duchess. She received him coolly, and lectured him on his conduct to his wife. When the Duke asked her to lend him money, she answered that she would pay his expenses home, if he chose to go back to Liegnitz, but not one penny otherwise should he have. Not content with this refusal, the Duke went on to Nurnberg, where he sent Hans to the town council to invite them to lend him money; he asked for 4,000 florins. The council declined the honour. The two daughters of the Duke were in the charge of the Margrave of Anspach, their mother's brother. The Duke sent Hans to Anspach to urge the Margrave to send the little girls to him, or invite him to visit Anspach to see them. He was shy of visiting his brother-in-law uninvited, because of the box in the ear and the black eye. He confided to Hans that if he got his children at Nurnberg, he would not return them to their uncle, without a loan or a honorarium.

This shabby transaction was not to Schweinichen's taste, but he was obliged to undertake it. It proved unsuccessful, the Margrave refused to give up the children till the Duke returned to his wife and duchy and set a better example.

Whilst Hans was away, the Duke won a large sum of money at play, enough to pay his own bill, but instead of doing this with it, he had it melted up and[Pg 78] made into silver cups. When he came to leave Nurnberg he was unable to pay his inn bill, and obliged to leave in pawn with the taverner a valuable jewel. Then he and his suite went to Augsburg and settled into an inn till the town council could agree to lend him money.

One day, whilst there, Hans was invited to a wedding. The Duke wanted to go also, but, as he was not invited, he went as Hans' servant, but got so drunk that Hans was obliged to carry him home to the tavern, after which he returned to the wedding. In the evening, when dancing began, the Duke reappeared, he had slept off his drunkenness and was fresh for more entertainment. He was now recognized, and according to etiquette, two town councillors, in robes of office and gold chains, danced solemnly before his Highness. Hans tells us that it was customary for all dances to be led by two persons habited in scarlet with white sleeves, and these called the dance and set the figures, no one might execute any figure or do anything which had not been done by the leaders. Now as Hans vows he never saw so many pretty girls anywhere as on that evening, he tipped the leaders with half a thaler to kiss each other, whereupon the two solemn dancing councillors had also to kiss each other, and the Duke, nothing loth, his partner, and Hans, with zest, his. That evening he gave plenty of kisses, and what with the many lights, and the music and the dancing and the pretty girls he thought himself in Paradise. Shortly after this, the Duke was invited to dine with Fugger, the merchant prince, who showed him his[Pg 79] treasury, gold to the worth of a million, and one tower lined within from top half way down with nothing but silver thalers. The Duke's mouth watered, and he graciously invited Fugger to lend him £5,000; this the merchant declined, but made him a present of 200 crowns and a good horse. The town council consented to lend the Duke £1,200 on his I.O.U. for a year; and then to pay his host he melted up his silver mugs again, pawned his plate and gave him a promissory note for two months.

From Augsburg the Duke went about the abbeys, trying to squeeze loans out of the abbots, but found that they had always the excuse ready, that they would not lend to Lutheran princes. Then he stuck on in the abbeys, eating up all their provisions and rioting in their guest-apartments, till the abbots were fain to make him a present to be rid of him.

All at once an opening offered for the Duke to gain both renown and money. Henry I. of Condé was at the court of the Elector Palatine at Heidelsberg, soliciting assistance in behalf of the Huguenots against the King of France. The Elector agreed to send a force under his son John Casimir, and the Duke of Liegnitz offered his services, which were readily accepted. He was to lead the rearguard, and to receive a liberal pay for his services. Whilst he was collecting this force and getting underway, John Casimir and the Prince of Condé marched through Lorraine to Metz, and Hans went with John Casimir. He trusted he was now on his way to fortune. But it was not so to be. The Duke, his master, insisted that he should return to him, and Hans, on doing so, found[Pg 80] him rioting and gambling away, at Frankfort and Nassau, the money paid him in advance for his useless services. Almost the first duty imposed on Hans, on his return, was to negociate a loan for £5,000 with the magistrates of Frankfort, which was peremptorily refused; whereupon the Duke went to Cologne and stayed there seven months, endeavouring to cajole the town council there into advancing him money.

But we can not follow any further the miserable story of the degradation of the Silesian Duke, till at the beginning of the new year, 1577, the Duke ran away from the town of Emmerich, leaving his servants to pay his debts as best they could. Hans sold the horses and whatever was left, and then, not sorry to be quit of such a master, returned on foot to his Silesian home.

It is, perhaps, worth while quoting Duke Henry's letter, which Hans found in the morning announcing his master's evasion.

"Dear Hans,—Here is a chain, do what you can with it. Weigh it and sell it, also the horses for ready money; I will not pillow my head in feathers till, by God's help, I have got some money, to enable me to clear out of this vile land, and away from these people. Good morning, best-loved Hans.

"With mine own hand, HENRY, DUKE."

As he neared home, sad news reached Hans. The Ducal creditors had come down on his father, who had made himself responsible, and had seized the family estates; whereat the old man's heart broke, and he had died in January. When Hans heard this, he sat for two hours on a stone beside the road, utterly unmanned, before he could recover himself sufficiently to pursue his journey.

[Pg 81]

In the meantime an Imperial commission had sat on the Duke, deposed him, and appointed his brother Frederick duke in his room. Schweinichen's fidelity to Duke Henry ensured his disfavour with Duke Frederick, and he was not summoned to court, but was left quietly at Mertschütz to do his best along with his brother to bring the family affairs into some sort of order. His old master did not, however, allow him much rest. By the Imperial decision, he was to be provided with a daily allowance of money, food and wine.

This drew Duke Henry home, and no sooner was he back in Silesia than he insisted on Hans returning to his service, and for some years more he led the faithful soul a troubled life, and involved him in miserable pecuniary perplexities. This was the more trying to Hans as he had now fallen in love with Margaret von Schellendorff, whom he married eventually. The tenderness and goodness of Schweinichen's heart break out whenever he speaks of his dear Margaretta, and of the children which came and were taken from him. His sorrows as he lingered over the sick-beds of his little ones, and the closeness with which he was drawn by domestic bereavements and pecuniary distresses, to his Margaretta, come out clearly in his narrative. The whole story is far too long to tell in its entirety. Hans was a voluminous diarist. His memoirs cease at the year 1602, when he was suffering from gout, but he lived on some years longer.

In the church of S. John at Liegnitz was at one time his monument, with life-sized figure of Hans von Schweinichen, and above it his banner and an inscription[Pg 82] stating that he died on the 23rd Aug., 1616. Alas! the hand of the destroyer has been there. The church and monument are destroyed, and we can no longer see what manner of face Hans wore; but of the inner man, of a good, faithful, God fearing, and loving soul, strong and true, he has himself left us the most accurate portrait in his precious memoirs.

[Pg 83]
The Locksmith Gamain.

Among the many episodes of the French Revolution there is one which deserves to be somewhat closely examined, because of the gravity of the accusation which it involves against the King and Queen, and because a good deal of controversy has raged round it. The episode is that of the locksmith Gamain, whom the King and Queen are charged with having attempted to poison.

That the accusation was believed during "the Terror" goes without saying; the heated heads and angry hearts at that time were in no condition to sift evidence with impartiality. Afterwards, the charge was regarded as preposterous, till the late M. Paul Lacroix—better known as le Bibliophile Jacob—a student of history, very careful and diligent as a collector, gave it a new spell of life in 1836, when he reformulated the accusation in a *feuilleton* of the *Siècle*. Not content to let it sleep or die in the ephemeral pages of a newspaper, he republished the whole story in 1838, in his "Dissertations sur quelques points curieux de l'histoire de France." This he again reproduced in his "Curiosités de l'histoire de France," in 1858. M. Louis Blanc, convinced that the case was made out, has reasserted the charge in his work on the French Revolution, and it has since been accepted by popular writers—as [Pg 84]Décembre-Alonnier—who seek to justify the execution of the King and Queen, and to glorify the Revolution.

M. Thiers rejected the accusation; M. Eckard pointed out the improbabilities in the story in the "Biographie Universelle," and M. Mortimer-Ternaux has also shown its falsity in his "Histoire de la Terreur;" and finally, M. Le Roy, librarian of Versailles, in 1867, devoted his special attention to it, and completely disproved the poisoning of Gamain. But in spite of disproval the slanderous accusation does not die, and no doubt is still largely believed in Paris.

So tenacious of life is a lie—like the bacteria that can be steeped in sulphuric acid without destroying their vitality—that the story has been again recently raked up, and given to the public, from Lacroix, in a number of the Cornhill Magazine (December, 1887); the writer of course knew only Lacroix' myth, and had never seen how it had been disproved. It is well now to review the whole story.

François Gamain was born at Versailles on August 29, 1751. He belonged to an hereditary locksmith family. His father Nicolas had been in the same trade, and had charge of the locks in the royal palaces in Versailles and elsewhere.

The love of Louis XVI. for mechanical works is well known. He had a little workshop at Versailles, where he amused himself making locks, assisted by François Gamain, to whom he was much attached, and with whom he spent many hours in projecting and executing mechanical contrivances. The story is told of the Intendant Thierry, that when one day the King showed him a lock he had made, he replied,[Pg 85] "Sire, when kings occupy themselves with the works of the common people, the common people will assume the functions of kings," but the *mot* was probably made after the fact.

After the terrible days of the 5th and 6th of October, 1789, the King was brought to Paris. Gamain remained at Versailles, which was his home, and retained the King's full confidence.

When, later, the King was surrounded by enemies, and he felt the necessity for having some secret place where he could conceal papers of importance which might yet fall into the hands of the rabble if the palace was again invaded, as it had been at Versailles, he sent for Gamain to make for him an iron chest in a place of concealment, that could only be opened by one knowing the secret of the lock.

Unfortunately, the man was not as trustworthy as Louis XVI. supposed. Surrounded by those who had adopted the principles of the Revolution, and being a man without strong mind, he followed the current, and in 1792 he was nominated member of the Council General of the Commune of Versailles, and on September 24 he was one of the commissioners appointed "to cause to disappear all such paintings, sculptures, and inscriptions from the monuments of the Commune as might serve to recall royalty and despotism."

The records of the debates of the Communal Council show that Gamain attended regularly and took part in the discussions, which were often tumultuous.

The Queen heard of Gamain's Jacobinism, and[Pg 86] warned the King, who, however, could not believe that Gamain would betray him. Marie Antoinette insisted on the most important papers being removed from the iron chest, and they were confided to Mme. de Campan.

When the trial of the King was begun, on November 20, Gamain went to Roland, Minister of the Interior, and told him the secret of the iron chest. Roland, alarmed at the consequences of such a discovery, hastened to consult his wife, who was in reality more minister than himself.

From August 10, a commission had been appointed to collect all the papers found in the Tuileries; this commission, therefore, ought to be made acquainted with the discovery; but here lay the danger. Mme. Roland, as an instrument of the Girondins, feared that among the papers in the chest might be discovered some which would show in what close relations the Girondins stood to the Court. She decided that her husband should go to the Tuileries, accompanied by Gamain, an architect, and a servant. The chest was opened by the locksmith, Roland removed all the papers, tied them up in a napkin, and took them home. They were taken the same day to the Convention; and the commission charged the minister with having abstracted such papers as would have been inconvenient to him to deliver up.

When Roland surrendered the papers he declared, without naming Gamain, that they had been discovered in a hole in the wall closed by an iron door, behind a wainscot panel, in so secret a place "that they could not have been found had not the secret[Pg 87] been disclosed by the workman who had himself made the place of concealment."

On December 24 following, Gamain was summoned to Paris by the Convention to give his evidence to prove that a key discovered in the desk of Thierry de Ville-d'Avray fitted the iron chest.

After the execution of the King, on January 21, 1793, the Convention sent deputies into all the departments "to stimulate the authorities to act with the energy requisite under the circumstances." Crassous was sent into the department of Seine-et-Oise; and not finding the municipality of Versailles, of which Gamain was a member, "up to the requisite pitch," he discharged them from office; and by a law of September 17, all such discharged functionaries were declared to be "suspected persons," who were liable to be brought before the revolutionary tribunal on that charge alone.

Thus, in spite of all the proofs he had given of his fidelity to the principles of the Revolution, Gamain was at any moment liable to arrest, and to being brought before that terrible tribunal from which the only exit was to the guillotine. Moreover, Gamain had lost his place and emoluments as Court locksmith; he had fallen into great poverty, was without work, and without health.

On April 27, 1794, he presented a petition to the Convention which was supported by Musset, the deputy and constitutional curé. "It was not enough," said Musset from the tribune, "that the last of our tyrants should have delivered over thousands of citizens to be slain by the sword of the enemy. You[Pg 88] will see by the petition I am about to read that he was familiarised with the most refined cruelty, and that he himself administered poison to the father of a family, in the hopes thereby of destroying evidence of his perfidy. You will see that his ferocious mind had adopted the maxim that to a king everything is permissible."

After this preamble Musset read the petition of Gamain, which is as follows: "François Gamain, locksmith to the cabinets and to the laboratory of the late King, and for three years member of the Council General of the Commune of Versailles, declares that at the beginning of May 1792 he was ordered to go to Paris. On reaching it, Capet required him to make a cupboard in the thickness of one of the walls of his room, and to fasten it with an iron door; and he further states that he was thus engaged up to the 22nd of the said month, and that he worked in the King's presence. When the chest was completed, Capet himself offered citizen Gamain a large tumbler of wine, and asked him to drink it, as he, the said Gamain, was very hot.

"*A few hours later* he was attacked by a violent colic, which did not abate till he had taken two spoonfuls of elixir, which made him vomit all he had eaten and drunk that day. This was the prelude to a terrible illness, which lasted fourteen months, during which he lost the use of his limbs, and which has left him at present without hope of recovering his full health, and of working so as to provide for the necessities of his family."

After reading the petition Musset added: "I hold[Pg 89] in my hands the certificate of the doctors, that testifies to the bad state of the health of the citizen petitioner.

"Citizens! If wickedness is common to kings, generosity is the prerogative of the free people. I demand that this petition be referred to the Committee of Public Assistance to be promptly dealt with. I demand that after the request all the papers relating to it be deposed in the national archives, as a monument of the atrocity of tyrants, and be inserted in the bulletin, that all those who have supposed that Capet did evil only at the instigation of others may know that crime was rooted in his very heart." This proposition was decreed. On May 17, 1794, the representative Peyssard mounted the tribune, and read the report of the Committee, which we must condense.

"Citizens! At the tribunal of liberty the crimes of the oppressors of the human race stand to be judged. To paint a king in all his hideousness I need name only Louis XVI. This name sums in itself all crimes; it recalls a prodigy of iniquity and of perfidy. Hardly escaped from infancy, the germs of the ferocious perversity which characterise a despot appeared in him. His earliest sports were with blood, and his brutality grew with his years, and he delighted in wreaking his ferocity on all the animals he met. He was known to be cruel, treacherous, and murderous. The object of this report is to exhibit him to France cold-bloodedly offering a cup of poison to the unhappy artist whom he had just employed to construct a cupboard in which to conceal the plots of tyranny. It was no stranger he marked as his victim,[Pg 90] but a workman whom he had employed for five-and-twenty years, and the father of a family, his own instructor in the locksmith's art. Monsters who thus treat their chosen servants, how will they deal with the rest of men?"

The National Convention thereupon ordered that "François Gamain, poisoned by Louis Capet on May 22, 1792, should enjoy an annual pension of the sum of 1,200 livres, dating from the day on which he was poisoned."

It will be noticed by the most careless reader that the evidence is *nil*. Gamain does not feel the colic till some hours after he has drunk the wine; he had eaten or drunk other things besides during the day; and finally the testimony of the doctors is, not that he was poisoned, but that, at the time of his presenting the petition, he was in a bad state of health. Accordingly, all reasonable historians, unblinded by party passion, have scouted the idea of an attempt on Gamain's life by the King. Thus the matter would have remained had not M. Paul Lacroix taken it up and propped the old slander on new legs. We will take his account, which he pretends to have received from several persons to whom Gamain related it repeatedly. This is his *mise en scène*.

"The old inhabitants of Versailles will remember with pity the man whom they often encountered alone, bowed on his stick like one bent with years. Gamain was aged only fifty-eight when he died, but he bore all the marks of decrepitude."

Here is a blunder, to begin with; he died, as the Versailles registers testify, on May 8, 1795, and was[Pg 91] accordingly only forty-four years old,—that is, he died *one* year after the grant of the annuity. M. Parrott, in his article on Gamain in the "Dictionnaire de la Révolution Française," says that he died in 1799, five years after having received his pension; but the Versailles registers are explicit.

M. Lacroix goes on: "His hair had fallen off, and the little that remained had turned white over a brow furrowed deeply; the loss of his teeth made his cheeks hollow; his dull eyes only glared with sombre fire when the name of Louis XVI was pronounced. Sometimes even tears then filled them. Gamain lived very quietly with his family on his humble pension, which, notwithstanding the many changes of government, was always accorded him. It was not suppressed, lest the reason of its being granted should again be raked up before the public."

As we have seen, Gamain died under the Government which granted the pension. M. Lacroix goes on to say "that the old locksmith bore to his dying day an implacable hatred of Louis XVI., whom he accused of having been guilty of an abominable act of treachery."

"This act of treachery was the fixed and sole idea in Gamain's head, he recurred to it incessantly, and poured forth a flood of bitter and savage recriminations against the King. It was Gamain who disclosed the secret of the iron chest in the Tuileries, and the papers it contained, which furnished the chief accusation against Louis XVI.; it was he, therefore, who had, so to speak, prepared the guillotine for the royal head; it was he, finally, who provoked the[Pg 92] decree of the Convention which blackened the memory of the King as that of a vulgar murderer. But this did not suffice the hate of Gamain, who went about everywhere pursuing the dead beyond the tomb, with his charge of having attempted murder as payment of life-long and devoted service. Gamain ordinarily passed his evenings in a cafe at Versailles, the name of which I have been told, but which I do not divulge lest I should make a mistake. He was generally in the society of two old notaries, who are still alive (in 1836), and of the doctor Lameyran, who attended him when he was poisoned. These three persons were prepared to attest all the particulars of the poisoning which had been proved at the *procès verbal*. Gamain, indeed, lacked witnesses to establish the incidents of the 22nd May, 1792, at the Tuileries; but his air of veracity and expression of pain, his accent of conviction, his face full of suffering, his burning eyes, his pathetic pantomime, were the guarantees of good faith."

These three men, the notaries and the doctor, which latter M. Lacroix hints was living when he wrote, were his authorities for what follows. The notaries he does not name, nor the café where they met. His account published in the *Siècle* at once attracted attention, and M. Lacroix was challenged to produce his witnesses. As for M. Lameyran, the doctor, he had died in 1811; consequently his testimony was not to be had in 1836. The other doctor who had attended Gamain was M. Voisin, who died in 1823, but M. Le Roy asserts positively that in 1813 M. Voisin told him, "Never was Gamain poisoned. Lameyran and I had long[Pg 93] attended him for chronic malady of the stomach. This is all we testified to in our certificate, when he applied for a pension. In our certificate we stated that he was in weak health—not a word was in it about poisoning, which existed only in his fancy."

These certificates are no longer in existence. They were not preserved in the archives of the Convention. Even this fact is taken as evidence in favour of the attempt. M. Emile Bonnet, in an article on Gamain in the "Intermédiaire des Chercheurs," declares that they have been substracted since the Restoration of Charles;[8] but there is no trace in the archives of them ever having been there. Moreover, we have M. Le Roy's word that M. Voisin assured him he had not testified to poisoning, and, what is more important, we have Musset's declaration before the Convention that the certificate of the doctors "asserted the ill-health of the claimant." If there had been a word about poison in it, he would assuredly have said so.

M. Lacroix was asked to name his authorities—the two advocates who, as M. Lameyran was dead, were alive and would testify to the fact that they had heard the story from the lips of Gamain. He remained silent. He would not even name the café where they met, and which might lead to the identification. M. Eckard, who wrote the notice on Gamain in the "Biographie Universelle," consulted the family of the locksmith on the case, and was assured by them that the bad health of Gamain was due to no other cause than disappointment at the loss of his fortune, the[Pg 94] privations he underwent, and, above all, his terror for his life after his dismissal from the Communal Council.

We will now continue M. Lacroix's account, which he proceeds, not a little disingenuously, to put into the mouth of Gamain himself, so that the accusation may not be charged on the author.

"On May 21, 1792," says Gamain, according to the "Bibliophile Jacob," "whilst I was working in my shop, a horseman drew up at my door and called me out. His disguise as a carter did not prevent me from recognising Durey, the King's forge assistant. I refused. I congratulated myself that evening at having done so, as the rumour spread in Versailles that the Tuileries had been attacked by the mob, but this did not really take place till a month later. Next morning Durey returned and showed me a note in the King's own hand, entreating me to lend my assistance in a difficult job past his unaided powers. My pride was flattered. I embraced my wife and children, without telling them whither I was going, but I promised to return that night. It was not without anxiety that they saw me depart with a stranger for Paris."

We need merely point out that Durey was no stranger to the family: he had been for years associated daily with Gamain.

"Durey conducted me to the Tuileries, where the King was guarded as in a prison. We went at once to the royal workshop, where Durey left me, whilst he went to announce my arrival. Whilst I was alone, I observed an iron door, recently forged, a mortise lock, well executed, and a little iron box with a secret[Pg 95] spring which I did not at once discover. Then in came Durey with the King. 'The times are bad,' said Louis XVI., 'and I do not know how matters will end.' Then he showed me the works I had noticed, and said, 'What do you say to my skill? It took me ten days to execute these things. I am your apprentice, Gamain.' I protested my entire devotion. Then the King assured me that he always had confidence in me, and that he did not scruple to trust the fate of himself and his family in my hands. Thereupon he conducted me into the dark passage that led from his room to the chamber of the Dauphin. Durey lit a taper, and removed a panel in the passage, behind which I perceived a round hole, about two feet in diameter, bored in the wall. The King told me he intended to secrete his money in it, and that Durey, who had helped to make it, threw the dust and chips into the river during the night. Then the King told me that he was unable to fit the iron door to the hole unassisted. I went to work immediately. I went over all the parts of the lock, and got them into working order; then I fashioned a key to the lock, then made hinges and fastened them into the wall as firmly as I could, without letting the hammering be heard. The King helped as well as he was able, entreating me every moment to strike with less noise, and to be quicker over my work. The key was put in the little iron casket, and this casket was concealed under a slab of pavement in the corridor."

It will be seen that this story does not agree with the account in the petition made by Gamain to the Convention. In that he said he was summoned to[Pg 96] Paris at the beginning of the month of May, and that "Capet ordered him to make a cupboard in the thickness of the wall of his apartment, and to close it with an iron door, the whole of which was not accomplished till the 22nd of the same month." He was three weeks over the job, not a few hours. "I had been working," continues Gamain, or M. Lacroix for him, "for eight consecutive hours. The sweat poured from my brow; I was impatient to repose, and faint with hunger, as I had eaten nothing since I got up."

But, according to his account before the Convention, the elixir made him throw up "all he had eaten and drunk during the day."

"I seated myself a moment in the King's chamber, and he asked me to count for him two thousand double louis and tie them up in four leather bags. Whilst so doing I observed that Durey was carrying some bundles of papers which I conjectured were destined for the secret closet; and, indeed, the money-counting was designed to distract my attention from what Durey was about."

What a clumsy story! Why were not the papers hidden after Gamain was gone? Was it necessary that this should be done in his presence, and he set to count money, so as not to observe what was going on?

"As I was about to leave, the Queen suddenly entered by a masked door at the foot of the King's bed, holding in her hands a plate, in which was a cake (brioche) and a glass of wine. She came up to me, and I saluted her with surprise, because the King had assured me that she knew nothing about the[Pg 97] fabrication of the chest. 'My dear Gamain,' said she in a caressing tone, 'how hot you are! Drink this tumbler of wine and eat this

39

cake, and they will sustain you on your journey home.' I thanked her, confounded by this consideration for a poor workman, and I emptied the tumbler to her health. I put the cake in my pocket, intending to take it home to my children."

Here again is a discrepancy. In his petition Gamain says that the King gave him a glass of wine, and makes no mention of the Queen.

On leaving the Tuileries, Gamain set out on foot for Versailles, but was attacked by a violent colic in the Champs Elysées. His agonies increased; he was no longer able to walk; he fell, and rolled on the ground, uttering cries and moans. A carriage that was passing stopped, and an English gentleman got out—wonderful to relate!—extraordinary coincidence!—a physician, and an acquaintance.

"The Englishman took me to his carriage, and ordered the coachman to drive at full gallop to an apothecary's shop. The conveyance halted at last before one in the Rue de Bac; the Englishman left me alone, whilst he prepared an elixir which might counteract the withering power of the poison. When I had swallowed this draught I ejected the venomous substances. An hour later nothing could have saved me. I recovered in part my sight and hearing; the cold that circulated in my veins was dissipated by degrees, and the Englishman judged that I might be safely removed to Versailles, which we reached at two o'clock in the morning. A physician, M. de[Pg 98] Lameyran, and a surgeon, M. Voisin, were called in; they recognised the unequivocal tokens of poison.

"After three days of fever, delirium, and inconceivable suffering, I triumphed over the poison, but suffered ever after from a paralysis almost complete, and a general inflammation of the digestive organs.

"A few days after this catastrophe the servant maid, whilst cleaning my coat, which I had worn on the occasion of my accident, found my handkerchief, stained black, and the cake. She took a bite of the latter, and threw the rest into the yard, where a dog ate it and died. The girl, who had consumed only a morsel of the cake, fell dangerously ill. The dog was opened by M. Voisin, and a chemical analysis disclosed the presence of poison, both on my kerchief stained by my vomit, and in the cake. The cake alone contained enough corrosive sublimate to kill ten persons."

So—the poison was found. But how is it that in Gamain's petition none of this occurs? According to that document, Gamain was offered a goblet of wine by the King himself. "A few hours later he was attacked by a violent colic. This was the prelude to a terrible illness." Only a vague hint as to poison, no specific statement that he had been poisoned, and that the kind of poison had been determined.

Now, corrosive sublimate, when put in red wine, forms a violet precipitate, and alters the taste of the wine, giving it a characteristic metallic, harsh flavour, so disagreeable that it insures its immediate rejection. Gamain tasted nothing. Again, the action of corrosive sublimate is immediate or very nearly so; but[Pg 99] Gamain was not affected till several hours after having drunk the wine.

According to the petition, Gamain asserted that he was paralysed in all his limbs for fourteen months, from May 22, 1792; but the Communal registers of Versailles show that he attended a session of the Council and took part in the discussion on June 4 following, that is, less than a fortnight after; that he was present at the sessions of June 8, 17, 20, and on August 22, and that he was sufficiently hearty and active to be elected on the commission which was to obliterate the insignia of monarchy on September 24 following, which certainly would not have been the case had he been a sick man paralysed in all his members.

Why, we may further inquire, did not Louis the XVI. or Queen Marie Antoinette attempt to poison Durey also, if they desired to make away with all those who knew the secret of the iron locker?

Now, Durey was alive in 1800, and Eckard, who wrote the article on Gamain in the "Biographie Universelle," knew him and saw him at that date, and Durey told him that Gamain's story was a lie; the iron safe was made, not in 1792, but in May, 1791; and this is probable, as it would have been easier for the King to have the locker made before his escape to Varennes, than in 1792, when he was under the closest supervision.

According to the version attributed to Gamain by M. Paul Lacroix, Gamain was paralysed for five months only. Why this change? Because either M. Lacroix or the locksmith had discovered that it was[Pg 100] an anachronism for him to appear in November before Roland, and assist him in opening the case which he had made in May—five months before, and afterwards to declare that he was paralysed in all his members from May till the year following. We think this correction is due to the Bibliophile. But he was not acquainted with the Versailles archives proving him to have been at a session a few days after the pretended poisoning.

There is not much difficulty in discovering Gamain's motive for formulating the accusation against the King. He betrayed his king, who trusted him, and then, to excuse his meanness, invented an odious calumny against him.

But what was M. Lacroix's object in revivifying the base charge? We are not sure that he comes cleaner out of the slough than the despicable locksmith. He gave the story a new spell of life; he based his "facts" on testimonies, who, he said, were ready at any moment to vouch for the truth. When challenged to produce them he would not do so. His "facts" were proved again and again to be fables, and yet he dared to republish his slanderous story again and again, without a word of apology, explanation, or retractation. M. Lacroix died only a year or two ago, and it may seem ungenerous to attack a dead man, but one is forced to do this in defence of the honour of a dead Queen whom he grossly calumniated. The calumny was ingeniously put. M. Lacroix set it in the mouth of Gamain, thinking thereby to free himself from responsibility, but the responsibility sticks when he refuses to withdraw what has been demonstrated to be false.

[Pg 101]

There is something offensive to the last degree in the pose of M. Lacroix as he opens his charge. "For some years I have kept by me, with a sort of terror, the materials for an historic revelation, without venturing to use them, and yet the fact, now almost unknown, on which I purpose casting a sinister light, is one that has been the object of my most active preoccupations. For long I condemned myself to silence and to fresh research, hitherto fruitless, hoping that the truth would come to light.... Well! now, at the moment of lifting the veil which covers a half-effaced page of history, with the documents I have consulted and the evidence I have gleaned lying before me, surrounded by a crowd of witnesses, one sustaining the testimony of the other, relying on my conscience and on my sentiments as a man of honour—still I hesitate to open my mouth and call up the remembrance of an event monstrous in itself, that has not found an echo even in the writings of the blindest partisans of a hideous epoch. Yes, I feel a certain repugnance in seeming to associate in thought, though not in act, with the enemies of Louis XVI. I have just re-read the sublime death of this unhappy political martyr; I have felt my eyes moisten with tears at the contemplation of the picture of the death inflicted by an inexorable state necessity, and I felt I must break my pen lest I should mix my ink with the yet warm blood of the innocent victim. Let my hand wither rather than rob Louis XVI. of the mantle of probity and goodness, which the outrages of '93 succeeded neither in staining nor in rending to rags." And so on—M. Lacroix is only acting under a high[Pg 102] sense of the sacred duty of seeking the truth, "of forcing the disclosure of facts, before it be too late," which may establish the innocence of Louis XVI. Now, be it noted that M. Lacroix is the first to accuse the Queen of attempting the murder; his assault is on her as much as, more than, on the poor King—in the sacred interests of historic truth!

What are his evidences, his crowd of witnesses, his documents that he has collected? What proof is there of his active preoccupations and fresh researches? He produced nothing that can be called proof, and refused the names of his witnesses when asked for them. We can quite understand that the Bibliophile Jacob may have heard some gossiping story such as he narrates, and may have believed it when he wrote the story; but then, where are the high sense of honour, the tender conscience, the enthusiasm for truth, when his story is proved to be a tissue of improbabilities and impossibilities, that permit him to republish, and again republish at intervals of years, this cruel and calumnious fabrication?

FOOTNOTE:

[8] Le Bibliophile Jacob says the same: "Les—pièces—détournées maladroitement par la Restauration."

[Pg 103]
Abram the Usurer.[9]

In the reign of Heraclius, when Sergius was patriarch of Constantinople, there lived in Byzantium a merchant named Theodore, a good man and just, fearing God, and serving him with all his heart. He went on a voyage to the ports of Syria and Palestine with his wares, in a large well-laden vessel, sold his goods to profit, and turned his ship's head homewards with a good lading of silks and spices, the former some of the produce of the looms of distant China, brought in caravans through Persia and Syria to the emporiums on the Mediterranean.

It was late in the year when Theodore began his voyage home, the equinoctial gales had begun to blow, and prudence would have suggested that he should winter in Cyprus; but he was eager to return to Byzantium to his beloved wife, and to prepare for another adventure in the ensuing spring.

But he was overtaken by a storm as he was sailing up the Propontis, and to save the vessel he was obliged to throw all the lading overboard. He[Pg 104] reached Constantinople in safety, but with the loss of his goods. His grief and despair were excessive. His wife was unable to console him. He declared that he was weary of the world, his loss was sent him as a warning from heaven not to set his heart on Mammon, and that he was resolved to enter a monastery, and spend the rest of his days in devotion.

"Hasten, husband mine," said the wife, "put this scheme into execution at once; for if you delay you may change your mind."

The manifest impatience of his wife to get rid of him somewhat cooled the ardour of Theodore for the monastic profession, and before taking the irrevocable step, he consulted a friend. "I think, dearest brother, nay, I am certain, that this misfortune came on me as the indication of the finger of Providence that I should give up merchandise and care only for the saving of my soul."

"My friend," answered the other, "I do not see this in the same light as you. Every merchant must expect loss. It is one of the ordinary risks of sailors. It is absurd to despair. Go to your friends and borrow of them sufficient to load your vessel again, and try your luck once more. You are known as a merchant, and trusted as an honest man, and will have no difficulty in raising the sum requisite."

Theodore rushed home, and announced to his wife that he had already changed his mind, and that he was going to borrow money.

"Whatever pleases you is right in my eyes," said the lady.

Theodore then went the round of his acquaintances,[Pg 105] told them of his misfortune, and then asked them to lend him enough to restock his vessel, promising to pay them a good percentage on the money lent. But the autumn had been fatal to more vessels than that of Theodore, and he found that no one was disposed to advance him the large sum he required. He went from door to door, but a cold refusal met him everywhere. Disappointed, and sick at heart, distressed at finding friends so unfriendly, he returned home, and said to his wife, "Woman! the world is hard and heartless, I will have nothing more to do with it. I will become a monk."

"Dearest husband, do so by all means, and I shall be well pleased," answered the wife.

Theodore tossed on his bed all night, unable to sleep; before dawn an idea struck him. There was a Jew named Abram who had often importuned him to trade with his money, but whom he had invariably refused. He would try this man as a last resource.

So when morning came, Theodore rose and went to the shop of Abram. The Hebrew listened attentively to his story, and then said, smiling, "Master Theodore, when thou wast rich, I often asked thee to take my money and trade with it in foreign parts, so that I might turn it over with advantage. But I always met with refusal. And now that thou art poor, with only an empty ship, thou comest to me to ask for a loan. What if again tempest should fall on thee, and wreck and ruin be thy lot, where should I look for my money? Thou art poor. If I were to sell thy house it would not fetch much. Nay, if I am to lend thee money thou must provide a surety, to whom I[Pg 106] may apply, and who will repay me, should accident befall thee. Go, find security, and I will find the money."

So Theodore went to his best friend, and told him the circumstances, and asked him to stand surety for him to the Jew.

"Dear friend," answered he, "I should be most happy to oblige you; but I am a poor man, I have not as much money in the world as would suffice. The Hebrew would not accept me as surety, he knows the state of my affairs too well. But I will do for you what little I can. We will go together to some merchants, and together beseech them to stand security for you to the Jew."

So the two friends went to a rich merchant with whom they were acquainted, and told him what they wanted; but he blustered and turned red, and said, "Away with you, fellows; who ever heard of such insolence as that two needy beggars should ask a man of substance like me to go with them to the den of a cursed infidel Jew. God be thanked! I have no dealings with Jews. I never have spoken to one in my life, and never give them a greeting when I pass any in street or market-place. A man who goes to the Jews to-day, goes to the dogs to-morrow, and to the devil the day after."

The friends visited other merchants, but with like ill-success. Theodore had spent the day fasting, and he went supperless to bed, very hopeless, and with the prospect growing more distinct of being obliged to put on the cowl of the monk, a prospect which somehow or other he did not relish.

[Pg 107]

Next morning he started from home to tell Abram his failure. His way was through the great square called the Copper-Market before the Imperial palace. Now there stood there a porch consisting of four pillars, which supported a dome covered with brazen tiles, the whole surmounted by a cross, on the east side of which, looking down on the square, and across over the sparkling Bosphorus to the hills of Asia, was a large, solemn figure of the Crucified. This porch and cross had been set up by Constantine the Great,[10] and had been restored by Anastasius.

As Theodore sped through the Copper-Market in the morning, he looked up; the sky was of the deepest gentian blue. Against it, glittering like gold in the early sun, above the blazing, brazen tiles, stood the great cross with the holy form thereon. Theodore halted, in his desolation, doubt and despair, and looked up at the figure. It was in the old, grave Byzantine style, very solemn, without the pain expressed in Mediæval crucifixes, and like so many early figures of the sort was probably vested and crowned.

A sudden inspiration took hold of the ruined man. He fell on his knees, stretched his hands towards the[Pg 108] shining form, and cried, "Lord Jesus Christ! the hope of the whole earth, the only succour of all who are cast down, the sure confidence of those that look to Thee! All on whom I could lean have failed me. I have none on earth on whom I can call. Do Thou, Lord, be surety for me, though I am unworthy to ask it." Then filled with confidence he rose from his knees, and ran to the house of Abram, and bursting in on him said, "Be of good cheer, I have found a Surety very great and noble and mighty. Trust thy money, He will keep it safe."

Abram answered, "Let the man come, and sign the deed and see the money paid over."

"Nay, my brother," said Theodore; "come thou with me. I have hurried in thus to bring thee to him."

Then Abram went with Theodore, who led him to the Copper-Market, and bade him be seated, and then raising his finger, he pointed to the sacred form hanging on the cross, and, full of confidence, said to the Hebrew, "There, friend, thou could'st not have a better security than the Lord of heaven and earth. I have besought Him to stand for me, and I know He is so good that He will not deny me."

The Jew was perplexed. He said nothing for a moment or two, and then, wondering at the man's faith, answered, "Friend, dost thou not know the difference between the faith of a Christian and of a Hebrew? How can'st thou ask me to accept as thy surety, One whom thou believest my people to have rejected and crucified? However, I will trust thee, for thou art a God-fearing and an honest man, and I will risk my money."

[Pg 109]

So they twain returned to the Jew's quarters, and Abram counted out fifty pounds of gold, in our money about £2,400. He tied the money up in bags, and bade his servants bear it after Theodore. And Abram and the glad merchant came to the Copper-Market, and then the Jew ordered that the money bags should be set down under the Tetrastyle where was the great crucifix. Then said the Hebrew usurer, "See, Theodore, I make over to thee the loan here before thy God." And there, in the face of the great image of his Saviour, Theodore received the loan, and swore to deal faithfully by the Jew, and to restore the money to him with usury.

After this, the merchant bought a cargo for his vessel, and hired sailors, and set sail for Syria. He put into port at Tyre and Sidon, and traded with his goods, and bought in place of them many rich Oriental stuffs, with spices and gums, and when his ship was well laden, he sailed for Constantinople.

But again misfortune befell him. A storm arose, and the sailors were constrained to throw the bales of silk, and bags of costly gums, and vessels of Oriental chasing into the greedy waves. But as the ship began to fill, they were obliged to get into the boat and escape to land. The ship keeled over and drifted into shallow water. When the storm abated they got to her, succeeded in floating her, and made the best of their way in the battered ship to Constantinople, thankful that they had preserved their lives. But

Theodore was in sad distress, chiefly because he had lost Abram's money. "How shall I dare to face the man who dealt so generously by me?" he said to[Pg 110] himself. "What shall I say, when he reproaches me? What answer can I make to my Surety for having lost the money entrusted to me?"

Now when Abram heard that Theodore had arrived in Constantinople in his wrecked vessel with the loss of all his cargo, he went to him at once, and found the man prostrate in his chamber, the pavement wet with his tears of shame and disappointment. Abram laid his hand gently on his shoulder, and said, in a kind voice, "Rise, my brother, do not be downcast; give glory to God who rules all things as He wills, and follow me home. God will order all for the best."

Then the merchant rose, and followed the Jew, but he would not lift his eyes from the ground, for he was ashamed to look him in the face. Abram was troubled at the distress of his friend, and he said to him, as he shut the door of his house, "Let not thy heart be broken with overmuch grief, dearest friend, for it is the mark of a wise man to bear all things with firm mind. See! I am ready again to lend thee fifty pounds of gold, and may better fortune attend thee this time. I trust that our God will bless the money and multiply it, so that in the end we shall lose nothing by our former misadventure."

"Then," said Theodore, "Christ shall again stand security for me. Bring the money to the Tetrastyle."

Therefore again the bags of gold were brought before the cross, and when they had then been made over to the merchant, Abram said, "Accept, Master Theodore, this sum of fifty pounds of gold, paid over to thee before thy Surety, and go in peace. And may the[Pg 111] Lord God prosper thee on thy journey, and make plain the way before thee. And remember, that before this thy Surety thou art bound to me for a hundred pounds of gold."

Having thus spoken, Abram returned home. Theodore repaired and reloaded his ship, engaged mariners and made ready to sail. But on the day that he was about to depart, he went into the Copper-Market, and kneeling down, with his face towards the cross, he prayed the Lord to be his companion and captain, and to guide him on his journey, and bring him safe through all perils with his goods back to Byzantium once more.

Then he went on to the house of Abram to bid him farewell. And the Jew said to him, "Keep thyself safe, brother, and beware now of trusting thy ship to the sea at the time of equinoctial gales. Thou hast twice experienced the risk, run not into it again. Winter at the place whither thou goest, and that I may know how thou farest, if thou hast the opportunity, send me some of the money by a sure hand. Then there is less chance of total ruin, for if one portion fails, the other is likely to be secure."

Theodore approved of this advice, and promised to follow it; so then the Jew and the Christian parted with much affection and mutual respect, for each knew the other to be a good and true man, fearing God, and seeking to do that which is right. This time Theodore turned his ship's head towards the West, intending to carry his wares to the markets of Spain. He passed safely through the Straits of Hercules, and sailed North. Then a succession of[Pg 112] steady strong breezes blew from the South and swept him on so that he could not get into harbour till he reached Britain. He anchored in a bay on the rugged Cornish coast, in the very emporium of tin and lead, in the Cassiterides famed of old for supplying ore precious in the manufacture of bronze. He readily disposed of all his merchandise, and bought as much tin and lead as his ship would hold. His goods had sold so well, and tin and lead were so cheap that he found he had fifty pounds in gold in addition to the cargo.

The voyage back from Britain to Byzantium was long and dangerous, and Theodore was uneasy. He found no other ships from Constantinople where he was, and no means presented themselves for sending back the money in part, as he had promised. He was a conscientious man, and he wished to keep his word.

He set sail from Cornwall before the summer was over, passed safely through the straits into the Mediterranean, but saw no chance of reaching Constantinople before winter. He would not again risk his vessel in the gales of the equinox, and he resolved to winter in Sicily. He arrived too late in the year to be able to send a message and the money to Abram. His promise troubled him, and he cast about in his mind how to keep his word.

At last, in the simple faith which coloured the whole life of the man, he made a very solid wooden box and tarred it well internally and externally. Then he inclosed in it the fifty pounds of gold he had made by his goods in Britain over and above his[Pg 113] lading of lead and tin, and with the money he put a letter, couched in these terms:

"In the name of my heir and God, my Lord and Saviour Jesus Christ who is also my Surety for a large sum of money, I, Theodore, humbly address my master Abram, who, with God, is my benefactor and creditor.

"I would have thee know, Master Abram, that we all, by the mercy of God, are in good health. God has verily prospered us well and brought our merchandise to a good market. And now, see! I send thee fifty pounds of gold, which I commit to the care of my Surety, and He will convey the money safely to thy hands. Receive it from me and do not forget us. Farewell."

Then he fastened up the box, and raised his eyes to heaven, and prayed to God, saying: "O Lord Jesus Christ, Mediator between God and Man, Who dwellest in Heaven, but hast respect unto the lowly; hear the voice of thy servant this day; because Thou hast proved Thyself to me a good and kind Surety, I trust to Thee to return to my benefactor and creditor, Abram, the money I promised to send him. Trusting in Thee, Lord, I commit this little box to the sea!"

So saying he flung the case containing the gold and the letter into the waves; and standing on a cliff watched it floating on the waters, rising and falling on the glittering wavelets, gradually drifting further and further out to sea, till it was lost to his sight, and then, nothing doubting but that the Lord Christ would look after the little box and guide it over the waste of waters to its proper destination, he went[Pg 114] back to his lodging, and told the ship pilot what he had done. The sailor remained silent wondering in his mind at the great faith of his master. Then his rough heart softened, and he knelt down and blessed and praised God.

That night Theodore had a dream, and in the morning he told it to the pilot.

"I thought," said he, "that I was back in Byzantium, and standing in the Copper-Market before the great cross with Christ on it. And I fancied in my dream that Abram was at my side. And I looked, and saw him hold up his hands, and receive the box in them, and the great figure of Christ said, 'See, Abram, I give thee what Theodore committed to my trust.' And, thereupon, I awoke trembling. So now I am quite satisfied that the gold is in safe keeping, and will infallibly reach its destination."

The summer passed, the storms of autumn had swept over the grey sea, and torn away from the trees the last russet leaves; winter had set in; yet Abram had received no news of Theodore.

He did not doubt the good faith of his friend, but he began to fear that ill-luck attended him. He had risked a large sum, and would feel the loss severely should this cargo be lost like the former one. He talked the matter over with his steward, and considered it from every imaginable point of view. His anxiety took him constantly to the shore to watch the ships that arrived, hoping to hear news by some of them, and to recover part of his money. He hardly expected the return of Theodore after the injunctions he had given him not to risk his vessel in a stormy season.

[Pg 115]

One day he was walking with his steward by the sea-side, when the waves were more boisterous than usual. Not a ship was visible. All were in winter quarters. Abram drew off his sandals, and began to wash his feet in the sea water. Whilst so doing he observed something floating at a little distance. With the assistance of his steward he fished out a box black with tar, firmly fastened up, like a solid cube of wood. Moved by curiosity he carried the box home, and succeeded with a little difficulty in forcing it open. Inside he found a letter, not directed, but marked with three crosses, and a bag of gold. It need hardly be said that this was the box Theodore had entrusted to Christ, and his Surety had fulfilled His trust and conveyed it to the hands of the creditor.

Next spring Theodore returned to Constantinople in safety. As soon as he had disembarked, he hastened to the house of Abram to tell him the results of his voyage.

The Jewish usurer, wishing to prove him, feigned not to understand, when Theodore related how he had sent him fifty pounds of gold, and made as though he had not received the money. But the merchant was full of confidence, and he said, "I cannot understand this, brother, for I enclosed the money in a box along with a letter, and committed it to the custody of my Saviour Christ, Who has acted as Surety for me unworthy. But as thou sayest that thou hast not received it, come with me, and let us go together before the crucifix, and say before it that thou hast not had the money conveyed to thee, and then I will believe thy word."

[Pg 116]

Abram promised to accompany his friend, and rising from their seats, they went together to the Copper-Market. And when they came to the Tetrastyle, Theodore raised his hands to the Crucified, and said, "My Saviour and Surety, didst Thou not restore the gold to Abram that I entrusted to Thee for that purpose?"

There was something so wonderful, so beautiful, in the man's faith, that Abram was overpowered; and withal there was the evidence that it was not misplaced so clear to the Jew, that the light of conviction like a dazzling sunbeam darted into his soul, and Theodore saw the Hebrew usurer fall prostrate on the pavement, half fainting with the emotion which oppressed him.

Theodore ran and fetched water in his hands and sprinkled his face, and brought the usurer round. And Abram said, "As God liveth, my friend, I will not enter into my house till I have taken thy Lord and Surety for my Master." A crowd began to gather, and it was bruited abroad that the Jewish usurer sought baptism. And when the story reached the ears of the Emperor Heraclius, he glorified God. So Abram was put under instruction, and was baptised by the patriarch Sergius.[11]

And after seven days a solemn procession was instituted through the streets of Constantinople to the Copper-Market, in which walked the emperor and the patriarch, and all the clergy of the city; and the box which had contained the money was conveyed[Pg 117] by them to the Tetrastyle and laid up, along with the gold and the letter before the image, to be a memorial of what had taken place to all generations. And thenceforth the crucifix received the common appellation of Antiphonetos, or the Surety.

As for the tin and lead with which the vessel of Theodore was freighted, it sold for a great price, so that both he and Abram realised a large sum by the transaction. But neither would keep to himself any portion of it, but gave it all to the Church of S. Sophia, and therewith a part of the sanctuary was overlaid with silver. Then Theodore and his wife, with mutual consent, gave up the world and retired into monastic institutions.

Abram afterwards built and endowed an oratory near the Tetrastyle, and Sergius ordained him priest and his two sons deacons.

Thus ends this strange and very beautiful story, which I have merely condensed from the somewhat prolix narrative of the Byzantine preacher. The reader will probably agree with me that if sermons in the 19th century were as entertaining as this of the 10th, fewer people would be found to go to sleep during their delivery.

I have told the tale as related by the preacher. But there are reasons which awaken suspicion that he somewhat erred as to his dates; but that, nevertheless the story is really not without a foundation of fact. Towards the close of the oration the preacher points to the ambone, and the thusiasterion, and bids his hearers remark how they are overlaid with silver, and this he says was the silver that Abram, the wealthy Jewish[Pg 118]usurer, and Theodore, the merchant, gave to the Church of S. Sophia.

Now it happens that we have got a contemporary record of this overlaying of the sanctuary with silver; we know from the pen of Procopius of Gaza that it took place in the reign of Justinian in A.D. 537.[12]

This was preparatory to the dedication of the great Church, when the Emperor and the wealthy citizens of Byzantium were lavishly contributing to the adornment of the glorious building.

We can quite understand how that the new convert and the grateful merchant were carried away by the current of the general enthusiasm, and gave all their silver to the plating of the sanctuary of the new Church. Procopius tells us that forty thousand pounds of silver were spent in this work. Not all of this, however, could have been given by Abram and Theodore.

If this then were the date of the conversion of Abram, for Heraclius we must read Justinian, and for Sergius we must substitute Mennas. As the sermon was not preached till four hundred years after, the error can be accounted for, one imperial benefactor of the Church was mistaken for another.

Now about the time of Justinian, we know from other sources that there was a converted Jew named Abram who founded and built a church and monastery in Constantinople, and which in after times was known as the Abramite Monastery. We are told this by John Moschus. We can not fix the exact date of the foundation, Moschus heard about[Pg 119] A.D. 600 from the abbot John Rutilus, who had heard it from Stephen the Moabite, that the Monastery of the Abramites had been constructed by Abram who afterwards was raised to the metropolitan See of Ephesus. We may put then the foundation of the monastery at about A.D. 540.

Now Abram of Ephesus succeeded Procopius who was bishop in 560; and his successor was Rufinus in 597. The date of the elevation of Abram to the metropolitan throne of Ephesus is not known exactly, but it was probably about 565.

There is, of course, much conjecture in thus identifying the usurer Abram with Abram, Bishop of Ephesus; but there is certainly a probability that they were identical; and if so, then one more pretty story of the good man survives. After having built the monastery in Constantinople, Moschus tells us that Abram went to Jerusalem, the home to which a Jewish heart naturally turns, and there he set to work to erect another monastery. Now there was among the workmen engaged on the building a mason who ate but sparingly, conversed with none, but worked diligently, and prayed much in his hours of relaxation from labour.

Abram became interested in the man, and called him to him, and learned from him his story. It was this. The mason had been a monk in the Theodorian Monastery along with his brother. The brother weary of the life, had left and fallen into grave moral disorders. Then this one now acting as mason had gone after him, laid aside his cowl and undertaken the same daily toil as the erring brother, that he[Pg 120] might be with him, waiting his time when by means of advice or example he might draw the young man from his life of sin. But though he had laid aside the outward emblems of his monastic profession, he kept the rule of life as closely as he was able, cultivating prayer and silence and fasting. Then Abram deeply moved, said to the monk-mason: "God will look on thy fraternal charity; be of good courage, He will give thee thy brother at thy petition."

FOOTNOTES:

[9] This account is taken from a sermon preached in the Church of St. Sophia at Constantinople on Orthodoxy Sunday, printed by Combefisius (Auctuarium novum, pars post. col. 644), from a MS. in the National Library at Paris. Another copy of the sermon is in the Library at Turin. The probable date of the composition is the tenth century. Orthodoxy Sunday was not instituted till 842.

[10] This famous figure was cast down and broken by Leo the Isaurian in 730, a riot ensued, the market-women interfering with the soldiers, who were engaged on pulling down the figure, they shook the ladders and threw down one who was engaged in hacking the face of the figure. This led to the execution of ten persons, among them Gregory, head of the bodyguard, and Mary, a lady of the Imperial family. The Empress Irene set up a mosaic figure in its place. This was again destroyed by Leo the Armenian, and again restored after his death by Theophilus in 829.

[11] Sergius was patriarch of Constantinople between 610 and 638. He embraced the Monothelite heresy.

[12] Fabricius, Bibl. Græca, Ed. Harles, T.X. p. 124, 125.

[Pg 121]

Sophie Apitzsch.

"Some are born great," said Malvolio, strutting in yellow stockings, cross-gartered, before Olivia, "some achieve greatness," and with a smile, "some have greatness thrust upon them."

Of the latter was Sophie Sabine Apitzsch. She was not born great, she was the daughter of an armourer. She hardly can be said to have achieved greatness, though she did attain to notoriety; what greatness she had was thrust on her, not altogether reluctant to receive it. But the greatness was not much, and was of an ambiguous description. She was treated for a while as a prince in disguise, and then became the theme of an opera, of a drama, and of a novel. For a hundred years her top-boots were preserved as historical relics in the archives of the House of Saxony, till in 1813 a Cossack of the Russian army passing through Augustenburg, saw, desired, tried on, and marched off with them; and her boots entered Paris with the Allies.

About five-and-twenty miles from Dresden lived in 1714 a couple of landed proprietors, the one called Volkmar, and the other von Günther, who fumed with fiery hostility against each other, and the cause of disagreement was, that the latter wrote himself von Günther. Now, to get a *von* before the name makes a great deal of difference: it purifies, nay, it alters[Pg 122] the colour of the blood, turning it from red to blue. No one in Germany can prefix *von* to his name as any one in England can append Esq. to his. He must receive authorisation by diploma of nobility from his sovereign.

George von Günther had been, not long before, plain George Günther, but in 1712 he had obtained from the Emperor Charles VI. a patent of nobility, or gentility, they are the same abroad, and the motive that moved his sacred apostolic majesty to grant the patent was—as set forth therein—that an ancestor of George Günther of the same name "had sat down to table with the elector John George II. of Saxony;" and it was inconceivable that a mere citizen could have been suffered to do this, unless there were some nobility in him. George von Günther possessed an estate which was a manor, a knight's fee, at Jägerhof, and he was moreover upper Forester and Master of the Fisheries to the King-elector of Saxony, and Sheriff of Chemnitz and Frankenberg. He managed to marry his daughters to men blessed with *von* before their names, one to von Bretschneider, Privy-Councillor of War, the other to a Major von Wöllner.

Now, all this was gall and wormwood to Councillor-of-Agriculture, Daniel Volkmar, who lived on his paternal acres at Hetzdorf, of which he was hereditary chief magistrate by virtue of his lordship of the acres. This man had made vain efforts to be ennobled. He could not find that any ancestor of his had sat at table with an elector; and, perhaps, he could not scrape together sufficient money to induce his sacred apostolic majesty to overlook this defect. As he[Pg 123] could not get his diploma, he sought how he might injure his more fortunate neighbour, and this he did by spying out his acts, watching for neglect of his duties to the fishes or the game, and reporting him anonymously to head-quarters. Günther knew well enough who it was that sought to injure him, and, as Volkmar believed, had invited some of the gamekeepers to shoot him; accordingly, Volkmar never rode or walked in the neighbourhood of the royal forests and fish-ponds unarmed, and without servants carrying loaded muskets.

One day a brother magistrate, Pöckel by name, came over to see him about a matter that puzzled him. There had appeared in the district under his jurisdiction a young man, tall, well-built, handsome, but slightly small-pox-pitted, who had been arrested by the police for blowing a hunting-horn. Now ignoble lips might not touch a hunting-horn, and for any other than breath that issued out of noble lungs to sound a note on such a horn was against the laws.

"Oh," said Volkmar, "if he has done this, and is not a gentleman—lock him up. What is his name?"

"He calls himself Karl Marbitz."

"But I, even I, may not blow a blast on a horn—that scoundrel Günther may. Deal with the fellow Marbitz with the utmost severity."

"But—suppose he may have the necessary qualification?"

"How can he without a von before his name?"

"Suppose he be a nobleman, or something even higher, in disguise?"

[Pg 124]

"What, in disguise? Travelling incognito? Our Crown Prince is not at Dresden."[13]

"Exactly. All kinds of rumours are afloat concerning this young man, who is, indeed, about the Crown Prince's age; he has been lodging with a baker at Aue, and there blowing the horn."

"I'll go with you and see him. I will stand bail for him. Let him come to me. Hah-hah! George von Günther, hah-hah!"

So Volkmar, already more than half disposed to believe that the horn-blower was a prince in disguise, rode over to the place where he was in confinement, saw him, and lost what little doubt he had. The upright carriage, the aristocratic cast of features, the stand-off manners, all betokened the purest of blue blood—all were glimmerings of that halo which surrounds sovereignty.

The Crown Prince of Saxony was away—it was alleged, in France—making the grand tour, but, was it not more likely that he was going the round of the duchy of Saxony, inquiring into the wants and wrongs of the people? If so, who could better assist him to the knowledge of these things, than he, Volkmar, and who could better open his eyes to the delinquencies of high-placed, high-salaried officials—notably of the fisheries and forests?

"There is one thing shakes my faith," said Pöckel: "our Crown Prince is not small-pox marked."

"That is nothing," answered Volkmar eagerly.[Pg 125] "His Serenity has caught the infection in making his studies among the people."

"And then—he is so shabbily dressed."

"That is nothing—it is the perfection of disguise."

Volkmar carried off the young man to his house, and showed him the greatest respect, insisted on his sitting in the carriage facing the horses, and would on no account take a place at his side, but seated himself deferentially opposite him.

On reaching Hetzdorf, Volkmar introduced his wife and his daughter Joanna to the distinguished prince, who behaved to them very graciously, and with the most courtly air expressed himself charmed with the room prepared for him.

Dinner was served, and politics were discussed; the reserve with which the guest treated such subjects, the caution with which he expressed an opinion, served to deepen in Volkmar's mind the conviction that he had caught the Crown Prince travelling incog. After the servants had withdrawn, and when a good deal of wine—the best in the cellar—had been drunk, the host said confidentially in a whisper, "I see clearly enough what you are."

"Indeed," answered the guest, "I can tell you what I am—by trade an armourer."

"Ah, ha! but by birth—what?" said Volkmar, slyly, holding up his glass and winking over it.

"Well," answered the guest, "I will admit this—I am not what I appear."

"And may I further ask your—I mean you—where you are at home?"

"I am a child of Saxony," was the answer.

[Pg 126]

Afterwards, at the trial, the defendant insisted that this was exactly the reply made, whereas Volkmar asserted that the words were, "I am a child of the House of Saxony." But there can be no doubt that his imagination supplemented the actual words used with those he wished to hear.

"The small-pox has altered you since you left home," said Volkmar.

"Very likely. I have had the small-pox since I left my home."

Volkmar at once placed his house, his servants, his purse, at the disposal of his guest, and his offer was readily accepted.

It is now advisable to turn back and explain the situation, by relating the early history of this person, who passed under the name of Karl Marbitz, an armourer; but whom a good number of people suspected of being something other than what he gave himself out to be, though only Volkmar and Pöckel and one or two others supposed him to be the Crown Prince of Saxony.

Sophie Sabine Apitzsch was born at Lunzenau in Saxony in 1692, was well brought up, kept to school, and learned to write orthographically, and to have a fair general knowledge of history and geography. When she left school she was employed by her father in his trade, which was that of an armourer. She was tall and handsome, somewhat masculine—in after years a Cossack got into her boots—had the small-pox, which,

51

however, only slightly disfigured her. In 1710 she had a suitor, a gamekeeper, Melchior Leonhart. But Sophie entertained a rooted dislike[Pg 127] to marriage, and she kept her lover off for three years, till her father peremptorily ordered her to marry Melchior, and fixed the day for the wedding. Then Sophie one night got out of her own clothing, stepped into her father's best suit, and walked away in the garments of a man, and shortly afterwards appeared in Anspach under a feigned name, as a barber's assistant. Here she got into difficulties with the police, as she had no papers of legitimation, and to escape them, enlisted. She carried a musket for a month only, deserted, and resumed her vagabond life in civil attire, as a barber's assistant, and came to Leipzig, where she lodged at the Golden Cock. How she acquired the art, and how those liked it on whose faces she made her experiments with the razor, we are not told.

At the Golden Cock lodged an athletic lady of the name of Anna Franke, stout, muscular, and able to lift great weights with her teeth, and with a jerk throw them over her shoulders. Anna Franke gave daily exhibitions of her powers, and on the proceeds maintained herself and her daughter, a girl of seventeen. The stout and muscular lady also danced on a tight rope, which with her bounces acted like a taut bowstring, projecting the athlete high into the air.

The Fräulein Franke very speedily fell in love with the fine young barber, and proposed to her mother that Herr Karl should be taken into the concern, as he would be useful to stretch the ropes, and go round for coppers. Sophie was nothing loth to have her inn bill paid on these terms, but when finally the bouncing mother announced that her daughter's hand[Pg 128] was at the disposal of Karl, then the situation became even more embarrassing than that at home from which Sophie had run away. The barber maintained her place as long as she could, but at last, when the endearments of the daughter became oppressive, and the urgency of the mother for speedy nuptials became vexatious, she pretended that the father, who was represented as a well-to-do citizen of Hamburg, must first be consulted. On this plea Sophie borrowed of Mother Franke the requisite money for her journey and departed, promising to return in a few weeks. Instead of fulfilling her promise, Sophie wrote to ask for a further advance of money, and when this was refused, disappeared altogether from the knowledge of the athlete and her daughter.

On this second flight from marriage, Sophie Apitzsch met with an armourer named Karl Marbitz, and by some means or other contrived to get possession of his pass, leaving him instead a paper of legitimation made out under the name of Karl Gottfried, which old Mother Franke had induced the police to grant to the young barber who was engaged to marry her daughter.

In June 1714, under the name of Marbitz, Sophie appeared among the Erz-Gebirge, the chain of mountains that separate Saxony from Bohemia, and begged her way from place to place, pretending to be a schoolmaster out of employ. After rambling about for some time, she took up her quarters with a baker at Elterlein. Here it was that for the first time a suspicion was aroused that she was a person of greater consequence than she gave out. The rumour reached[Pg 129] the nearest magistrate that there was a mysterious stranger there who wore a ribbon and star of some order, and he at once went to the place to make inquiries, but found that Sophie had neither ribbon nor order, and that her papers declared in proper form who and what she was. At this time she fell ill at the baker's house, and the man, perhaps moved by the reports abroad concerning her, was ready to advance her money to the amount of £6 or £7. When recovered, she left the village where she had been ill, and went to another one, where she took up her abode with another baker, named Fischer, whom she helped in his trade, or went about practising upon the huntsman's horn.

This amusement it was which brought her into trouble. Possibly she may not have known that the horn was a reserved instrument that might not be played by the ignoble.

At the time that Volkmar took her out of the lockup, and carried her off to his mansion in his carriage, she was absolutely without money, in threadbare black coat, stockings ill darned, and her hair very much in want of powder.

Hitherto her associates had been of the lowest classes; she had been superior to them in education, in morals, and in character, and had to some extent imposed on them. They acknowledged in her an undefined dignity and quiet reserve, with unquestioned superiority in attainments and general tone of mind, and this they attributed to her belonging to a vastly higher class in society.

Now, all at once she was translated into another[Pg 130] condition of life, one in which she had never moved before; but she did not lose her head; she maintained the same caution and reserve in it, and never once exposed her ignorance so as to arouse suspicion that she was not what people insisted on believing her to be. She was sufficiently shrewd never by word to compromise herself, and afterwards, when brought to trial, she insisted that she had not once asserted that she was other than Karl Marbitz the armourer. Others had imagined she was a prince, but she had not encouraged them in their delusion by as much as a word. That, no doubt, was true, but she accepted the honours offered and presents made her under this erroneous impression, without an attempt to open the eyes of the deluded to their own folly.

Perhaps this was more than could be expected of her. "Foolery," said the clown in "Twelfth Night," "does walk about the orb, like the sun; it shines everywhere"—and what are fools but the natural prey of the clever?

Sophie had been ill, reduced to abject poverty, was in need of good food, new clothes, and shelter; all were offered, even forced upon her. Was she called upon to reject them? She thought not.

Now that Volkmar had a supposed prince under his roof he threw open his house to the neighbourhood, and invited every gentleman he knew—except the von Günthers. He provided the prince with a coat of scarlet cloth frogged and laced with gold, with a new hat, gave him a horse, filled his purse, and provided him with those identical boots in which a century later a Cossack marched into Paris.

[Pg 131]

She was addressed by her host and hostess as "Your Highness," and "Your Serenity," and they sought to kiss her hand, but she waived away these exhibitions of servility, saying, "Let be—we will regard each other as on a common level." Once Volkmar said slyly to her, "What would your august father say if he knew you were here?"

"He would be surprised," was all the answer that could be drawn from her. One day the newspaper contained information of the Crown Prince's doings in Paris with his tutor and attendants. Volkmar pointed it out to her with a twinkle of the eye, saying, "Do not suppose I am to be hoodwinked by such attempts to deceive the public as that."

In the mornings when the pseudo prince left the bedroom, outside the door stood Herr Volkmar, cap in hand, bowing. As he offered her a pinch of snuff from a gold *tabatière* one day, he saw her eyes rest on it; he at once said, "This belonged formerly to the Königsmark."

"Then," she replied, "it will have the double initials on it. 'A' for Aurora."

Now, argued Volkmar, how was it likely that his guest should know the scandalous story of Augustus I. and the fair Aurora of Königsmark, mother of the famous French

53

marshal, unless he had belonged to the royal family of Saxony?[14] He left out of account that Court scandal is talked about everywhere, and is in the mouths of all. Then he presented her with the snuff-box. Next he purchased for her a set of silver[Pg 132]plate for her cover, and ordered a ribbon and a star of diamonds, because it became one of such distinguished rank not to appear without a decoration! As the girl said afterwards at her trial, she had but to hint a desire for anything, and it was granted her at once. Her host somewhat bored her with political disquisitions; he was desirous of impressing on his illustrious guest what a political genius he was, and in his own mind had resolved to become prime minister of Saxony in the place of the fallen Beichlingen, who was said to have made so much money out of the State that he could buy a principality, and who, indeed, struck a medal with his arms on it surmounted by a princely crown.

But Volkmar's ambition went further. As already stated he had a daughter—the modest Joanna; what a splendid opportunity was in the hands of the scheming parents! If the young prince formed an attachment for Joanna, surely he might get the emperor to elevate her by diploma to the rank of a princess, and thus Volkmar would see his Joanna Queen of Poland and Electress of Saxony. He and Frau Volkmar were far too good people to scheme to get their daughter such a place as the old Königsmark had occupied with the reigning sovereign. Besides, Königsmark had been merely created a countess, and who would crave to be a countess when she might be Queen? and a favourite, when, by playing her cards well, she might become a legitimate wife?

So the old couple threw Joanna at the head of their guest, and did their utmost to entangle him. In the meantime the von Günthers were flaming with[Pg 133] envy and rage. They no more doubted that the Volkmars had got the Crown Prince living with them, than did the Volkmars themselves. The whole neighbourhood flowed to the entertainments given in his honour at Hetzdorf; only the von Günthers were shut out. But von Günther met the mysterious stranger at one or two of the return festivities given by the gentry who had been entertained at Hetzdorf, and he seized on one of these occasions boldly to invite his Highness to pay him also a visit at his "little place;" and what was more than he expected, the offer was accepted.

In fact, the Apitzsch who had twice run away from matrimony, was becoming embarrassed again by the tenderness of Joanna and the ambition of the parents.

The dismay of the Volkmars passes description when their guest informed them he was going to pay a visit to the hated rivals.

Sophie was fetched away in the von Günther carriage, and by servants put into new liveries for the occasion, and was received and entertained with the best at Jägerhof. Here, also, presents were made; among others a silver cover for table was given her by the daughter of her host, who had married a major, and who hoped, in return, to see her husband advanced to be a general.

She was taken to see the royal castle of Augustusburg, and here a little difference of testimony occurs as to the observation she made in the chapel, which was found to be without an organ. At her trial it was asserted that she had said, "I must order an organ," but she positively swore she had said, "An[Pg 134] organ ought to be provided." She was taken also to the mansion of the Duke of Holstein at Weisenburg, where she purchased one of his horses—that is to say, agreed to take it, and let her hosts find the money.

The visit to the von Günthers did not last ten days, and then she was back again with the Volkmars, to their exuberant delight. Why she remained so short a time at Jägerhof does not appear. Possibly she may have been there more in fear of detection than at Hetzdorf. Now that the Volkmars had her back they would not let her out of their sight. They gave her two servants in livery to attend her; they assured her that her absence had so affected Joanna that the girl had done nothing but weep, and had refused to eat. They began to press in their daughter's interest for a declaration of intentions, and that negotiations with the Emperor should be opened that a title of princess of the Holy Roman Empire might be obtained for her as preliminary to the nuptials.

Sophie Apitzsch saw that she must again make a bolt to escape the marriage ring, and she looked about for an opportunity. But there was no evading the watch of the Volkmars, who were alarmed lest their guest should again go to the hated von Günthers.

Well would it have been for the Volkmars had they kept the "prince" under less close surveillance, and allowed him to succeed in his attempts to get away. It would have been to their advantage in many ways.

A fortnight or three weeks passed, and the horse bought of the Duke of Holstein had not been sent[Pg 135] In fact the Duke, when the matter was communicated to him, was puzzled. He knew that the Crown Prince was in Paris, and could not have visited his stables, and promised to purchase his horse. So he instituted inquiries before he consented to part with the horse, and at once the bubble burst. Police arrived at Hetzdorf to arrest the pretender, and convey her to Augustusburg, where she was imprisoned, till her trial. This was in February, 1715. In her prison she had an apoplectic stroke, but recovered. Sentence was pronounced against her by the court at Leipzig in 1716, that she should be publicly whipped out of the country. That is to say, sent from town to town, and whipped in the market-place of each, till she was sent over the frontier. In consideration of her having had a stroke, the king commuted the sentence to whipping in private, and imprisonment at his majesty's pleasure.

She does not seem to have been harshly treated by the gaoler of Waldheim, the prison to which she was sent. She was given her own room, she dined at the table of the gaoler, continued to wear male clothes, and was cheerful, obedient, and contented. In 1717 both she and her father appealed to the king for further relaxation of her sentence, but this was refused. The prison authorities gave her the best testimony for good conduct whilst in their hands.

In the same year, 1717, the unfortunate Volkmar made a claim for the scarlet coat—which he said the moths were likely to eat unless placed on some one's back—the gold snuff-box, the silver spoons, dishes, forks, the horse, the watch, and various other things[Pg 136] he had given Sophie, being induced to do so by false representations. The horse as well as the plate, the star, the snuff-box, the coat and the boots had all been requisitioned as evidence before her trial. The question was a hard one to solve, whether Herr Volkmar could recover presents, and it had to be transmitted from one court to another. An order of court dated January, 1722, required further evidence to be produced before purse, coat, boots, &c., could be returned to Volkmar—that is, *seven* years after they had been taken into the custody of the Court. The horse must have eaten more than his cost by this time, and the coat must have lost all value through moth-eating. The cost of proceedings was heavy, and Volkmar then withdrew from his attempt to recover the objects given to the false prince.

But already—long before, by decree of October 1717—Sophie Apitzsch had been liberated. She left prison in half male, half female costume, and in this dress took service with a baker at Waldheim; and we hear no more of her, whether she married, and when she died.

FOOTNOTES:

[13] Augustus the Strong was King of Poland and Elector of Saxony.

[14] Aurora v. Königsmark went out of favour in 1698—probably then sold the gold snuff-box. She died in 1728.

[Pg 137]
Peter Nielsen.

On the 29th day of April in the year 1465, died Henry Strangebjerg, bishop of Ribe in Denmark, after having occupied the See for just ten years. For some days before his decease public, official prayer had been made for his recovery by the Cathedral Chapter, but in their hearts the Canons were impatient for his departure. Not, be it understood, that the Bishop was an unworthy occupant of the See of Liafdag the Martyr—on the contrary, he had been a man of exemplary conduct; nor because he was harsh in his rule—on the contrary, he had been a lenient prelate. The reason why, when official prayer was made for his recovery, it was neutralised by private intercession for his removal, was solely this—his removal opened a prospect of advancement.

The Cathedral Chapter of Ribe consisted of fifteen Canons, and a Dean or Provost, all men of family, learning and morals. Before the doctors had shaken their heads over the sick bed of Henry Strangebjerg, it was known throughout Ribe that there would be four candidates for the vacant throne. It was, of course, impossible for more than one man to be elected; but as the election lay entirely and uncontrolledly in the hands of the Chapter, it was quite possible for a Canon to make a good thing out of an election without being himself elected. The bishops nominated[Pg 138] to many benefices, and there existed then no law against pluralities. The newly chosen prelate, if he had a spark of gratitude, must reward those faithful men who had made him bishop.

At 4 p.m. on April 29th the breath left the body of Henry Strangebjerg. At 4.15 p.m. the Chapter were rubbing their hands and drawing sighs of relief. But Thomas Lange, the Dean, rubbed his hands and drew his sigh of relief ten minutes earlier, viz., at 4.5 p.m., for he stood by the bed of the dying bishop. At 3.25 p.m. Thomas Lange's nerves had received a great shock, for a flicker as of returning life had manifested itself in the sick man, and for a few minutes he really feared he might recover. At 4.10 p.m. Hartwig Juel, the Archdeacon, who had been standing outside the bishop's door, was seen running down the corridor with a flush in his cheeks. Through the keyhole he had heard the Dean exclaim: "Thank God!" and when he heard that pious ejaculation, he knew that all dread of the Bishop's restoration was over. It was not till so late as 4.20 p.m. that Olaf Petersen knew it. Olaf was kneeling in the Cathedral, in the Chapel of St. Lambert, the yellow chapel as it was called, absorbed in devotion, consequently the news did not reach him till five minutes after the Chapter, twenty minutes after the vacation of the See. Olaf Petersen was a very holy man; he was earnest and sincere. He was, above everything, desirous of the welfare of the Church and the advancement of religion. He was ascetic, denying himself in food, sleep and clothing, and was profuse in his alms and in his devotions. He saw the[Pg 139] worldliness, the self-seeking, the greed of gain and honours that possessed his fellows, and he was convinced that one thing was necessary for the salvation of Christianity in Ribe, and that one thing was his own election to the See.

The other candidates were moved by selfish interests. He cared only for true religion. Providence would do a manifest injustice if it did not take cognizance of his integrity and interfere to give him the mitre. He was resolved to use no unworthy means to secure it. He would make no promises, offer no bribes—that is, to his fellow Canons, but he promised a silver candlestick to St. Lambert, and bribed St. Gertrude to intervene with the assurance of a pilgrimage to her shrine.

We have mentioned only three of the candidates. The fourth was Jep Mundelstrup, an old and amiable man, who had not thrust himself forward, but had been put forward by his friends, who considered him sufficiently malleable to be moulded to their purposes.

Jep was, as has been said, old; he was so old that it was thought (and hoped), if chosen, his tenure of office would be but brief. Four or five years—under favourable circumstances, such as a changeable winter, a raw spring with east winds—he might drop off even sooner, and leave the mitre free for another scramble.

The Kings of Denmark no longer nominated to the Sees, sent no *congé d'élire* to the Chapter. They did not even appoint to the Canonries. Consequently the Canons had everything pretty much their own way, and had only two things to consider, to guide their determination—the good of the Church and[Pg 140] their own petty interests. The expression "good of the Church" demands comment. "The good of the Church" was the motive, the only recognised motive, on which the Chapter were supposed to act. Practically, however, it was non-existent as a motive. It was a mere figure of speech used to cloak selfish ambition.

From this sweeping characterisation we must, however, exclude Olaf Petersen, who did indeed regard pre-eminently the good of the Church, but then that good was, in his mind, inextricably involved with his own fortunes. He was the man to make religion a living reality. He was the man to bring the Church back to primitive purity. He could not blind his eyes to the fact that not one of the Canons beside himself cared a farthing for spiritual matters; therefore he desired the mitre for his own brows.

The conclave at which the election was to be made was fixed for the afternoon of the day on which Henry Strangebjerg was to be buried, and the burial was appointed to take place as soon as was consistent with decency.

The whole of the time between the death and the funeral was taken up by the Canons with hurrying to and from each other's residences, canvassing for votes.

Olaf Petersen alone refrained from canvassing, he spent his whole time in fasting and prayer, so anxious was he for the welfare of the Church and the advancement of true religion.

At length—Boom! Boom! Boom! The great bell of the minster tower summoned the Chapter to the[Pg 141] hall of conclave. Every Canon was in his place, fifteen Canons and the provost, sixteen in all. It was certain that the provost, although chairman, would claim his right to vote, and exercise it, voting for himself. It was ruled that all voting should be open, for two reasons—that the successful candidate might know who had given him their shoulders on which to mount, and so reward these shoulders by laying many benefices upon them, and secondly, that he might know who had been his adversaries, and so might exclude them from preferments. Every one believed he would be on the winning side, no one supposed the other alternative possible.

The candidates, as already intimated, were four. Thomas Lange, the Dean, who belonged to a good, though not wealthy family. He had been in business before taking orders, and brought with him into the Church practical shrewdness and business habits. He had husbanded well the resources of the Chapter, and had even enlarged its revenue by the purchase of three farms and a manor.

The second candidate, Hartwig Juel, was a member of a powerful noble family. His brother was at Court and highly regarded by King Christian. His election would gratify the king. Hartwig Juel was Archdeacon.

The third candidate was the good old Jep Mundelstrup; and the fourth was the representative of the ascetic, religious party, which was also the party of reform, Olaf Petersen.

The Dean was, naturally, chairman. Before taking the chair he announced his intention of voting.[Pg 142] The four candidates were proposed, and the votes taken.

The Dean numbered 4.

Hartwig Juel numbered 4.
Jep Mundelstrup numbered 4.
Olaf Petersen numbered 4.
Moreover, each candidate had voted for himself.

What was to be done? The Chapter sat silent, looking about them in each others' faces.

Then the venerable Jep Mundelstrup, assisted by those who sat by him, staggered to his feet, and leaning on his staff, he mumbled forth this address: "My reverend brothers, it was wholly without my desire and not in furtherance of any ambition of mine, that my name was put up as that of a candidate for the vacant mitre of the Holy See of Ribe. I am old and infirm. With the patriarch Jacob I may say, 'Few and evil have been the days of the years of my life.' and I am not worthy to receive so great an honour. Evil my days have been, because I have had only my Canonry and one sorry living to support me; and there are comforts I should desire in my old age which I cannot afford. My health is not sound. I shrink from the responsibilities and labours of a bishopric. If I withdraw my candidature, I feel confident that the successful candidate will not forget my infirmities, and the facility I have afforded for his election. I decline to stand, and at the same time, lest I should seem to pose in opposition to three of my excellent brethren, I decline also to vote." Then he sat down, amidst general applause.

Here was an unexpected simplification of matters.[Pg 143] The Dean and Hartwig Juel cast kindly, even affectionate glances at those who had previously voted for Jep, Olaf Petersen looked up to heaven and prayed.

Again, the votes were taken, and again the chairman claimed his right to vote.

When taken they stood thus:
The Dean, 5.
Hartwig Juel, 5.
Olaf Petersen, 5.

What was to be done? Again the Chapter sat silent, rubbing their chins, and casting furtive glances at each other. The Chapter was adjourned to the same hour on the morrow. The intervening hours were spent in negociations between the several parties, and attempts made by the two first in combination to force Olaf Petersen to resign his candidature. But Olaf was too conscientious a man to do this. He felt that the salvation of souls depended on his staying the plague like Phinehas with his censer.

Boom! Boom! Boom! The Cathedral bell again summoned the conclave to the Chapter House.

Before proceeding to business the Dean, as chairman, addressed the electors. He was an eloquent man, and he set in moving words before them the solemnity of the duty imposed on them, the importance of considering only the welfare of the Church, and the responsibility that would weigh on them should they choose an unworthy prelate. He conjured them in tones vibrating with pathos, to put far from them all self-seeking thoughts, and to be guided only by conscience. Then he sat down. The votes were again taken. Jep Mundelstrup again[Pg 144] shaking his head, and refusing to vote. When counted, they stood thus.

Thomas Lange, 5.
Hartwig Juel, 5.
Olaf Petersen, 5.

Then up started the Dean, very red in the face, and said, "Really this is preposterous! Are we to continue this farce? Some of the brethren must yield for the general good. I would cheerfully withdraw my candidature, but for one consideration. You all know that the temporal affairs of the See have fallen into confusion. Our late excellent prelate was not a man of business, and there has been alienation, and underletting, and racking out of church lands, which I have marked with anxiety, and which I am desirous to remedy. You all know that I have this one good quality, I am a business man, understand account keeping, and look sharp after the pecuniary interests of the Chapter lands. It is essential that the lands of the See should be attended to by some practical man like myself, therefore I do not withdraw from my candidature, but therefore only—"

Then up sprang Hartwig Juel, and said, "The very Reverend the Dean has well said, this farce must not continue. Some must yield if a bishop is to be elected. I would cheerfully withdraw from candidature but for one little matter. I hold in my hand a letter received this morning from my brother, who tells me that his most gracious majesty, King Christian, expressed himself to my brother in terms of hope that I should be elected. You, my reverend brothers, all know that we are living in a critical[Pg 145] time when it is most necessary that a close relation, a cordial relation, should be maintained between the Church and the State. Therefore, in the political interests of the See, but only in these interests, I cannot withdraw my candidature."

Then all eyes turned on Olaf Petersen. His face was pale, his lips set. He stood up, and leaning forward said firmly, "The pecuniary and the political interests of the See are as nothing to me, its spiritual interests are supreme. Heaven is my witness, I have no personal ambition to wear the mitre. I know it will cause exhausting labour and terrible responsibilities, from which I shrink. Nevertheless, seeing as I do that this is a period in the history of the Church when self-seeking and corruption have penetrated her veins and are poisoning her life-blood, seeing as I do that unless there be a revival of religion, and an attempt at reform be made within the Church, there will ensue such a convulsion as will overthrow her, therefore, and only therefore do I feel that I can not withdraw from my candidature."

"Very well," said the Dean in a crusty tone. "There is nothing for it but for us to vote again. Now at least we have clear issues before us, the temporal, the political, and the spiritual interests of the Church." The votes were again taken, and stood thus.

The temporal interests, 5.

The political interests, 5.

The spiritual interests, 5.

Here was a dead lock. It was clear that parties were exactly divided, and that none would yield.

[Pg 146]

After a pause of ten minutes, Jep Mundelstrup was again helped to his feet. He looked round the Chapter with blinking eyes, and opened and shut his mouth several times before he came to speak. At last he said, in faltering tones, "My reverend brethren, it is clear to me that my resignation has complicated, rather than helped matters forward. Do not think I am about to renew my candidature, *that* I am not, but I am going to make a proposition to which I hope you will give attentive hearing. If we go on in this manner, we shall elect no one, and then his Majesty, whom God bless, will step in and nominate."

"Hear, hear!" from the adherents of Hartwig Juel.

"I do not for a moment pretend that the nominee of his Majesty would not prove an excellent bishop, but I do fear that a nomination by the crown would be the establishment of a dangerous precedent."

"Hear! hear!" from the adherents of Olaf Petersen.

"At the same time it must be borne in mind that the temporal welfare of the See ought to be put in the hands of some one conversant with the condition into which they have been allowed to lapse."

"Hear! hear!" from the adherents of Thomas Lange.

"I would suggest, as we none of us can agree, that we refer the decision to an umpire."

General commotion, and whispers, and looks of alarm.

"How are we to obtain one at once conversant with the condition of the diocese, and not a partizan?" asked the Dean.

"There is a wretched little village in the midst of[Pg 147] the Roager Heath, cut off from communication with the world, in which lives a priest named Peter Nielsen on his cure, a man who is related to no one here, belongs, I believe, to no gentle family, and, therefore, would have no family interests one way or the other to bias him. He has the character of being a shrewd man of business, some of the estates of the Church are on the Roager Heath, and he knows how they have been treated, and I have always heard that he is a good preacher and an indefatigable parish priest. Let him be umpire. I can think of none other who would not be a partizan."

The proposition was so extraordinary and unexpected that the Chapter, at first, did not know what to think of it. Who was this Peter Nielsen? No one knew of him anything more than what Jep Mundelstrup had said, and he, it was believed, had drawn largely on his imagination for his facts. Indeed, he was the least known man among the diocesan clergy. It was disputed whether he was a good preacher. Who had heard him? no one. Was it true that he was not a gentleman by birth? No one knew to what family he belonged. In default of any other solution to the dead lock in which the Chapter stood, it was agreed by all that the selection of a bishop for Ribe should be left to Peter Nielsen of Roager.

That same day, indeed as soon after the dissolution of the meeting as was possible, one of the Canons mounted his horse, and rode away to the Roager Heath.

The village of Ro or Raa-ager, literally the rough or barren field, lay in the dead flat of sandy heath[Pg 148] that occupies so large a portion of the centre and west coast of Jutland, and which goes by various names, as Randböll Heath and Varde Moor. In many places it is mere fen, where the water lies and stagnates. In others it is a dry waste of sand strewn with coarse grass and a few scant bushes. The village itself consisted of one street of cottages thatched with turf, and with walls built of the same, heather and grass sprouting from the interstices of the blocks. The church was little more dignified than the hovels. It was without tower and bell. Near the church was the parsonage.

The Canon descended from his cob; he had ridden faster than was his wont, and was hot. He drew his sleeve across his face and bald head, and then threw the bridle over the gate-post.

In the door of the parsonage stood a short, stout, rosy-faced, dark-eyed woman, with two little children pulling at her skirts. This was Maren Grubbe, the housekeeper of the pastor, at least that was her official designation. She had been many years at Roager with Peter Nielsen, and was believed to manage him as well as the cattle and pigs and poultry of the glebe. From behind her peered a shock-headed boy of about eight years with a very dirty face and cunning eyes.

The Canon stood and looked at the woman, then at the children, and the woman and children stood and looked at him.

"Is this the house of the priest, Peter Nielsen?" he asked.

"Certainly, do you want him?" inquired the housekeeper.

[Pg 149]
"I have come from Ribe to see him on diocesan business."

"Step inside," said the housekeeper curtly. "His reverence is not in the house at this moment, he is in the church saying his offices."

"That's lies!" shouted the dirty boy from behind. "Dada is in the pigstye setting a trap for the rats."

"Hold your tongue, Jens!" exclaimed the woman, giving the boy a cuff which knocked him over. Then to the Canon she said, "Take a seat and I will go to the church after him."

She went out with the two smaller children staggering at her skirts, tumbling, picking themselves up, going head over heels, crowing and squealing.

When she was outside the house, the dirty boy sat upright on the floor, winked at the Canon, crooked his fingers, and said, "Follow me, and I will show you Dada."

The bald-headed ecclesiastic rose, and guided by the boy went into a back room, through a small window in which he saw into the pig-styes, and there, without his coat, in a pair of stained and patched breeches, and a blue worsted night-cap, over ankles in filth, was the parish priest engaged in setting a rat-trap. Outside, in the yard, the pigs were enjoying their freedom. Leisurely round the corner came the housekeeper with the satellites. "There, Peers!" said she, "There is a reverend gentleman from the cathedral come after thee."

"Then," said the pastor, slowly rising, "do thou, Maren, keep out of sight, and especially be careful[Pg 150] not to produce the brats. Their presence opens the door to misconstruction."

The Canon stole back to his seat, mopped his brow and head, and thought to himself that the Chapter had put the selection of a chief pastor into very queer hands. The nasty little boy began to giggle and snuffle simultaneously. "Have you seen Dada? Dada saying his prayers in there."

"Who are you?" asked the ecclesiastic stiffly of the child.

"I'm Jens," answered the boy.

"I know you are Jens, I heard your mother call you so. I presume that person is your mother."

"That is my mother, but Dada is not my dada."

"O, Jens, boy, Jens! Truth above all things. Magna est veritas et prævalebit." The Reverend Peter Nielsen entered, clean, in a cassock, and with a shovel hat on his head.

"The children whom you have seen," said Peter Nielsen, "are the nephews and nieces of my worthy housekeeper, Maria Grubbe. She is a charitable woman, and as her sister is very poor, and has a large family, my Maren, I mean my housekeeper, takes charge of some of the overflow."[15]

"It is a great burden to you," said the Canon.

Peter Nielsen shrugged his shoulders. "To clothe[Pg 151] the naked and give food to the hungry are deeds of mercy."

"I quite understand, quite," said the Canon.

"I only mentioned it," continued the parish priest, "lest you should suppose—"

"I quite understand," said the Canon, interrupting him, with a bow and a benignant smile.

"And now," said Peter Nielsen, "I am at your service."

Thereupon the Canon unfolded to his astonished hearer the nature of his mission. The pastor sat listening attentively with his head bowed, and his hands planted on his knees. Then, when his visitor had done speaking, he thrust his left hand into his trouser pocket and produced a palmful of carraway seed. He put some into his mouth, and began to chew it; whereupon the whole room became scented with carraway.

"I am fond of this seed," said the priest composedly, whilst he turned over the grains in his hand with the five fingers of his right. "It is good for the stomach, and it clears the brain. So I understand that there are three parties?"

"Exactly, there is that of Olaf Petersen, a narrow, uncompromising man, very sharp on the morals of the clergy; there is also that of the Dean, Thomas Lange, an ambitious and scheming ecclesiastic; and there is lastly that of the Archdeacon Hartwig Juel, one of the most amiable men in the world."

"And you incline strongly to the latter?"

"I do—how could you discover that? Juel is not a man to forget a friend who has done him a favour."

[Pg 152]

"Now, see!" exclaimed Peter Nielsen, "See the advantage of chewing carraway seed. Three minutes ago I knew or recollected nothing about Hartwig Juel, but I do now remember that five years ago he passed through Roager, and did me the honour of partaking of such poor hospitality as I was able to give. I supplied him and his four attendants, and six horses, with refreshment. Bless my soul! the efficacy of carraway is prodigious! I can now recall all that took place. I recollect that I had only hogs' puddings to offer the Archdeacon, his chaplain, and servants, and they ate up all I had. I remember also that I had a little barrel of ale which I broached for them, and they drank the whole dry. To be sure!—I had a bin of oats, and the horses consumed every grain! I know that the Archdeacon regretted that I had no bell to my church, and that he promised to send me one. He also assured me he would not leave a stone unturned till he had secured for me a better and more lucrative cure. I even sent a side of bacon away with him as a present—but nothing came of the promises. I ought to have given him a bushel of carraway. You really have no notion of the poverty of this living. I cannot now offer you any other food than buck-wheat brose, as I have no meat in the house. I can only give you water to drink as I am without beer. I cannot even furnish you with butter and milk, as I have not a cow."

"Not even a cow!" exclaimed the Canon. "I really am thankful for your having spoken so plainly to me. I had no conception that your cure was so poor. That the Archdeacon should not have fulfilled[Pg 153] the promises he made you is due to forgetfulness. Indeed, I assure you, for the last five years I have repeatedly seen Hartwig Juel strike his brow and exclaim, 'Something troubles me. I have made a promise, and cannot recall it. This lies on my conscience, and I shall have no peace till I recollect and discharge it.' This is plain fact."

"Take him a handful of carraway," urged the parish priest.

"No—he will remember all when I speak to him, unaided by carraway."

"There is one thing I can offer you," said Peter Nielsen, "a mug of dill-water."

"Dill-water! what is that?"

"It is made from carraway. It is given to infants to enable them to retain their milk. It is good for adults to make them recollect their promises."

"My dear good friend," said the Canon rising, "your requirements shall be complied with to-morrow. I see you have excellent pasture here for sheep. Have you any?"

The parish priest shook his head.

"That is a pity. That however can be rectified. Good-bye, rely on me. *Qui pacem habet, se primum pacat.*"

When the Canon was gone, Peter Nielsen, who had attended him to the door, turned, and found Maren Grubbe behind him.

"I say, Peers!" spoke the housekeeper, nudging him, "What is the meaning of all this? What was that Latin he said as he went away?"

"My dear, good Maren," answered the priest, "he[Pg 154] quoted a saying familiar to us clergy. At the altar is a little metal plate with a cross on it, and this is called the Pax, or Peace. During the mass the priest kisses it, and then hands it to his assistant, who kisses it in turn and passes it on so throughout the attendance. The Latin means this, 'Let him who has the Pax bless himself with it before giving it out of his hands,' and means nothing more than this: 'Charity begins at Home,' or—put more boldly still, 'Look out for Number I.'"

"Now, see here," said the housekeeper, "you have been too moderate, Peers, you have not looked out sufficiently for Number I. Leave the next comer to me. No doubt that the Dean will send to you, in like manner as the Archdeacon sent to-day."

"As you like, Maren, but keep the children in the background. Charity that thinketh no ill, is an uncommon virtue."

Next morning early there arrived at the parsonage a waggon laden with sides of bacon, smoked beef, a hogshead of prime ale, a barrel of claret, and several sacks of wheat. It had scarcely been unloaded when a couple of milch cows arrived; half an hour later came a drove of sheep. Peter Nielsen disposed of everything satisfactorily about the house and glebe. His eye twinkled, he rubbed his hands, and said to himself with a chuckle, "He who blesses, blesses first himself."

In the course of the morning a rider drew up at the house door. Maren flattened her nose at the little window of the guest-room, and scrutinized the arrival before admitting him. Then she nodded her[Pg 155] head, and whispered to the priest to disappear. A moment later she opened the door, and ushered a stout red-faced ecclesiastic into the room.

"Is the Reverend Pastor at home?" he asked, bowing to Maren Grubbe; "I have come to see him on important business."

"He is at the present moment engaged with a sick parishioner. He will be here in a quarter of an hour. He left word before going out, that should your reverence arrive before his return—"

"What! I was expected!"

"The venerable the Archdeacon sent a deputation to see my master yesterday, and he thought it probable that a deputation from the very Reverend the Dean would arrive to-day."

"Indeed! So Hartwig Juel has stolen a march on us."

"Hartwig Juel had on a visit some little while ago made promises to my master of a couple of cows, a herd of sheep, some ale, wine, wheat, and so on, and he took advantage of the occasion to send all these things to us."

"Indeed! Hartwig Juel's practice is sharp."

"Thomas Lange will make up no doubt for dilatoriness."

"Humph! and Olaf Petersen, has he sent?"

"His deputation will, doubtless, come to-morrow, or even this afternoon."

The Canon folded his hands over his ample paunch, and looked hard at Maren Grubbe. She was attired in her best. Her cheeks shone like quarendon apples, as red and glossy; full of health—with a threat of[Pg 156] temper, just as a hot sky has in it indications of a tempest. Her eyes were dark as sloes, and looked as sharp. She was past middle age, but ripe and strong; for all that.

The fat Canon sat looking at her, twirling his thumbs like a little windmill, over his paunch, without speaking. She also sat demurely with her hands flat on her knees, and looked him full and firm in the face.

"I have been thinking," said the Canon, "how well a set of silver chains would look about that neck, and pendant over that ample bosom."

"Gold would look better," said Maren, and shut her mouth again.

"And a crimson silk kerchief—"

"Would do," interrupted the housekeeper, "for one who has not expectations of a crimson silk skirt."

"Quite so." A pause, and the windmills recommenced working. Presently squeals were heard in the back premises. One of the children had fallen and hurt itself.

"Cats?" asked the Canon.

"Cats," answered Maren.

"Quite so," said the Canon. "I am fond of cats.'

"So am I," said Maren.

Then ensued an uproar. The door burst open, and in tumbled little Jens with one child in his arms, the other clinging to the seat of his pantaloons. These same articles of clothing had belonged to the Reverend Peter Nielsen, till worn out, when at the request of Maren, they had been given to her and cut down in length for Jens. In length they answered.[Pg 157] The waistband was under the arms, indeed, but the legs were not too long. In breadth and capacity they were uncurtailed.

"I cannot manage them, mother," said the boy. "It is of no use making me nurse. Besides, I want to see the stranger."

"These children," said Maren, looking firmly in the face of the Canon, "call me mother, but they are the offspring of my sister, whose husband was lost last winter at sea. Poor thing, she was left with fourteen, and I—"

She put her apron to her eyes and wept.

"O, noble charity!" said the fat priest enthusiastically. "You—I see it all—you took charge of the little orphans. You sacrifice your savings for them, your time is given to them. Emotion overcomes me. What is their name?"

"Katts."

"Cats?"

"John Katts, and little Kristine and Sissely Katts."

"And the worthy pastor assists in supporting these poor orphans?"

"Yes, in spite of his poverty. And now we are on this point, let me ask you if you have not been struck with the meanness of this parsonage house. I can assure you, there is not a decent room in it, upstairs the chambers are open to the rafters, unceiled."

"My worthy woman," said the Canon, "I will see to this myself. Rely upon it, if the Dean becomes Bishop, he will see that the manses of his best clergy are put into thorough repair."

"I should prefer to see the repairs begun at once,"[Pg 158] said Maren. "When the Dean becomes Bishop he will have so much to think about, that he might forget our parsonage house."

"Madam," said the visitor, as he rose, "they shall be executed at once. When I see the charity shown in this humble dwelling, by pastor and housekeeper alike, I feel that it demands instantaneous acknowledgment."

Then in came Peter Nielsen, and said, "I have not sufficient cattle-sheds. Sheep yards are also needed."

"They shall be erected."

Then the Canon caught up little Kirsten and little Sissel, and kissed their dirty faces. Maren's radiant countenance assured the Canon that the cause of Thomas Lange was won with Maren Grubbe.

He took the parish priest by the hand, pressed it, and said in a low tone, "*Qui pacem habet, se primum pacat.* You understand me?"

"Perfectly," answered Peter Nielsen, with a smile.

Next morning early there arrived at Roager a party of masons from Ribe, ready to pull down the old parsonage and build one more commodious and extensive. The pastor went over the plans with the master mason, suggested alterations and enlargements, and then, with a chuckle, he muttered to himself, "That is an excellent saying, *Qui pacem habet, se primum pacat.*" Then looking up, he saw before him an ascetic, hollow-eyed, pale-faced priest.

"I am Olaf Petersen," said the new comer. "I thought best to come over and see you myself; I think the true condition of the Church ought to be set before you, and that you should consider the[Pg 159] spiritual welfare of the poor sheep in the Ribe fold, and give them a chief pastor who will care for the sheep and not for the wool."

"I have got a flock of sheep already," said Peter Nielsen, coldly. "Hartwig Juel sent it me."

"I think," continued Olaf, "that you should consider the edification of the spiritual building."

"I am going to have a new parsonage erected," said Peter Nielsen, stiffly; "Thomas Lange has seen to that."

"The Bishop needed for this diocese," Olaf Petersen went on, "should combine the harmlessness of the dove with the wisdom of the serpent."

"If he does that," said Nielsen, roughly, "he will be half knave and half fool. Let us have the wisdom, that is what we want now; and one of the first maxims of wisdom in Church and State is, *Qui pacem habet, se primum pacat.* You take me?"

Olaf sighed, and shook his head.

"Do you see this plan," said Peter Nielsen. "I am going to have a byre fashioned on that, with room for a dozen oxen. I have but two cows; stables for two horses, I have not one; a waggon shed, I am without a wheeled conveyance. I shall have new rooms, and have no furniture to put in them. Now, to stock and furnish farm and parsonage will cost much money. I have not a hundred shillings in the world. What am I to do? The man who would be Bishop of Ribe should consider the welfare of one of the most influential, learned, and moral of the priests in the diocese, and do what he can to make him comfortable. Before we choose a cow we go over her,[Pg 160] feel her, examine her parts; before we purchase a horse we look at the teeth and explore the hoofs, and try the wind. When we select a bishop we naturally try the stuff of which he is made, if liberal, generous, open-handed, amiable. You understand me?"

Olaf sighed, and drops of cold perspiration stood on his brow. A contest was going on within. Simony was a mortal sin. Was there a savour of simony in offering a present to the man in whose hands the choice of a chief pastor lay? He feared so. But then—did not the end sometimes justify the means? As these questions rose in his mind and refused to be answered, something heavy fell at his feet. His hand had been plucking at his purse, and in his nervousness he had detached it from his girdle, and had let it slip through his fingers. He did not look down. He seemed not to notice his loss, but he moved away without another word, with bent head and troubled conscience. When he was gone, Peter Nielsen bowed himself, picked up the pouch, counted the gold coins in it, laughed, rubbed his hands, and said, "He who blesses, blesses first himself."

Next day a litter stayed at the parsonage gate, and out of it, with great difficulty, supported on the arms of two servants, came the aged Jep Mundelstrup. He entered the guest-room and was accommodated with a seat. When he got his breath, he said, extending a roll of parchment to the incumbent of Roager, "You will not fail to remember that it was at *my* suggestion that the choice of a bishop was left with you. You are deeply indebted to me. But for me[Pg 161] you would not have been visited and canvassed by the Dean, the Arch-deacon, and the Ascetic, either in person or by their representatives. You will please to remember that I was nominated, but seeing so many others proposed, I withdrew my name. I think you will allow that this exhibited great humility and shrinking from honour. In these worldly, self-seeking days such an example deserves notice and reward. I am old, and perhaps unequal to the labours of office, but I think I ought to be considered; although I did formally withdraw my candidature, I am not sure that I would refuse the mitre were it pressed on me. At all events it would be a compliment to offer it me and I might refuse it. *Qui pacem habet, se primum pacat.* You will not regret the return courtesy."

* * * * * *

Boom! Boom! Boom! The cathedral bell was summoning all Ribe to the minster to be present at the nomination of its bishop. All Ribe answered the summons.

The cathedral stands on a hill called the Mount of Lilies, but the mount is of so slight an elevation that it does not protect the cathedral from overflow, and a spring tide with N.W. wind has been known to flood both town and minster and leave fishes on the sacred floor. The church is built of granite, brick and sandstone; originally the contrast may have been striking, but weather has smudged the colours together into an ugly brown-grey. The tower is lofty, narrow, and wanting a spire. It resembles a square ruler set up on end; it is too tall for its base. The church is stately, of early architecture with transepts, and the[Pg 162] choir at their intersection with the nave, domed over, and a small semi-circular apse beyond, for the altar. The nave was crowded, the canons occupied the stalls in their purple tippets edged with crimson; purple, because the chapter of a cathedral; crimson edged, because the founder of the See was a martyr. Fifteen, and the Dean, sixteen in all, were in their places. On the altar steps, in the apse, in the centre, sat Peter Nielsen in his old, worn cassock, without surplice. On the left side of the altar stood the richly-sculptured Episcopal throne, and on the seat was placed the jewelled mitre, over the arm the cloth of gold cope was cast, and against the back leaned the pastoral crook of silver gilt, encrusted with precious stones.

When the last note of the bell sounded, the Dean rose from his stall, and stepping up to the apse, made oath before heaven, the whole congregation and Peter Nielsen, that he was prepared to abide by the decision of this said Peter, son of Nicolas, parish priest of Roager. Amen. He was followed by the Archdeacon, then by each of the canons to the last.

Then mass was said, during which the man in whose hands the fortunes of the See reposed, knelt with unimpassioned countenance and folded hands.

At the conclusion he resumed his seat, the crucifix was brought forth and he kissed it.

A moment of anxious silence. The moment for the decision had arrived. He remained for a short while seated, with his eyes fixed on the ground, then he turned them on the anxious face of the Dean, and after having allowed them to rest scrutinisingly there for a minute, he looked at Hartwig Juel, then at Olaf[Pg 163] Petersen, who was deadly white, and whose frame shook like an aspen leaf. Then he looked long at Jep Mundelstrup and rose suddenly to his feet.

The fall of a pin might have been heard in the cathedral at that moment.

He said—and his voice was distinctly audible by every one present—"I have been summoned here from my barren heath, into this city, out of a poor hamlet, by these worthy and reverend fathers, to choose for them a prelate who shall be at once careful of the temporal and the spiritual welfare of the See. I have scrupulously considered the merits of all those who have been presented to me as candidates for the mitre. I find that in only one man are all the requisite qualities combined in proper proportion and degree—not in Thomas Lange," the Dean's head fell on his bosom, "nor in Hartwig Juel," the Archdeacon sank back in his stall; "nor in Olaf Petersen," the man designated uttered a faint cry and dropped on his knees, "nor in Jep Mundelstrup—but in myself. I therefore nominate Peter, son of Nicolas, commonly called Nielsen, Curate of Roager, to be Bishop of Ribe, twenty-ninth in descent from Liafdag the martyr. *Qui pacem habet, se primum pacat*. Amen. He who has to bless, blesses first himself."

Then he sat down.

For a moment there was silence, and then a storm broke loose. Peter sat motionless, with his eyes fixed on the ground, motionless as a rock round which the waves toss and tear themselves to foam.

Thus it came about that the twenty-ninth bishop of Ribe was Peter Nielsen.

FOOTNOTE:

[15] In Norway, Denmark, Sweden, and Iceland, clerical celibacy was never enforced before the Reformation. Now and then a formal prohibition was issued by the bishops, but it was generally ignored. The clergy were married, openly and undisguisedly.

[Pg 164]

The Wonder-Working Prince Hohenlohe.

In the year 1821, much interest was excited in Germany and, indeed, throughout Europe by the report that miracles of healing were being wrought by Prince Leopold Alexander of Hohenlohe-Waldenburg-Schillingsfürst at Würzburg, Bamberg, and elsewhere. The wonders soon came to an end, for, after the ensuing year, no more was heard of his extraordinary powers.

At the time, as might be expected, his claims to be a miracle-worker were hotly disputed, and as hotly asserted. Evidence was produced that some of his miracles were genuine; counter evidence was brought forward reducing them to nothing.

The whole story of Prince Hohenlohe's sudden blaze into fame, and speedy extinction, is both curious and instructive. In the Baden village of Wittighausen, at the beginning of this century, lived a peasant named Martin Michel, owning a farm, and in fairly prosperous circumstances. His age, according to one authority, was fifty, according to another sixty-seven, when he became acquainted with Prince Hohenlohe. This peasant was unquestionably a devout, guileless man. He had been afflicted in youth with a rupture, but, in answer to continuous and earnest prayer, he asserted that he had been completely[Pg 165] healed. Then, for some while he prayed over other afflicted persons, and it was rumoured that he had effected several miraculous cures. He emphatically and earnestly repudiated every claim to superior sanctity. The cures, he declared, depended on the faith of the patient, and on the power of the Almighty. The most solemn promises had been made in the gospel to those who asked in faith, and all he did was to act upon these evangelical promises.

The Government speedily interfered, and Michel was forbidden by the police to work any more miracles by prayer or faith, or any other means except the recognised pharmacopœia.

He had received no payment for his cures in money or in kind, but he took occasion through them to impress on his patients the duty of prayer, and the efficacy of faith.

By some means he met Prince Alexander Hohenlohe, and the prince was interested and excited by what he heard, and by the apparent sincerity of the man. A few days later the prince was in Würzburg, where he called on the Princess Mathilde Schwarzenberg, a young girl of seventeen who was a cripple, and who had already spent a year and a half at Würzburg, under the hands of the orthopædic physician Heine, and the surgeon Textor. She had been to the best medical men in Vienna and Paris, and the case had been given up as hopeless. Then Prince Schwarzenberg placed her under the treatment of Heine. She was so contracted, with her knees drawn up to her body, that she could neither stand nor walk.

Prince Hohenlohe first met her at dinner, on June[Pg 166] 18, 1821, and the sight of her distortion filled him with pity. He thought over her case, and communicated with Michel, who at his summons came to Würzburg. As Würzburg is in Bavaria, the orders of the Baden Government did not extend to it, and the peasant might freely conduct his experiments there.

Prince Alexander called on the Princess at ten o'clock in the morning of June 20, taking with him Michel, but leaving him outside the house, in the court. Then Prince Hohenlohe began to speak to the suffering girl of the power of faith, and mentioned the wonders wrought by the prayers of Michel. She became interested, and the Prince asked her if she would like to put the powers of Michel to the test, warning her that the man could do nothing unless she had full and perfect belief in the mercy of God. The Princess expressed her eagerness to try the new remedy and assured her interrogator that she had the requisite faith. Thereupon he went to the window, and signed to the peasant to come up.

What follows shall be given in the Princess's own words, from her account written a day or two later:—"The peasant knelt down and prayed in German aloud and distinctly, and, after his prayer, he said to me, 'In the Name of Jesus, stand up. You are whole, and can both stand and walk!' The peasant and the Prince then went into an adjoining room, and I rose from my couch, without assistance, in the name of God, well and sound, and so I have continued to this moment."

A much fuller and minuter account of the proceedings was published, probably from the pen of the[Pg 167] governess, who was present at the time; but as it is anonymous we need not concern ourselves with it.

The news of the miraculous recovery spread through the town; Dr. Heine heard of it, and ran to the house, and stood silent and amazed at what he saw. The Princess descended the stone staircase towards the garden, but hesitated, and, instead of going into the garden, returned upstairs, leaning on the arm of Prince Hohenlohe.

Next day was Corpus Christi. The excitement in the town was immense, when the poor cripple, who had been seen for more than a year carried into her carriage and carried out of it into church, walked to church, and thence strolled into the gardens of the palace.

On the following day she visited the Julius Hospital, a noble institution founded by one of the bishops of Würzburg. On the 24th she called on the Princess Lichtenstein, the Duke of Aremberg, and the Prince of Baar, and moreover, attended a sermon preached by Prince Hohenlohe in the Haugh parish church. Her recovery was complete.

Now, at first sight, nothing seems more satisfactorily established than this miracle. Let us, however, see what Dr. Heine, who had attended her for nineteen months, had to say on it. We cannot quote his account in its entirety, as it is long, but we will take the principal points in it:—"The Princess of Schwarzenberg came under my treatment at the end of October, 1819, afflicted with several abnormities of the thorax, with a twisted spine, ribs, &c. Moreover, she could not rise to her feet from a sitting posture,[Pg 168]nor endure to be so raised; but this was not in consequence of malformation or weakness of the system, for when sitting or lying down she could freely move her limbs. She complained of acute pain when placed in any other position, and when she was made to assume an angle of 100° her agony became so intense that her extremities were in a nervous quiver, and partial paralysis ensued, which, however, ceased when she was restored to her habitual contracted position.

"The Princess lost her power of locomotion when she was three years old, and the contraction was the result of abscesses on the loins. She was taken to France and Italy, and got so far in Paris as to be able to hop about a room supported on crutches. But she suffered a relapse on her return to Vienna in 1813, and thenceforth was able neither to stand nor to move about. She was placed in my hands, and I contrived an apparatus by which the angle at which she rested was gradually extended, and her position gradually changed from horizontal to vertical. At the same time I manipulated her almost daily, and had the satisfaction by the end of last April to see her occupy an angle of 50°, without complaining of suffering. By the close of May further advance was made, and she was able to assume a vertical position, with her feet resting on the ground, but with her body supported, and to remain in this position for four or five hours. Moreover, in this situation I made her go through all the motions of walking. The extremities had, in every position, retained their natural muscular powers and movements, and the contraction was[Pg 169] simply a nervous affection. I made no attempt to force her to walk unsupported, because I would not do this till I was well assured such a trial would not be injurious to her.

"On the 30th of May I revisited her, after having been unable, on account of a slight indisposition, to see my patients for several days. Her governess then told me that the Princess had made great progress. She lay at an angle of 80°. The governess placed herself at the foot of the couch, held out her hands to the Princess, and drew her up into an upright position, and she told me that this had been done several times of late during my enforced absence. Whilst she was thus standing I made the Princess raise and depress her feet, and go through all the motions of walking. Immediately on my return home I set to work to construct a machine which might enable her to walk without risk of a fall and of hurting herself. On the 19th of June, in the evening, I told the Princess that the apparatus was nearly finished. Next day, a little after 10 A.M., I visited her. When I opened her door she rose up from a chair in which she was seated, and came towards me with short, somewhat uncertain steps. I bowed myself, in token of joy and thanks to God.

"At that moment a gentleman I had never seen before entered the room and exclaimed, 'Mathilde! you have had faith in God!' The Princess replied, 'I have had, and I have now, entire faith.' The gentleman said, 'Your faith has saved and healed you. God has succoured you.' Then I began to suspect that some strange influence was at work, and[Pg 170]that something had been going on of which I was not cognizant. I asked the gentleman what was the meaning of this. He raised his right hand to heaven, and replied that he had prayed and thought of the Princess that morning at mass, and that Prince Wallerstein was privy to the whole proceeding. I was puzzled and amazed. Then I asked the Princess to walk again. She did so, and shortly after I left, and only then did I learn that the stranger was the Prince of Hohenlohe.

"Next month, on July 21, her aunt, the Princess Eleanor of Schwarzenberg, came with three of the sisters of Princess Mathilde to fetch her away and to take her back to her father. Her Highness did me the honour of visiting me along with the Princesses on the second day after their arrival, to thank me for the pains I had taken to cure the Princess Mathilde. Before they left, Dr. Schäfer, who had attended her at Ratisbon, Herr Textor, and myself were allowed to examine the Princess. Dr. Schäfer found that the condition of the thorax was mightily improved since she had been in my hands. I, however, saw that her condition had retrograded since I had last seen her on June 20, and it was agreed that the Princess was to occupy her extension-couch at night, and by day wear the steel apparatus for support I had contrived for her. At the same time Dr. Schäfer distinctly assured her and the Princess, her aunt, that under my management the patient had recovered the power of walking *before* the 19th of June."

This account puts a different complexion on the cure, and shows that it was not in any way [Pg 171]miraculous. The Prince and the peasant stepped in and snatched the credit of having cured the Princess from the doctor, to whom it rightly belonged.

Before we proceed, it will be well to say a few words about this Prince Alexander Hohenlohe. The Hohenlohe family takes its name from a bare elevated plateau in Franconia. About the beginning of the 16th century it broke into two branches; the elder is Hohenlohe-Neuenstein, the younger is Hohenlohe-Waldenburg.

The elder branch has its sub-ramifications—Hohenlohe-Langenburg, which possesses also the county of Gleichen; and the Hohenlohe-Oehringen and the Hohenlohe-Kirchberg sub-branches. The second main branch of Hohenlohe-Waldenburg has also its lateral branches, as those of Hohenlohe-Bartenstein and Hohenlohe-Schillingsfürst; the last of these being Catholic.

Prince Leopold Alexander was born in 1794 at Kupferzell, near Waldenburg, and was the eighteenth child of Prince Karl Albrecht and his wife Judith, Baroness Reviczky. His father never became reigning prince, from intellectual incapacity, and Alexander lost him when he was one year old. He was educated for the Church by the ex-Jesuit Riel, and went to school first in Vienna, then at Berne; in 1810 he entered the Episcopal seminary at Vienna, and finished his theological studies at Ellwangen in 1814. He was ordained priest in 1816, and went to Rome.

Dr. Wolff, the father of Sir Henry Drummond Wolff, in his "Travels and Adventures," which is really his autobiography, says (vol i. p. 31):—

[Pg 172]
"Wolff left the house of Count Stolberg on the 3rd April, 1815, and went to Ellwangen, and there met again an old pupil from Vienna, Prince Alexander Hohenlohe-Schillingsfürst, afterwards so celebrated for his miracles—to which so many men of the highest rank and intelligence have borne witness that Wolff dares not give a decided opinion about them. But Niebuhr relates that the Pope said to him himself, speaking about Hohenlohe in a sneering manner, '*Questo* far dei miracoli!' *This* fellow performing miracles!

"It may be best to offer some slight sketch of Hohenlohe's life. His person was beautiful. He was placed under the direction of Vock, the Roman Catholic parish priest at Berne. One Sunday he was invited to dinner with Vock, his tutor, at the Spanish ambassador's. The next day there was a great noise in the Spanish embassy, because the mass-robe, with the silver chalice and all its appurtenances, had been stolen. It was advertised in the paper, but nothing could be discovered, until Vock took Prince Hohenlohe aside, and said to him, 'Prince, confess to me; have you not stolen the mass-robe?' He at once confessed it, and said that he made use of it every morning in practising the celebration of the mass in his room; which was true." (This was when Hohenlohe was twenty-one years old.) "He was afterwards sent to Tyrnau, to the ecclesiastical seminary in Hungary, whence he was expelled, on account of levity. But, being a Prince, the Chapter of Olmütz, in Moravia, elected him titulary canon of the cathedral; nevertheless, the Emperor Francis was too[Pg 173] honest to confirm it. Wolff taught him Hebrew in Vienna. He had but little talent for languages, but his conversation on religion was sometimes very charming; and at other times he broke out into most indecent discourses. He was ordained priest, and Sailer[16] preached a sermon on the day of his ordination, which was published under the title of 'The Priest without Reproach.' On the same day money was collected for building a Roman Catholic Church at Zürich, and the money collected was given to Prince Hohenlohe, to be remitted to the parish priest of Zürich (Moritz Mayer); but the money never reached its destination. Wolff saw him once at the bed of the sick and dying, and his discourse, exhortations, and treatment of these sick people were wonderfully beautiful. When he mounted the pulpit to preach, one imagined one saw a saint of the Middle Ages. His devotion was penetrating, and commanded silence in a church where there were 4,000 people collected. Wolff one day called on him, when Hohenlohe said to him, 'I never read any other book than the Bible. I never look in a sermon-book by anybody else, not even at the sermons of Sailer.' But Wolff after this heard him preach, and the whole sermon was copied from one of Sailer's, which Wolff had read only the day before.

"With all his faults, Hohenlohe cannot be charged with avarice, for he give away every farthing he got, perhaps even that which he obtained dishonestly.[Pg 174] They afterwards met at Rome, where Hohenlohe lodged with the Jesuits, and there it was said he composed a Latin poem. Wolff, knowing his incapacity to do such a thing, asked him boldly, 'Who is the author of this poem?' Hohenlohe confessed at once that it was written by a Jesuit priest. At that time Madame Schlegel wrote to Wolff: 'Prince Hohenlohe is a man who struggles with heaven and hell, and heaven will gain the victory with him.' Hohenlohe was on the point of being made a bishop at Rome, but, on the strength of his previous knowledge of him, Wolff protested against his consecration. Several princes, amongst them Kaunitz, the ambassador, took Hohenlohe's part on this occasion; but the matter was investigated, and Hohenlohe walked off from Rome without being made a bishop. In his protest against the man, Wolff stated that Hohenlohe's pretensions to being a canon of Olmütz were false; that he had been expelled the seminary of Tyrnau; that he sometimes spoke like a saint, and at others like a profligate."

And now let us return to Würzburg, and see the result of the cure of Princess Schwarzenberg. The people who had seen the poor cripple one day carried into her carriage and into church, and a day or two after saw her walk to church and in the gardens, and who knew nothing of Dr. Heine's operations, concluded that this was a miracle, and gave the credit of it quite as much to Prince Hohenlohe as to the peasant Michel.

The police at once sent an official letter to the Prince, requesting to be informed authoritatively what[Pg 175] he had done, by what right he had interfered, and how he had acted. He replied that he had done nothing, faith and the Almighty had wrought the miracle. "The instantaneous cure of the Princess is a *fact*, which cannot be disputed; it was the result of a living faith. That is the truth. It happened to the Princess according to her faith." The peasant Michel now fell into the background, and was forgotten, and the Prince stood forward as the worker of miraculous cures. Immense excitement was caused by the restoration of the Princess Schwarzenberg, and patients streamed into Würzburg from all the country round, seeking health at the hands of Prince Alexander. The local papers published marvellous details of his successful cures. The blind saw, the lame walked, the deaf heard. Among the deaf who recovered was His Royal Highness the Crown Prince of Bavaria, three years later King Ludwig I., grandfather of the late King of

Bavaria. Unfortunately we have not exact details of this cure, but a letter of the Crown Prince written shortly after merely states that he heard *better* than before. Now the spring of 1821 was very raw and wet, and about June 20 there set in some dry hot weather. It is therefore quite possible that the change of weather may have had to do with this cure. However, we can say nothing for certain about it, as no data were published, merely the announcement that the Crown Prince had recovered his hearing at the prayer of Prince Hohenlohe. Here are some better-authenticated cases, as given by Herr Scharold, an eye-witness; he was city councillor and secretary.

[Pg 176]
"The Prince had dined at midday with General von D———. All the entrances to the house from two streets were blocked by hundreds of persons, and they said that he had already healed four individuals crippled with rheumatism in this house. I convinced myself on the spot that one of these cases was as said. The patient was the young wife of a fisherman, who was crippled in the right hand, so that she could not lift anything with it, or use it in any way; and all at once she was enabled to raise a heavy chair, with the hand hitherto powerless, and hold it aloft. She went home weeping tears of joy and thankfulness.

"The Prince was then entreated to go to another house, at another end of the town, and he consented. There he found many paralysed persons. He began with a poor man whose left arm was quite useless and stiff. After he had asked him if he had perfect faith, and had received a satisfactory answer, the Prince prayed with folded hands and closed eyes. Then he raised the kneeling patient; and said, 'Move your arm.' Weeping and trembling in all his limbs the man did as he was bid; but as he said that he obeyed with difficulty, the Prince prayed again, and said, 'Now move your arm again.' This time the man easily moved his arm forwards, backwards, and raised it. The cure was complete. Equally successful was he with the next two cases. One was a tailor's wife, named Lanzamer. 'What do you want?' asked the Prince, who was bathed in perspiration. Answer: 'I have had a paralytic stroke, and have lost the use of one side of my body, so that I cannot walk unsupported.' 'Kneel down!' But[Pg 177] this could only be effected with difficulty, and it was rather a tumbling down of an inert body, painful to behold. I never saw a face more full of expression of faith in the strongly marked features. The Prince, deeply moved, prayed with great fervour, and then said, 'Stand up!' The good woman, much agitated, was unable to do so, in spite of all her efforts, without the assistance of her boy, who was by her, crying, and then her lame leg seemed to crack. When she had reached her feet, he said, 'Now walk the length of the room without pain.' She tried to do so, but succeeded with difficulty, yet with only a little suffering. Again he prayed, and the healing was complete; she walked lightly and painlessly up and down, and finally out of the room; and the boy, crying more than before, but now with joy, exclaimed, 'O my God! mother can walk, mother can walk!' Whilst this was going on, an old woman, called Siebert, wife of a bookbinder, who had been brought in a sedan-chair, was admitted to the room. She suffered from paralysis and incessant headaches that left her neither night nor day. The first attempt made to heal her failed. The second only brought on the paroxysm of headache worse than ever, so that the poor creature could hardly keep her feet or open her eyes. The Prince began to doubt her faith, but when she assured him of it, he prayed again with redoubled earnestness. And, all at once, she was cured. This woman left the room, conducted by her daughter, and all present were filled with astonishment." This account was written on June 26. On June 28 Herr Scharold wrote a further account of other cures he had[Pg 178]witnessed; but those already given are sufficient. That this witness was convinced and sincere appears from his description, but how far valuable his evidence is we are not so well assured.

A curious little pamphlet was published the same year at Darmstadt, entitled, "Das Mährchen vom Wunder," that professed to be the result of the observations of a medical man who attended one or two of these *séances*. Unfortunately the pamphlet is anonymous, and this deprives it of most of its authority. Another writer who attacked the genuineness of the miracles was Dr. Paulus, in his "Quintessenz aus den Wundercurversuchen durch Michel und Hohenlohe," Leipzig, 1822; but this author also wrote anonymously, and did not profess to have seen any of the cures. On the other hand, Scharold and a Dr. Onymus, and two or three priests published their testimonies as witnesses to their genuineness, and gave the names and particulars of those cured.

Those who assailed the Prince and his cures dipped their pens in gall. It is only just to add that they cast on his character none of the reflections for honesty which Dr. Wolff flung on him.

The author of the Darmstadt pamphlet, mentioned above, says that when he was present the Prince was attended by two sergeants of police, as the crowd thronging on him was so great that he needed protection from its pressure. He speaks sneeringly of him as spending his time in eating, smoking, and miracle-working, when not sleeping, and says he was plump and good-looking, "A girl of eighteen, who was paralysed in her limbs, was brought from a [Pg 179]carriage to the feet of the prophet. After he had asked her if she believed, and he had prayed for about twelve seconds, he exclaimed in a threatening rather than gentle voice, 'You are healed!' But I observed that he had to thunder this thrice into the ear of the frightened girl, before she made an effort to move, which was painful and distressing; and, groaning and supported by others, she made her way to the rear. 'You will be better shortly—only believe!' he cried to her. I, who was looking on, observed her conveyed away as much a cripple as she came.

"The next case was a peasant of fifty-eight, a cripple on crutches. Without his crutches he was doubled up, and could only shuffle with his feet on the ground. After the Prince had asked the usual questions and had prayed, he ordered the kneeling man to stand up, his crutches having been removed. As he was unable to do so, the miracle-worker seemed irritated, and repeated his order in an angry tone. One of the policemen at the side threw in 'Up! in the name of the Trinity,' and pulled him to his feet. The man seemed bewildered. He stood, indeed, but doubled as before, and the sweat streamed from his face, and he was not a ha'porth better than previously; but as he had come with crutches, and now stood without them, there arose a shout of 'A miracle!' and all pressed round to congratulate the poor wretch. His son helped him away. 'Have faith and courage!' cried to him the Prince; and the policeman added, 'Only believe, and rub in a little spirits of camphor!' Many pressed alms into the man's hand, and he smiled; this was regarded as a token of his perfect[Pg 180] cure. I saw, however, that his knees were as stiff as before, and that the rogue cast longing eyes at his crutches, which had been taken away, but which he insisted on having back. No one thought of asking how it fared with the poor wretch later, and, as a fact, he died shortly after.

"The next to come up was a deaf girl of eighteen. The wonder-worker was bathed in perspiration, and evidently exhausted with his continuous prayer night and day. After a few questions as to the duration of her infirmity, the Prince prayed, then signed a cross over the girl, and, stepping back from her, asked her questions, at each in succession somewhat lowering his tone; but she only heard those spoken as loudly as before the experiment was made, and she remained for the most part staring stupidly at the wonder-worker. To cut the matter short, he declared her healed. I took the mother aside soon after, and inquired what was the result. She assured me that the girl heard no better than before.

"In her place came a stone-deaf man of twenty-five. The result was very similar; but as the Prince, when bidding him depart healed, made a sign of withdrawal with his hand, the man rose and departed, and this was taken as evidence that he had heard the command addressed to him."

The author gives other cases that he witnessed, not one of which was other than a failure, though they were all declared to be cures.

On June 29 the Prince practised his miracle-working at the palace, in the presence of the Crown Prince and of Prince Esterhazy, the Austrian ambassador[Pg 181] who was on his way to London to attend the coronation of George IV. in July. The attempts were probably as great failures as those described in the Darmstadt pamphlet. The Prince was somewhat discouraged at the invitation of the physicians attached to the Julius Hospital; he had visited that institution the day before, and had experimented on twenty cases, and was unsuccessful in every one. Full particulars of these were published in the "Bamberger Briefe," Nos. 28-33. We will give only a very few:—

"1. Barbara Uhlen, of Oberschleichach, aged 39, suffering from dropsy. The Prince said to her, 'Do you sincerely believe that you can be helped and are helped?' The sick woman replied, 'Yes. I had resolved to leave the hospital, where no good has been done to me, and to seek health from God and the Prince.' He raised his eyes to heaven and prayed; then assured the patient of her cure. Her case became worse rapidly, instead of better.

"7. Margaretta Löhlein, of Randersacher, aged 56. Suffering from dropsy owing to disorganisation of the liver. Another failure. Shortly after the Prince left, she had to be operated on to save her from suffocation.

"10. Susanna Söllnerin, servant maid of Aub, aged 22, had already been thirteen weeks in hospital, suffering from roaring noises in the head and deafness. The Prince, observing the fervour of her faith, cried out, 'You shall see now how speedily she will be cured!' Prayers, blessing, as before, and—as before, no results.

[Pg 182]
"11. George Forchheimer, butcher, suffering from rheumatism. One foot is immovable, and he can only walk with the assistance of a stick. During the prayer of the Prince the patient wept and sobbed, and was profoundly agitated. The Prince ordered him to stand up and go without his stick. His efforts to obey were unavailing; he fell several times on the ground, though the Prince repeated over him his prayers."

These are sufficient as instances; not a single case in the hospital was more successfully treated by him.

On July 5 Prince Hohenlohe went to Bamberg, where he was eagerly awaited by many sick and credulous persons. The Burgomaster Hornthal, however, interfered, and forbade the attempt at performing miracles till the authorities at Baireuth had been instructed of his arrival, and till a commission had been appointed of men of judgment, and physicians to take note of the previous condition of every patient who was submitted to him, and of the subsequent condition. Thus hampered the Prince could do nothing; he failed as signally as in the Julius Hospital at Würzburg, and the only cases of cures claimed to have been wrought were among a mixed crowd in the street to whom he gave a blessing from the balcony of his lodging.

Finding that Bamberg was uncongenial, he accepted a call to the Baths of Brückenau, and thence news reached the incredulous of Bamberg and Würzburg that extraordinary cures had been wrought at the prayers of the Prince. As, however, we have no details respecting these, we may pass them over.

[Pg 183]

Hohenlohe, who had no notion of hiding his light under a bushel, drew up a detailed account of over a hundred cures which he claimed to have worked, had them attested by witnesses, and sent this precious document to the Pope, who, with good sense, took no notice of it; at least no public notice, though it is probable that he administered a sharp private reprimand, for Hohenlohe collapsed very speedily.

From Brückenau the Prince went to Vienna, but was not favourably received there, so he departed to Hungary, where his mother's relations lived. Though he was applied to by sick people who had heard of his fame, he did not make any more direct attempts to heal them. He, however, gave them cards on which a day and hour were fixed, and a prayer written, and exhorted them to pray for recovery earnestly on the day and at the hour indicated, and promised to pray for them at the same time. But this was also discontinued, having proved inefficacious, and Hohenlohe relapsed into a quiet unostentatious life. He was appointed, through family interest, Canon of Grosswardein, and in 1829 advanced to be Provost of the Cathedral. His powers as a preacher long survived his powers of working miracles. He spent his time in good works, and in writing little manuals of devotion. In 1844 he was consecrated titular Bishop of Sardic*in partibus*, that is, without a See. He died at Vöslau, near Vienna, in 1849. That Hohenlohe was a conscious hypocrite we are far from supposing. He was clearly a man of small mental powers, very conceited, and wanting in judgment.[Pg 184] We must not place too much reliance on the scandalous gossip of Dr. Wolff. Probably Hohenlohe's vanity received a severe check in 1821, when both the Roman See and the world united to discredit his miracles; and he had sufficient good sense to accept the verdict.

FOOTNOTE:

[16] Johann M. Sailer was a famous ex-Jesuit preacher, at this time Professor at the University of Landshut, afterwards Bishop of Ratisbon. He died, 1832.

[Pg 185]

The Snail-Telegraph.

The writer well remembers, as a child, the sense of awe not unmixed with fear, with which he observed the mysterious movements of the telegraph erected on church towers in France along all the main roads.

Many a beautiful tower was spoiled by these abominable erections. There were huge arms like those of a windmill, painted black, and jointed, so as to describe a great number of cabalistic signs in the air. Indeed, the movements were like the writhings of some monstrous spider.

Glanvil who wrote in the middle of the 17th century says, "To those that come after us, it may be as ordinary to buy a pair of wings to fly into the remotest regions, as now a pair of boots to ride a journey. *And to confer, at the distance of the Indies, by sympathetic conveyances*, may be as usual to future times as to us is literary correspondence." He further remarks, "Antiquity would not have believed the almost incredible force of our cannons, and would as coldly have entertained the wonders of the telescope. In these we all condemn antique incredulity. And it is likely posterity will have as much cause to pity ours. But those who are acquainted with the diligent and ingenious endeavours of true philosophers will despair of nothing."

In 1633 the Marquis of Worcester suggested a[Pg 186] scheme of telegraphing by means of signs. Another, but similar scheme, was mooted in 1660 by the Frenchman

Amonton. In 1763 Mr. Edgeworth erected for his private use a telegraph between London and Newmarket. But it was in 1789 that the Optical Telegraph came into practical use in France—Claude Chappe was the inventor. When he was a boy, he contrived a means of communication by signals with his brothers at a distance of two or three miles. He laid down the first line between Lille and Paris at a cost of about two thousand pounds, and the first message sent along it was the announcement of the capture of Lille by Condé. This led to the construction of many similar lines communicating with each other by means of stations. Some idea of the celerity with which messages were sent may be gained from the fact that it took only two minutes to reproduce in Paris a sign given in Lille at a distance of 140 miles. On this line there were 22 stations. The objections to this system lay in its being useless at night and in rainy weather. The French system of telegraph consisted of one main beam—the regulator, at the end of which were two shorter wings, so that it formed a letter Z. The regulator and its flags could be turned about in various ways, making in all 196 signs. Sometimes the regulator stood horizontally, sometimes perpendicularly.

Lord Murray introduced one of a different construction in England in 1795 consisting of two rows of three octangular flags revolving on their axis. This gave 64 different signs, but was defective in the[Pg 187] same point as that of Chappe. Poor Chappe was so troubled in mind because his claim to be the inventor of his telegraph was disputed, that he drowned himself in a well, 1805.

Besides the fact that the optical telegraph was paralysed by darkness and storm, it was very difficult to manage in mountainous and well-wooded country, and required there a great number of stations.

After that Sömmering had discovered at Munich in 1808 the means of signalling through the galvanic current obtained by decomposition of water, and Schilling at Canstadt and Ampère in Paris (1820) had made further advances in the science of electrology, and Oersted had established the deflexion of the magnetic needle, it was felt that the day of the cumbrous and disfiguring optical telegraph was over. A new power had been discovered, though the extent and the applicability of this power were not known. Gauss and Weber in 1833 made the first attempt to set up an electric telegraph; in 1837 Wheatstone and Morse utilised the needle and made the telegraph print its messages. In 1833 the telegraph of Gauss and Weber supplanted the optical contrivance on the line between Trèves and Berlin. The first line in America was laid from Washington to Baltimore in 1844. The first attempt at submarine telegraphy was made at Portsmouth in 1846, and in 1850 a cable was laid between England and France.

It was precisely in this year when men's minds were excited over the wonderful powers of the galvanic current, and a wide prospect was opened of its future advantage to men, when, indeed, the general public[Pg 188] understood very little about the principle and were in a condition of mind to accept almost any scientific marvel, that there appeared in Paris an adventurer, who undertook to open communications between all parts of the world without the expense and difficulty of laying cables of communication. The line laid across the channel in 1850 was not very successful; it broke several times, and had to be taken up again, and relaid in 1851. If it did not answer in conveying messages across so narrow a strip of water, was it likely to be utilized for Transatlantic telegraphy? The *Presse*, a respectable Paris paper, conducted by a journalist of note, M. de Girardin, answered emphatically, No. The means of communication was not to be sought in a chain. The gutta percha casing would decompose under the sea, and when the brine touched the wires, the cable would be useless. The Chappe telegraph was superseded by the electric telegraph which answered well on dry land, but fatal objections stood in the way of its answering for communication between places divided by belts of sea or oceans. Moreover, it was an intricate system. Now the tendency of science in modern times was towards simplification; and it was always found that the key to unlock difficulties which had puzzled the inventors of the past, lay at their hands. The electric telegraph was certainly more elaborate, complicated and expensive than the optical telegraph. Was it such a decided advance on it? Yes—in one way. It could be worked at all hours of night and day. But had the last word in telegraphy been spoken, when it was invented? Most assuredly not.

[Pg 189]

Along with electricity and terrestrial magnetism, another power, vaguely perceived, the full utility of which was also unknown, had been recognised—animal magnetism. Why should not this force be used as a means for the conveyance of messages?

M. Jules Allix after a long preamble in *La Presse*, in an article signed by himself, announced that a French inventor, M. Jacques Toussaint Benoît (de l'Hérault), and a fellow worker of Gallic origin, living in America, M. Biat-Chrétien, had hit on "a new system of universal intercommunication of thought, which operates instantaneously."

After a long introduction in true French rhodomontade, tracing the progress of humanity from the publication of the Gospel to the 19th century, M. Allix continued, "The discovery of MM. Benoît and Biat depends on galvanism, terrestrial and animal magnetism, also on natural sympathy, that is to say, the base of communication is a sort of special sympathetic fluid which is composed of the union or blending of the galvanic, magnetic and sympathetic currents, by a process to be described shortly. And as the various fluids vary according to the organic or inorganic bodies whence they are derived, it is necessary further to state that the forces or fluids here married are: (*a*) The terrestrial-galvanic current, (*b*) the animal-sympathetic current, in this case derived from *snails*, (*c*) the adamic or human current, or animal-magnetic current in man. Consequently, to describe concisely the basis of the new system of intercommunication, we shall have to call the force, '*The galvano-terrestrial-magnetic-animal and adamic*[Pg 190] *force!*'" Is not this something like a piece of Jules Verne's delicious scientific *hocus-pocus*? Will the reader believe that it was written in good faith? It was, there can be no question, written in perfect good faith. The character of *La Presse*, of the journalist, M. Jules Allix, would not allow of a hoax wilfully perpetrated on the public. We are quoting from the number for October 27th, 1850, of the paper.

"According to the experiments made by MM. Benoît and Biat, it seems that snails which have once been put in contact, are always in sympathetic communication. When separated, there disengages itself from them a species of fluid of which the earth is the conductor, which develops and unrolls, so to speak, like the almost invisible thread of the spider, or that of the silk worm, which can be uncoiled and prolonged almost indefinitely in space without its breaking, but with this vital difference that the thread of the escargotic fluid is invisible as completely and the pulsation along it is as rapid as the electric fluid.

"But, it may be objected with some plausibility, granted the existence in the snails of this sympathetic fluid, will it radiate from them in all directions, after the analogy of electric, galvanic and magnetic fluids, unless there be some conductor established between them? At first sight, this objection has some weight, but for all that it is more specious than serious." The solution of this difficulty is exquisitely absurd. We must summarise.

At first the discoverers of the galvanic current thought it necessary to establish a return wire, to complete the circle, till it was found to be sufficient[Pg 191] to carry the two ends of the wire in communication with the earth, when the earth itself completed the circle. There is no visible line between the ends underground, yet the current completes the circle through it. Moreover, it is impossible to think of two points without establishing, in idea, a line between them, indeed, according to Euclid's definition, a straight line is that which lies evenly between its extreme points, and a line is length without breadth or substance. So, if we conceive of two snails, we establish a line between them, an unsubstantial line, still a line along which the sympathetic current can travel. "Now MM. Benoît and Biat, by means of balloons in the atmosphere," had established beyond doubt that a visible tangible line of communication was only necessary when raised above the earth.

"Consequently, there remains nothing more to be considered than the means, the apparatus, whereby the transmission of thought is effected.

"This apparatus consists of a square box, in which is a Voltaic pile, of which the metallic plates, instead of being superposed, as in the pile of Volta, are disposed in order, attached in holes formed in a wheel or circular disc, that revolves about a steel axis. To these metallic plates used by Volta, MM. Benoît and Biat have substituted others in the shape of cups or circular basins, composed of zinc lined with cloth steeped in a solution of sulphate of copper maintained in place by a blade of copper riveted to the cup. At the bottom of each of these bowls, is fixed, by aid of a composition that shall be given presently, a living snail, whose sympathetic influence may unite and be[Pg 192] woven with the galvanic current, when the wheel of the pile is set in motion and with it the snails that are adhering to it.

"Each galvanic basin rests on a delicate spring, so that it may respond to every escargotic commotion. Now; it is obvious that such an apparatus requires a corresponding apparatus, disposed as has been described, and containing in it snails in sympathy with those in the other apparatus, so that the escargotic vibration may pass from one precise point in one of the piles to a precise point in the other and complementary pile. When these dispositions have been grasped the rest follows as a matter of course. MM. Benoît and Biat have fixed letters to the wheels, corresponding the one with the other, and at each sympathetic touch on one, the other is touched; consequently it is easy by this means, naturally and instantaneously, to communicate ideas at vast distances, by the indication of the letters touched by the snails. The apparatus described is in shape like a mariner's compass, and to distinguish it from that, it is termed the *pasilalinic—sympathetic compass*, as descriptive at once of its effects and the means of operation."

But, who were these inventors, Benoît and Biat-Chrétien? We will begin with the latter. As Pontoppidon in his History of Norway heads a chapter, "Of Snakes," and says, "Of these there are none," so we may say of M. Biat-Chrétien; there was no such man; at least he never rose to the surface and was seen. Apparently his existence was as much a hallucination or creation of the fancy of M. Benoît, as was Mrs. Harris a creature of the imagination of Mrs.[Pg 193] Betsy Gamp. Certainly no Biat-Chrétien was known in America as a discoverer.

Jacques Toussaint Benoît (de l'Hérault) was a man who had been devoted since his youth to the secret sciences. His studies in magic and astrology, in mesmerism, and electricity, had turned his head. Together with real eagerness to pursue his studies, and real belief in them, was added a certain spice of rascality.

One day Benoît, who had by some means made the acquaintance of M. Triat, founder and manager of a gymnasium in Paris for athletic exercises, came to Triat, and told him that he had made a discovery which would supersede electric telegraphy. The director was a man of common sense, but not of much education, certainly of no scientific acquirements. He was, therefore, quite unable to distinguish between true and false science. Benoît spoke with conviction, and carried away his hearer with his enthusiasm.

"What is needed for the construction of the machine?" asked M. Triat.

"Only two or three bits of wood," replied Benoît.

M. Triat took him into his carpenter's shop. "There, my friend," he said, "here you have wood, and a man to help you."

M. Triat did more. The future inventor of the instantaneous communication of thought was house-less and hungry. The manager rented a lodging for him, and advanced him money for his entertainment. Benoît set to work. He used a great many bits of wood, and occupied the carpenter a good part of his[Pg 194] time. Other things became necessary as well as wood, things that cost money, and the money was found by M. Triat. So passed a twelvemonth. At the end of that time, which had been spent at the cost of his protector, Benoît had arrived at no result. It was apparent that, in applying to M. Triat, he had sought, not so much to construct a machine already invented, as to devote himself to the pursuit of his favourite studies. The director became impatient. He declined to furnish further funds. Then Benoît declared that the machine was complete.

This machine, for the construction of which he had asked for two or three pieces of wood, was an enormous scaffold formed of beams ten feet long, supporting the Voltaic pile described by M. Allix, ensconced in the bowls of which were the wretched snails stuck to the bottom of the basins by some sort of glue, at intervals. This was the Pasilalinic-sympathetic compass. It occupied one end of the apartment. At the other end was a second, exactly similar. Each contained twenty-four alphabetic-sympathetic snails. These poor beasts, glued to the bottom of the zinc cups with little dribbles of sulphate of copper trickling down the sides of the bowls from the saturated cloth placed on them, were uncomfortable, and naturally tried to get away. They thrust themselves from their shells and poked forth their horns groping for some congenial spot on which to crawl, and came in contact with the wood on which was painted the letters. But if they came across a drop of solution of sulphate of copper, they went precipitately back into their shells.

Properly, the two machines should have been[Pg 195] established in different rooms, but no second room was available on the flat where Benoît was lodged, so he was forced to erect both vis-à-vis. That, however, was a matter wholly immaterial, as he explained to those who visited the laboratory. Space was not considered by snails. Place one in Paris, the other at the antipodes, the transmission of thought along their sympathetic current was as complete, instantaneous and effective as in his room on the *troisième*. In proof of this, Benoît undertook to correspond with his friend and fellow-worker Biat-Chrétien in America, who had constructed a similar apparatus. He assured all who came to inspect his invention that he conversed daily by means of the snails with his absent friend. When the machine was complete, the inventor was in no hurry to show it in working order; however M. Triat urged performance on him. He said, and there was reason in what he said, that an exhibition of the pasilalinic telegraph before it was perfected, would be putting others on the track, who might, having more means at their command, forestall him, and so rob him of the fruit of his labours. At last he invited M. Triat and M. Allix, as representative of an influential journal, to witness the apparatus in working order, on October 2nd. He assured them that since September 30, he had been in constant correspondence with Biat-Chrétien, who, without crossing the sea, would assist at the experiments conducted at Paris on Wednesday, October 2nd, in the lodging of M. Benoît.

On the appointed day, M. Triat and M. Allix were at the appointed place. The former at once objected[Pg 196] to the position of the two compasses, but was constrained to be satisfied with the reason given by the operator. If they could not be in different rooms, at least a division should be made in the apartment by means of a curtain, so that the operator at one compass could not see him at the other. But there was insuperable difficulty in doing this, so M. Triat had to waive this objection also. M. Jules Allix was asked to attend one of the compasses, whilst the inventor stood on the scaffold managing the other. M. Allix was to send the message, by touching the snails which represented the letters forming the words to be transmitted, whereupon the corresponding snail on M. Benoît's apparatus was supposed to thrust forth his horns. But, under one pretext or another, the inventor ran from one apparatus to the other, the whole time, so that it was not very difficult, with a little management, to reproduce on his animated compass the letters transmitted by M. Jules Allix.

The transmission, moreover, was not as exact as it ought to have been. M. Jules Allix had touched the snails in such order as to form the word *gymnase*; Benoît on his compass read the word *gymoate*. Then M. Triat, taking the place of the inventor, sent the words *lumiere divine* to M. Jules Allix, who read on his compass *lumhere divine*. Evidently the snails were bad in their orthography. The whole thing, moreover, was a farce, and the correspondence, such as it was, was due to the incessant voyages of the inventor from one compass to the other, under the pretext of supervising the mechanism of the two apparatuses.

[Pg 197]

Benoît was then desired to place himself in communication with his American friend, planted before his compass on the other side of the Atlantic. He transmitted to him the signal to be on the alert. Then he touched with a live snail he held in his hand the four snails that corresponded to the letters of the name BIAT; then they awaited the reply from America. After a few moments, the poor glued snails began to poke out their horns in a desultory, irregular manner, and by putting the letters together, with some accommodation CESTBIEN was made out, which when divided, and the apostrophe added, made *C'est bien*.

M. Triat was much disconcerted. He considered himself as hoaxed. Not so M. Allix. He was so completely satisfied, that on the 27th October, appeared the article from his pen which we have quoted. M. Triat then went to the inventor and told him point blank, that he withdrew his protection from him. Benoît entreated him not to throw up the matter, before the telegraph was perfected.

"Look here!" said M. Triat; "nothing is easier than for you to make me change my intention. Let one of your compasses be set up in my gymnasium, and the other in the side apartment. If that seems too much, then let a simple screen be drawn between the two, and do you refrain from passing between them whilst the experiment is being carried on. If under these conditions you succeed in transmitting a single word from one apparatus to the other, I will give you a thousand francs a day whilst your experiments are successful."

[Pg 198]

M. Triat then visited M. de Girardin who was interested in the matter, half believed in it, and had accordingly opened the columns of *La Presse* to the article of M. Allix. M. de Girardin wished to be present at the crucial experiment, and M. Triat gladly invited him to attend. He offered another thousand francs so long as the compasses worked. "My plan is this," said M. de Girardin: "If Benoît's invention is a success, we will hire the *Jardin d'hiver* and make Benoît perform his experiments in public. That will bring us in a great deal more than two thousand francs a day."

Benoît accepted all the conditions with apparent alacrity; but, before the day arrived for the experiment, after the removal of the two great scaffolds to the gymnasiums—he had disappeared. He was, however, seen afterwards several times in Paris, very thin, with eager restless eyes, apparently partly deranged. He died in 1852!

Alas for Benoît. He died a few years too soon. A little later, and he might have become a personage of importance in the great invasion of the table-turning craze which shortly after inundated Europe, and turned many heads as well as tables.

[Pg 199]

The Countess Goerlitz.

One of the most strange and terrible tragedies of this century was the murder of the Countess Goerlitz; and it excited immense interest in Germany, both because of the high position of the unfortunate lady, the mystery attaching to her death, and because the charge of having murdered her rested on her husband, the Count Goerlitz, Chamberlain to the Grand-Duke of Hesse, Privy Councillor, a man of fortune as well as rank, and of unimpeachable character. There was another reason why the case excited general interest: the solution remained a mystery for three whole years, from 1847 to 1850.

The Count Goerlitz was a man of forty-six, a great favourite at the Court, and of fine appearance. He had married, in 1820, the daughter of the Privy Councillor, Plitt. They had no children. The Countess was aged forty-six when the terrible event occurred which we are about to relate.

The Count and Countess lived in their mansion in the Neckarstrasse in Darmstadt—a large, palatial house, handsomely furnished. Although living under the same roof, husband and wife lived apart. She occupied the first floor, and he the parterre, or ground floor. They dined together. The cause of the unfriendly terms on which they lived was the fact that the Countess was wealthy, her family was of citizen[Pg 200] origin, and had amassed a large fortune in trade. Her father had been ennobled by the Grand-Duke, and she had been his heiress. The Count, himself, had not much of his own, and his wife cast this fact in his teeth. She loved to talk of the "beggar nobility," who were obliged to look out for rich burghers' daughters to gild their coronets. The Count may have been hot of temper, and have aggravated matters by sharpness of repartee; but, according to all accounts, it was her miserliness and bitter tongue which caused the estrangement.

There were but four servants in the house—the Count's valet, the coachman, a manservant of the Countess, and the cook.

Every Sunday the Count Goerlitz dined at the palace. On Sunday, June 13, 1847, he had dined at the Grand-Duke's table as usual. As we know from the letters of the Princess Alice, life was simple at that Court. Hours were, as usual in South Germany, early. The carriage took the Count to dinner at the palace at 3 P.M., and he returned home in it to the Neckar Street at half-past six. When he came in he asked the servant of the Countess, a man named John Stauff, whether his wife was at home, as he wanted to see her. As a matter of fact, he had brought away from the dinner-table at the palace some maccaroons and bonbons for her, as she had a sweet tooth, and he thought the attention might please her.

As John Stauff told him the Countess was in, he ascended the stone staircase. A glass door led into the anteroom. He put his hand to it and found it fastened. Thinking that his wife was asleep, or did[Pg 201] not want to be disturbed, he went downstairs to his own room, which was under her sitting-room. There he listened for her tread, intending, on hearing it, to reascend and present her with the bonbons. As he heard nothing, he went out for a walk. The time was half-past seven. A little before nine o'clock he returned from his stroll, drew on his dressing-gown and slippers, and asked for his supper, a light meal he was wont to take by himself in his own room, though not always, for the Countess frequently joined him. Her mood was capricious. As he had the bonbons in his pocket, and had not yet been able to present them, he sent her man Stauff to tell her ladyship that supper was served, and that it would give him great satisfaction if she would honour him with her presence. Stauff came back in a few moments to say that the Countess was not at home. "Nonsense!" said the husband, "of course she is at home. She may, however, be asleep. I will go myself and find her." Thereupon he ascended the stairs, and found, as before, the glass door to the anteroom fastened. He looked in, but saw nothing. He knocked, and received no answer. Then he went to the bedroom door, knocked, without result; listened, and heard no sound. The Count had a key to the dressing-room; he opened, and went in, and through that he passed into the bed-chamber. That was empty. The bed-clothes were turned down for the night, but were otherwise undisturbed. He had no key to the anteroom and drawing-room.

Then the Count went upstairs to the laundry, which was on the highest storey, and where were also[Pg 202] some rooms. The Countess was particular about her lace and linen, and often attended to them herself, getting up some of the collars and frills with her own hands. She was not in the laundry. Evidently she was, as Stauff had said, not at home. The Count questioned the manservant. Had his mistress intimated her intention of supping abroad? No, she had not. Nevertheless, it was possible she might have gone to intimate friends. Accordingly, he sent to the palace of Prince Wittgenstein, and to the house of Councillor von Storch, to inquire if she were at either. She had been seen at neither.

The Count was puzzled, without, however, being seriously alarmed. He bade Stauff call the valet, Schiller, and the coachman, Schämbs, who slept out of the house, and then go for a locksmith. Stauff departed. Presently the valet and coachman arrived, and, after, Stauff, without the locksmith, who, he said, was ill, and his man was at the tavern. The Count was angry and scolded. Then the coachman went forth, and soon came back with the locksmith's apprentice, who was set at once to open the locked doors in the top storey. The Countess was not in them. At the same time the young man noticed a smell of burning, but whence it came they could not decide. Thinking that this smell came from the kitchen on the first storey—that is, the floor above where the Count lived—they attacked the door of the kitchen, which was also locked. She was not there. Then the Count led the way to the private sitting-room of the Countess. As yet only the young locksmith had noticed the fire, the others were uncertain whether[Pg 203] they smelt anything unusual or not. The key of the apprentice would not fit the lock of the Countess' ante-room, so he ran home to get another. Then the Count went back to his own apartment, and on entering it, himself perceived the smell of burning. Accordingly, he went upstairs again, to find that the coachman had opened an iron stove door in the passage, and that a thick pungent smoke was pouring out of it. We must enter here into an explanation. In many cases the porcelain stove of a German house has no opening into the room. It is lighted outside through a door into the passage. Several stoves communicate with one chimney. The Count and his servants ran out into the courtyard to look at the chimney stack to see if smoke were issuing from it. None was. Then they returned to the house. The apprentice had not yet returned. Looking through the glass door, they saw that there was smoke in the room. It had been unperceived before, for it was evening and dusk. At once the Count's valet, Schiller, smashed the plate glass, and through the broken glass smoke rolled towards them.

The hour was half-past ten. The search had occupied an hour and a half. It had not been prosecuted with great activity; but then, no suspicion of anything to cause alarm had been entertained. If the Countess were at home, she must be in the sitting-room. From this room the smoke must come which pervaded the ante-chamber. The fire must be within, and if the Countess were there, she must run the danger of suffocation. Consequently, as the keys were not at hand, the doors ought to be broken open[Pg 204] at once. This was not done. Count Goerlitz sent the servants away. Stauff he bade run for a chimney-sweep, and Schiller for his medical man, Dr. Stegmayer. The coachman had lost his head and ran out into the street, yelling, "Fire! fire!" The wife of Schiller, who had come in, ran out to summon assistance.

The Count was left alone outside the glass door; and there he remained passive till the arrival of the locksmith's man with the keys. More time was wasted. None of the keys would open the door, and still the smoke rolled out. Then the apprentice beat the door open with a stroke of his hammer. He did it of his own accord, without orders from the Count. That was remembered afterwards. At once a dense, black, sickly-smelling smoke poured forth, and prevented the entrance of those who stood without.

In the meantime, the coachman and others had put ladders against the wall, one to the window of the ante-room, the other to that of the parlour. Seitz, the apprentice, ran up the ladder, and peered in. The room was quite dark. He broke two panes in the window, and at once a blue flame danced up, caught the curtains, flushed yellow, and shot out a fiery tongue through the broken window. Seitz, who seems to have been the only man with presence of mind, boldly put his arm through and unfastened the valves, and, catching the burning curtains, tore them down and flung them into the street. Then he cast down two chairs which were flaming from the window. He did not venture in because of the smoke.

[Pg 205]
In the meanwhile the coachman had broken the window panes of the ante-room. This produced a draught through the room, as the glass door had been broken in by Seitz. The smoke cleared sufficiently to allow of admission to the parlour door. This door was also found to be locked, and not only locked, but with the key withdrawn from it, as had been from the ante-chamber door. This door was also burst open, and then it was seen that the writing-desk of the Countess was on fire. That was all that could be distinguished at the first glance. The room was full of smoke, and the heat was so great that no one could enter.

Water was brought in jugs and pails, and thrown upon the floor. The current of air gradually dissipated the smoke, and something white was observed on the floor near the burning desk. "Good heavens!" exclaimed the Count, "there she lies!"

The Countess lay on the floor beside her writing-desk; the white object was her stockings.

Among those who entered was a smith called Wetzell; he dashed forward, flung a pail of water over the burning table, caught hold of the feet of the dead body, and dragged it into the ante-room. Then he sought to raise it, but it slipped through his hands. A second came to his assistance, with the same result. The corpse was like melted butter. When he seized it by the arm, the flesh came away from the bone.

The body was laid on a mat, and so transported into a cabinet. The upper portion was burnt to coal; one hand was charred; on the left foot was a shoe, the other was found, later, in another room. More[Pg 206] water was brought, and the fire in the parlour was completely quenched. Then only was it possible to examine the place. The fire had, apparently, originated at the writing-desk or secretaire of the Countess; the body had lain before the table, and near it was a chair, thrown over. From the drawing-room a door, which was found open, led into the boudoir. This boudoir had a window that looked into a side street. In the ante-room were no traces of fire. In the drawing-room only the secretaire and the floor beneath it had been burnt. On a chiffonier against the wall were candlesticks, the stearine candles in them had been melted by the heat of the room and run over the chiffonier.

In this room was also a sofa, opposite the door leading from the ante-chamber, some way from the desk and the seat of the fire. In the middle of the sofa was a hole fourteen inches long by six inches broad, burnt through the cretonne cover, the canvas below, and into the horse hair beneath. A looking-glass hung against the wall above; this glass was broken and covered with a deposit as of smoke. It was apparent, therefore, that a flame had leaped up on the sofa sufficiently high and hot to snap the mirror and obscure it.

Left of the entrance-door was a bell-rope, torn down and cast on the ground.

Beyond the parlour was the boudoir. It had a little corner divan. Its cover was burnt through in two places. The cushion at the back was also marked with holes burnt through. Above this seat against the wall hung an oil painting. It was blistered with[Pg 207]heat. Near it was an étagère, on which were candles; these also were found melted completely away. In this boudoir was found the slipper from the right foot of the Countess.

If the reader will consider what we have described, he will see that something very mysterious must have occurred. There were traces of burning in three distinct places—on the sofa, and at the secretaire in the parlour, and on the corner seat in the boudoir. It was clear also that the Countess had been in both rooms, for her one slipper was in the boudoir, the other on her foot in the drawing-room. Apparently, also, she had rung for assistance, and torn down the bell-rope.

Another very significant and mysterious feature of the case was the fact that the two doors were found locked, and that the key was not found with the body, nor anywhere in the rooms. Consequently, the Countess had not locked herself in.

Again:—the appearance of the corpse was peculiar. The head and face were burnt to cinder, especially the face, less so the back of the head. All the upper part of the body had been subjected to fire, as far as the lower ribs, and there the traces of burning ceased absolutely. Also, the floor was burnt in proximity to the corpse, but not where it lay. The body had protected the floor where it lay from fire.

The police were at once informed of what had taken place, and the magistrates examined the scene and the witnesses. This was done in a reprehensibly inefficient manner. The first opinion entertained was that the Countess had been writing at her[Pg 208]desk, and had set fire to herself, had run from room to room, tried to obtain assistance by ringing the bell, had failed, fallen, and died. Three medical men were called in to examine the body. One decided that this was a case of spontaneous combustion. The second that it was not a case of spontaneous combustion. The third simply stated that she had been burnt, but how the fire originated he was unable to say. No minute examination of the corpse was made. It was not even stripped of the half-burnt clothes upon it. It was not dissected. The family physician signed a certificate of "accidental death," and two days after the body was buried.

Only three or, at the outside, four hypotheses could account for the death of the Countess.

1. She had caught fire accidentally, whilst writing at her desk.
2. She had died of spontaneous combustion.
3. She had been murdered.

There is, indeed, a fourth hypothesis—that she had committed suicide; but this was too improbable to be entertained. The manner of death was not one to be reconciled with the idea of suicide.

The first idea was that in the minds of the magistrates. They were prepossessed with it. They saw nothing that could militate against it. Moreover, the Count was Chamberlain at Court, a favourite of the sovereign and much liked by the princes, also a man generally respected. Unquestionably this had something to do with the hasty and superficial manner in which the examination was gone through. The magistrates desired to have the tragedy hushed up.

[Pg 209]
A little consideration shows that the theory of accident was untenable. The candles were on the chiffonier, and no traces of candlesticks were found on the spot where the fire had burned. Moreover, the appearance of the secretaire was against this theory. The writing-desk and table consisted of a falling flap, on which the Countess wrote, and which she could close and lock. Above this table were several small drawers which contained her letters, receipted bills, and her jewelry. Below it were larger drawers. The upper drawers were not completely burnt; on the other hand, the lower drawers were completely consumed, and their bottoms and contents had fallen in cinders on the floor beneath, which was also burnt through to the depth of an inch and a half to two inches. It was apparent, therefore, that the secretaire had been set on fire from below. Moreover, there was more charcoal found under it than could be accounted for, by supposing it had fallen from above. Now it will be remembered that only the upper portion of the body was consumed. The Countess had not set fire to herself whilst writing, and so set fire to the papers on the desk. That was impossible.

The supposition that she had died of spontaneous combustion was also entertained by a good many. But no well-authenticated case of spontaneous combustion is known. Professor Liebig, when afterwards examined on this case, stated that spontaneous combustion of the human body was absolutely impossible, and such an idea must be relegated to the region of myths.

There remained, therefore, no other conclusion at which it was possible for a rational person to arrive[Pg 210] who weighed the circumstances than that the Countess had been murdered.

The Magisterial Court of the city of Darmstadt had attempted to hush-up the case. The German press took it up. It excited great interest and indignation throughout the country. It was intimated pretty pointedly that the case had been scandalously slurred over, because of the rank of the Count and the intimate relation in which he stood to the royal family. The papers did not shrink from more than insinuating that this was a case of murder, and that the murderer was the husband of the unfortunate woman. Some suspicion that this was so seems to have crossed the minds of the servants of the house. They recollected his dilatoriness in entering the rooms of the Countess; the time that was protracted in idle sending for keys, and trying key after key, when a kick of the foot or a blow of the hammer would have sufficed to give admission to the room where she lay. It was well known that the couple did not live on the best terms. To maintain appearances before the world, they dined and occasionally supped together. They rarely met alone, and when they did fell into dispute, and high words passed which the servants heard.

The Countess was mean and miserly, she grudged allowing her husband any of her money. She had, however, made her will the year before, leaving all her large fortune to her husband for life. Consequently her death released him from domestic and pecuniary annoyances. On the morning after the death he sent for the agent of the insurance company[Pg 211] with whom the furniture and other effects were insured and made his claim. He claimed, in addition to the value of the furniture destroyed, the worth of a necklace of diamonds and pearls which had been so injured by the fire that it had lost the greater part of its value. The pearls were quite spoiled, and the diamonds reduced in worth by a half. The agent refused this claim, as he contended that the jewelry was not included in the insurance, and the Count abstained from pressing it.

To the Count the situation became at length intolerable. He perceived a decline of cordiality in his reception at Court, his friends grew cold, and acquaintances cut him. He must clear himself of the charge which now weighed on him. The death of the Countess had occurred on June 13, 1847. On October 6, that is four months later, Count Goerlitz appeared before the Grand-Ducal Criminal Court of Darmstadt, and produced a bundle of German newspapers charging him with having murdered his wife, and set fire to the room to conceal the evidence of his crime. He therefore asked to have the case re-opened, and the witnesses re-examined. Nothing followed. The Court hesitated to take up the case again, and throw discredit on the magistrates' decision in June. Again, on October 16, the Count renewed his request, and desired, if this were refused, that he and his solicitor might be allowed access to the minutes of the examination, that they might be enabled to take decided measures for the clearing of the Count's character, and the chastisement of those who charged him with an atrocious crime. On[Pg 212] October 21, he received a reply, "that his request could not be granted, unless he produced such additional evidence as would show the Court that the former examination was defective."

On October 25, the Count laid a mass of evidence before the Court which, he contended, would materially modify, if not absolutely upset the conclusion arrived at by the previous investigation.

Then, at last, consent was given; but proceedings did not begin till November, and dragged on till the end of October in the following year, when a new law of criminal trial having been passed in the grand-duchy, the whole of what had gone before became invalid, save as preliminary investigation, and it was not till March 4, 1850—that is, not till *three years* after the death of the Countess—that the case was thoroughly sifted and settled. Before the promulgation of the law of October, 1848, all trials were private, then trial by jury, and in public, was introduced.

However, something had been done. In August 1848—that is, over a year after the burial of the Countess—the body was exhumed and submitted to examination. Two facts were then revealed. The skull of the Countess had been fractured by some blunt instrument; and she had been strangled. The condition in which the tongue had been found when the body was first discovered had pointed to strangulation, the state of the jaws when exhumed proved it.

So much, then, was made probable. A murderer had entered the room, struck the Countess on the head, and when that did not kill her, he had throttled her. Then, apparently, so it was argued, he had[Pg 213] burnt the body, and next, before it was more than half consumed, had placed it near the secretaire, and, finally, had set fire to the secretaire.

He had set fire to the writing-desk to lead to the supposition that the Countess had set fire to herself whilst writing at it; and this was the first conclusion formed.

86

That a struggle had taken place appeared from several circumstances. The bell-rope was torn down. Probably no servant had been in the house that Sunday evening when the bell rang desperately for aid. The seat flung over seemed to point to her having been surprised at the desk. One shoe was in the boudoir. The struggle had been continued as she fled from the sitting-room into the inner apartment.

Now, only, were the fire-marks on the divan and sofa explicable. The Countess had taken refuge first on one, then on the other, after having been wounded, and her blood had stained them. The murderer had burnt out the marks of blood.

She had fled from the sitting-room to the boudoir, and thence had hoped to escape through the next door into a corner room, but the door of that room was locked.

The next point to be determined was, where had her body been burnt.

In the sitting-room, the boudoir, and a locked corner room were stoves. The walls of these rooms met, and in the angles were the stoves. They all communicated with one chimney. They were all heated from an opening in the anteroom, marked *a*, which closed with an iron[Pg 214] door, and was covered with tapestry. The opening was large enough for a human being to be thrust through, and the fire-chamber amply large enough also for its consumption.

Much time had passed since a serious examination was begun, and it was too late to think of finding evidence of the burning of the body in this place. The stoves had been used since, each winter. However, some new and surprising evidence did come to light. At five minutes past eight on the evening that the mysterious death took place, Colonel von Stockhausen was on the opposite side of the street talking to a lady, when his attention was arrested by a dense black smoke issuing suddenly from the chimney of the Count Goerlitz' palace. He continued looking at the column of smoke whilst conversing with the lady, uncertain whether the chimney were on fire or not, and whether he ought to give the alarm. When the lady left him, after about ten minutes, or a quarter of an hour, he saw that smoke ceased to issue from the chimney. He accordingly went his way without giving notice of the smoke.

So far every piece of evidence went to show that the Countess had been murdered. The conclusion now arrived at was this: she had been struck on the head, chased from room to room bleeding, had been caught, strangled, then thrust into the fire-chamber of the stove over a fire which only half consumed her; taken out again and laid before the secretaire, and the secretaire deliberately set fire to, and all the blood-marks obliterated by fire. That something of this kind had taken place was evident. Who had[Pg 215] done it was not so clear. The efforts of the Count to clear himself had established the fact that his wife was murdered, but did not establish his innocence.

Suddenly—the case assumed a new aspect, through an incident wholly unexpected and extraordinary.

The result of inquiry into the case of the death of the Countess Goerlitz was, that the decision that she had come to her end by accident, given by the city magistrates, was upset, and it was made abundantly clear that she had been murdered. By whom murdered was not so clear.

Inquiry carried the conclusion still further. She had been robbed as well as murdered.

We have already described the writing-desk of the Countess. There were drawers below the flap, and other smaller drawers concealed by it when closed. In the smaller drawers she kept her letters, her bills, her vouchers for investments, and her jewelry. Among the latter was the pearl and diamond necklace, which she desired by her will might be sold, and the money given to a charitable institution. The necklace was indeed discovered seriously injured; but what had become of her bracelets, brooches, rings, her other necklets, her earrings? She had also a chain of pearls, which was nowhere to be found. All these articles were gone. No trace of them had been found in the cinders under the secretaire; moreover, the drawers in which she preserved them were not among those burnt through. In the first excitement and bewilderment caused by her death, the Count had not observed the loss, and the magistrates had not[Pg 216] thought fit to inquire whether any robbery had been committed.

A very important fact was now determined. The Countess had been robbed, and murdered, probably for the sake of her jewels. Consequently the murderer was not likely to be the Count.

When the case was re-opened, at Count Goerlitz's repeated demand, an "Inquirent" was appointed by the Count to examine the case—that is, an official investigator of all the circumstances; and on November 2, 1847, in the morning, notice was given to the Count that the "Inquirent" would visit his mansion on the morrow and examine both the scene of the murder and the servants. The Count at once convoked his domestics and bade them be in the house next day, ready for examination.

That same afternoon the cook, Margaret Eyrich by name, was engaged in the kitchen preparing dinner for the master, who dined at 4 P.M. At three o'clock the servant-man, John Stauff, came into the kitchen and told the cook that her master wanted a fire lit in one of the upper rooms. She refused to go because she was busy at the stove. Stauff remained a quarter of an hour there talking to her. Then he said it was high time for him to lay the table for dinner, a remark to which she gave an assent, wondering in her own mind why he had delayed so long. He took up a soup dish, observed that it was not quite clean, and asked her to wash it. She was then engaged on some sauce over the fire.

"I will wash it, if you will stir the sauce," she said. "If I leave the pan, the sauce will be burnt."

[Pg 217]

Stauff consented, and she went with the dish to the sink. Whilst thus engaged, she turned her head, and was surprised to see that Stauff had a small phial in his hand, and was pouring its contents into the sauce.

She asked him what he was about; he denied having done anything, and the woman, with great prudence, said nothing further, so as not to let him think that her suspicions were aroused. Directly, however, that he had left the kitchen, she examined the sauce, saw it was discoloured, and on trying it, that the taste was unpleasant. She called in the coachman and the housekeeper. On consultation they decided that this matter must be further investigated. The housekeeper took charge of the sauce, and carried it to Dr. Stegmayer, the family physician, who at once said that verdigris had been mixed with it, and desired that the police should be communicated with. This was done, the sauce was analysed, and found to contain 15½ grains of verdigris, enough to poison a man. Thereupon Stauff was arrested.

We see now that an attempt had been made on the life of the Count, on the day on which he had announced that an official inquiry into the murder was to be made in his house and among his domestics.

Stauff, then, was apparently desirous of putting the Count out of the way before that inquiry was made. At this very time a terrible tragedy had occurred in France, and was in all the papers. The Duke of Praslin had murdered his wife, and when he was about to be arrested, the duke had poisoned himself.

Did Stauff wish that the Count should be found poisoned that night, in order that the public might[Pg 218] come to the conclusion he had committed suicide to escape arrest? It would seem so.

John Stauff's arrest took place on November 3, 1847, four months and a half after the death of the Countess. He was, however, only arrested on a charge of attempting to poison the Count, and the further charge of having murdered the Countess was not brought against him till August 28, 1848. The body of the murdered woman, it will be remembered, was not exhumed and examined till August 11, 1848—eight months after the re-opening of the investigation! It is really wonderful that the mystery should have been cleared and the Count's character satisfactorily vindicated, with such dilatoriness of proceeding. One more instance of the stupid way in which the whole thing was managed. Although John Stauff was charged with the attempt to poison on November 3, 1847, he was not questioned on the charge till January 10, 1849, that is, till he had been fourteen months in prison.

It will be remembered that the bell-rope in the Countess's parlour was torn down. It would suggest itself to the meanest capacity that here was a point of departure for inquiry. If the bell had been torn down, it must have pealed its summons for help through the house. Who was in the house at the time? If anyone was, why did he not answer the appeal? Inconceivable was the neglect of the magistrates of Darmstadt in the first examination—they did not inquire. Only several months later was this matter subjected to investigation.

In the house lived the Count and Countess, the[Pg 219] cook, who also acted as chambermaid to the Countess, Schiller, the valet to the Count, Schämbs, the coachman, and the Countess's own servant-man, John Stauff. Of these Schiller and Schämbs did not sleep in the house.

June 13, the day of the murder, was a Sunday. The Count went as usual to the grand-ducal palace in his coach at 3 P.M. The coachman drove him; Stauff sat on the box beside the coachman. They left the Count at the palace and returned home. They were ordered to return to the palace to fetch him at 6 P.M. On Sundays, the Count usually spent his day in his own suite of apartments, and the Countess in hers. On the morning in question she had come downstairs to her husband with a bundle of coupons which she wanted him to cash for her on the morrow. He managed her fortune for her. The sum was small, only £30. At 2 P.M. she went to the kitchen to tell the cook she might go out for the afternoon, as she would not be wanted, and that she must return by 9P.M.

At three o'clock the cook left. The cook saw and spoke to her as she left. The Countess was then partially undressed, and the cook supposed she was changing her clothes. Shortly after this, Schiller, the Count's valet, saw and spoke with her. She was then upstairs in the laundry arranging the linen for the mangle. She was then in her morning cotton dress. Consequently she had not dressed herself to go out, as the cook supposed. At the same time the carriage left the court of the house for the palace. That was the last seen of her alive, except by John Stauff, and, if he was not the murderer, by one other.

[Pg 220]
About a quarter past three the coach returned with Schämbs and Stauff on the box. The Count had been left at the palace. The coachman took out his horses, without unharnessing them, and left for his own house, at half-past three, to remain there till 5 o'clock, when he must return, put the horses in, and drive back to the palace to fetch the Count. A quarter of an hour after the coachman left, Schiller went out for a walk with his little boy.

Consequently—none were in the house but the Countess and Stauff, and Stauff knew that the house was clear till 5 o'clock, when Schämbs would return to the stables. What happened during that time?

At a quarter past four, the wife of Schiller came to the house with a little child, and a stocking she was knitting. She wanted to know if her husband had gone with the boy to Eberstadt, a place about four miles distant. She went to the back-door. It was not fastened, but on being opened rang a bell, like a shop door. Near it were two rooms, one occupied by Schiller, the other by Stauff. The wife went into her husband's room and found it empty. Then she went into that of Stauff. It also was empty. She returned into the entrance hall and listened. Everything was still in the house. She stood there some little while knitting and listening. Presently she heard steps descending the backstairs, and saw Stauff, with an apron about him, and a duster in his hand. She asked him if her husband had gone to Eberstadt, and he said that he had. Then she left the house. Stauff, however, called to her from the window to hold up[Pg 221] the child to him, to kiss. She did so, and then departed.

Shortly after five, Schämbs returned to the stable, put in the horses, and drove to the palace without seeing Stauff. He thought nothing of this, as Stauff usually followed on foot, in time to open the coach door for the Count. On this occasion, Stauff appeared at his post in livery, at a quarter to six. At half-past six both returned with their master to the house in Neckar Street.

Accordingly, from half-past three to a quarter past four, and from half-past four to half-past five, Stauff was alone in the house with the Countess. But then, from a quarter to five to half-past five she was quite alone, and it was possible that the murder was committed at that time. The Count, it will be remembered, on his return, went upstairs and knocked at the door of the Countess' apartments, without meeting with a response. Probably, therefore, she was then dead.

At seven o'clock the coachman went away, and Stauff helped the Count to take off his court dining dress, and put on a light suit. He was with him till half-past seven, when the Count went out for a walk. The Count returned at half-past eight; during an hour, therefore, Stauff was alone in the house with the Countess, or—her corpse.

What occurred during that hour? Here two independent pieces of evidence come in to assist us in determining what took place. At five minutes past eight, Colonel von Stockhausen had seen the column of black smoke issue from the chimney of the house; it ascended, he said, some fifteen feet above the [Pg 222]chimney, and was so dense that it riveted his attention whilst he was talking to a lady.

At about a quarter-past eight the smoke ceased.

The reader may remember that the window of the inner boudoir did not look into the Neckar Street, but into a small side street. Immediately opposite lived a widow lady named Kekule. On the evening in question, her daughter, Augusta, a girl of eighteen, came in from a walk, and went upstairs to the room the window of which was exactly opposite, though at a somewhat higher level than the window of the boudoir. Looking out of her window, Augusta Kekule saw to her astonishment a flickering light like a lambent flame in the boudoir. A blind was down, so that she could see nothing distinctly. She was, however, alarmed, and called her brother Augustus, aged twenty years, and both watched the flames flashing in the room. They called their mother also, and all three saw it flare up high, then decrease, and go out. The time was 8.15. On examination of the spot, it was seen that the window of Miss Kekule commanded the corner of the boudoir, where was the divan partly burnt through in several places.

What was the meaning of these two appearances, the smoke and the flame? Apparently, from half-past seven to half-past eight the murderer was engaged in burning the body, and in effacing with fire the blood-stains on the sofas. During this time John Stauff was in the house, and, beside the Countess, alive or dead, John Stauff only.

Stauff was now subjected to examination. He was[Pg 223] required to account for his time on the afternoon and evening of Sunday, June 13.

He said, that after his return from the palace, that is, about ten minutes past three, he went into his room on the basement, and ate bread and cheese. When told that the wife of Schiller stated she had seen him come downstairs, he admitted that he had run upstairs to fetch a duster, to brush away the bread crumbs from the table at which he had eaten. After the woman left, according to his own account, he remained in his room below till five o'clock, when the Countess came to the head of the stairs and called him. He went up and found her on the topmost landing; she went into the laundry, and he stood in the door whilst she spoke to him, and gave him some orders for the butcher and baker. She wore, he said, a black stuff gown. Whilst he was talking to her, Schämbs drove away to fetch the Count. He gave a correct account of what followed, up to the departure of the Count on his walk. After that, he said, he had written a letter to his sweetheart, and at eight went out to get his supper at an outdoor restaurant where he remained till half-past nine. He was unable to produce evidence of anyone who had seen him and spoken to him there; but, of course, much cannot be made of this, owing to the distance of time at which the evidence was taken from the event of the murder. According to his account, therefore, no one was in the house at the time when the smoke rose from the chimney, and the flame was seen in the boudoir.

If we sum up the points determined concerning the[Pg 224] murder of the Countess, we shall see how heavily the evidence told against Stauff.

She had been attacked in her room, and after a desperate struggle, which went on in both parlour and boudoir, she had been killed.

Her secretaire had been robbed.

Her body had been burnt.

The blood-stains had been effaced by fire.

The secretaire had been set fire to; and, apparently, the body removed from where it had been partially consumed, and placed near it.

Now all this must have taken time. It could only be done by one who knew that he had time in which to effect it undisturbed.

John Stauff was at two separate times, in the afternoon and evening, alone in the house for an hour, knowing that during that time he would be undisturbed.

If his account were true, the murder must have been committed during his brief absence with the coach, and the burning of the body, and setting fire to the room, done when he went out to get his supper. But—how could the murderer suppose he would leave the house open and unprotected at eight o'clock? Was it likely that a murderer and robber, after having killed the Countess and taken her jewels at six o'clock, would hang about till eight, waiting the chance of getting back to the scene of his crime unobserved, to attempt to disguise it? not knowing, moreover, how much time he would have for effecting his purpose?

It was possible that this had been done, but it was not probable.

[Pg 225]

Evidence was forthcoming from a new quarter that served to establish the guilt of Stauff.

On October 6, 1847, an oilman, Henry Stauff, in Oberohmen, in Hesse Cassel, was arrested, because he was found to be disposing of several articles of jewelry, without being able to give a satisfactory account of where he got them. The jewelry consisted of a lump of molten gold, and some brooches, bracelets and rings.

Henry Stauff had been a whitesmith in his youth, then he became a carrier, but in the last few years, since the death of his wife, he had sold knives, and been a knife-grinder. He was very poor, and had been unable to pay his rates. In July of 1847, however, his affairs seemed to have mended; he wore a silver watch, and took out a licence to deal in oil and seeds. When he applied for the patent, the burgomaster was surprised, and asked him how he could get stock to set up business, in his state of poverty. Thereupon, Henry Stauff opened his purse and showed that it contained a good amount of silver, and—with the coins was a gold ring with, apparently, a precious stone in it.

The cause of his arrest was his offering the lump of gold to a silversmith in Cassel. It looked so much as if it was the melting up of jewelry, that the smith communicated with the police. On his arrest, Henry Stauff said he was the father of four children, two sons and two daughters; that his sons, one of whom was in the army, had sent him money, that his daughter in America had given him the jewelry, and that the gold he had had by him for several years, it[Pg 226] had been given him by a widow, who was dead. The silver watch he had bought in Frankfort. Henry Stauff had a daughter at home, name Anna Margaretta, who often received letters from Darmstadt. One of these letters had not been stamped, and as she declined to pay double for it, it lay in the post-office till opened to be returned. Then it was found to be dated September 29, 1847, and to be from her brother, John Stauff. It simply contained an inclosure to her father; this was opened; it contained an angry remonstrance with him for not having done what he was required, and sent the money at once to the writer.

Was it possible that this had reference to the disposal of the jewelry?

On July 7, three weeks after the death of the Countess, Henry Stauff was at Darmstadt, where one son, Jacob, was in the army; the other, John, was in service with the Goerlitz family.

This led the magistrates in Cassel to communicate with those in Darmstadt. On November 10, John Stauff was questioned with reference to his father. He said he had often sent him money. He was shown the jewelry, and asked if he recognised it. He denied having ever seen it, and having sent it to his father.

The jewelry was shown to Count Goerlitz, and he immediately identified it as having belonged to his wife. A former lady's-maid of the Countess also identified the articles. The Count, and a maid, asserted that these articles had always been kept by the deceased lady in the small upper drawers of her secretaire. The Countess was vain and miserly, and often looked over her jewelry. She would, certainly,[Pg 227] have missed her things had they been stolen before June 13.

The articles had not been stolen since, found among the ashes, and carried off surreptitiously, for they showed no trace of fire.

Here we must again remark on the extraordinary character of the proceedings in this case. The articles were identified and shown to John Stauff on November 10, 1847, but it was not till ten months after, on August 28, 1848, that he was told that he was suspected of the murder of the Countess, and of having robbed her of these ornaments. Another of the eccentricities of the administration of justice in Darmstadt consisted in allowing the father Henry, and his son John, to have free private communication with each other, whilst the latter was in prison, and thus allowing them to concoct together a plausible account of their conduct, with which, however, we need not trouble ourselves.

On September 1, 1848, on the fourth day after Stauff knew that he was charged with the murder of the Countess, he asked to make his statement of what really took place. This was the account he gave. It will be seen that, from the moment he knew the charge of murder was brought against him, he altered his defence.

He said, "On June 20, 1847," (that is, a week after the murder), "about ten o'clock in the evening, after the Count had partaken of his supper and undressed, he brought me a box containing jewelry, and told me he would give it to me, as I was so poor, and that it would place my father and me in comfortable [Pg 228]circumstances. I then told the Count that I did not know what to do with these jewels, whereupon he exhorted me to send them to my father, and get him to dispose of them. He told me that he required me solemnly to swear that I would not tell anyone about the jewels. I hid the box in a stocking and concealed it in some bushes on the Bessungen road. Later I told my brother Jacob where they were, and bade him give them to my father on his visit to Darmstadt."

When Stauff was asked what reason he could assign for the Count giving him the jewels, he said that the Count saw that he, John Stauff, suspected him of the murder, and he named several circumstances, such as observing blood on the Count's handkerchief on the evening of the murder, which had led him to believe that the Count was guilty, and the Count was aware of his suspicions.

On March 4, 1850, began the trial of John Stauff for the murder of the Countess, for robbery, for arson, and for attempt to poison the Count.

At the same time his father, Henry Stauff, and his brother, Jacob Stauff, were tried for concealment of stolen goods. The trial came to an end on April 11. As many as 118 witnesses were heard; among these was the Count Goerlitz, as to whose innocence no further doubts were entertained.

John Stauff was at that time aged twenty-six, he was therefore twenty-four years old at the time of the murder. He had been at school at Oberohmen, where he had shown himself an apt and intelligent scholar. In 1844 he had entered the grand-ducal army, and in May 1846 had become servant in the[Pg 229] Goerlitz house, as footman to the Countess. In his regiment he had behaved well; he had been accounted an excellent servant, and both his master and mistress placed confidence in him. Curiously enough, in the autumn of 1846, he had expressed a wish to a chambermaid of the Countess "that both the Countess and her pack of jewels, bracelets and all, might be burnt in one heap."

When the maid heard of the death of the Countess in the following year, "Ah!" she said, "now Stauff's wish has been fulfilled to the letter."

He was fond of talking of religion, and had the character among his fellow-servants of being pious. He was, however, deep in debt, and associated with women of bad character. Throughout the trial he maintained his composure, his lips closed, his colour pale, without token of agitation. But the man who could have stood by without showing emotion at the opening of the coffin of his mistress, at the sight of the half-burnt, half-decomposed remains of his victim, must have had powers of self-control of no ordinary description. During the trial he seemed determined to show that he was a man of some culture; he exhibited ease of manner and courtesy towards judges, jury, and lawyers. He never interrupted a witness, and when he questioned them, did so with intelligence and moderation. He often looked at the public, especially the women, who attended in great numbers, watching the effect of the evidence on their minds. When, as now and then happened, some ludicrous incident occurred, he laughed over it as heartily as the most innocent looker-on.

[Pg 230]

The jury unanimously found him "guilty" on every count. They unanimously gave a verdict of "guilty" against his father and brother. Henry Stauff was sentenced to six months' imprisonment; Jacob Stauff to detention for three months, and John to imprisonment for life. At that time capital punishment could not be inflicted in Hesse.

On June 3, he was taken to the convict prison of Marienschloss. On July 1, he appealed to the Grand-Duke to give him a free pardon, as he was innocent of the crimes for which he was sentenced. The appeal was rejected. Then he professed his intention of making full confession. He asked to see the Count. He professed himself a broken-hearted penitent, desirous of undoing, by a sincere confession, as much of the evil as was possible.

We will give his confession in his own words.

"When, at five o'clock, I went to announce to the Countess that I was about to go to the palace, I found both the glass door of the ante-room, and that into the sitting-room, open, and I walked in through them. I did not find the Countess in her parlour, of which the curtains were drawn. Nor was she in her boudoir. I saw the door into the little corner room ajar, so I presumed she was in there. The flap of her desk was down, so that I saw the little drawers, in which I knew she kept her valuables, accessible to my hand. Opportunity makes the thief. I was unable to resist the temptation to enrich myself by these precious articles. I opened one of the drawers, took out a gold bracelet, one of gold filigree, two of bronze, a pair of gold ear-rings, a gold brooch, and a[Pg 231] triple chain of beads or Roman pearls; and pocketed these articles, which my father afterwards had, and, for the most part, melted up.

"Most of these articles were in their cases. At that moment the Countess appeared on the threshold of her boudoir and rushed towards me. I do not remember what she exclaimed; fear for the consequences, and anxiety to prevent the Countess from making a noise and calling assistance, and thereby obtaining my arrest, prevailed in my mind, and I thought only how I might save myself. I grasped her by the neck, and pressed my thumbs into her throat. She struggled desperately. I was obliged to use all my strength to hold her. After a wrestle of between five and seven minutes, her eyes closed, her face became purple, and I felt her limbs relax.

"When I saw she was dead I was overcome with terror. I let the body fall, whereby the head struck the corner of the left side of the secretaire, and this made a wound which began to bleed. Then I ran and locked both the doors, hid what I had taken in my bed, and left the house. On my way to the palace, I stepped into Frey's tavern and drank three glasses of wine. I was afraid I should arrive too late at the palace, where I appeared, however, at half-past five. The Count did not return till half-past six, as dinner that day lasted rather longer than usual.

"When the Count went upstairs to see his wife and take her something good he had brought away with him from table, I was not uneasy at all, for I knew that he would knock and come away if he met with no response. So he did. He came down without[Pg 232]being discomposed, and remarked that he fancied the Countess had gone out. At half-past seven he left the house. In the mean time I had been considering what to do, and had formed my plan. Now my opportunity had arrived, and I hastened to put it into execution. My plan was to efface every trace of my deed by fire, and to commit suicide if interrupted.

"As the weather was chilly, the Count had some fire in his stove. I fetched the still glowing charcoal, collected splinters of firwood and other combustibles, and matches, and went upstairs with them. Only the wine sustained me through what I carried out. I took up the body. I put a chair before the open desk, seated the corpse on it, placed one arm on the desk, laid the head on the arm, so that the body reposed in a position of sleep, leaning on the flap of the desk. I threw the red hot charcoal down under the head, heaped matches, paper, and wood splinters over them; took one of the blazing bits of wood and threw it on the divan in the boudoir; locked both doors, and flung away the keys.

"Then I went to my own room and lighted a fire in the stove, and put the jewel cases on the fire. The fire would not burn well, and thick smoke came into the room. Then I saw that the damper was closed. I opened that, and the smoke flew up the chimney; this is what Colonel von Stockhausen saw. There were a lot of empty match-boxes also in the stove, and these burnt with the rest."

Such was the confession of Stauff. How far true, it is impossible to say. He said nothing about the bell-pull being torn down, nothing about the holes[Pg 233] burnt in the sofa of the sitting-room. According to the opinion of some experimentalists, the way in which he pretended to have burnt the Countess would not account for the appearance of the corpse.

His object was to represent himself as the victim of an over-mastering temptation—to show that the crime was wholly unpremeditated.

This was the sole plea on which he could appeal for sympathy, and expect a relaxation of his sentence.

That sentence was relaxed.

In 1872 he obtained a free pardon from the Grand-Duke, on condition that he left the country and settled in America. Including his imprisonment before his trial, he had, therefore, undergone twenty-five years of incarceration.

When released he went to America, where he probably still is.

[Pg 234]

A Wax-and-Honey-Moon.

In the history of Selenography, John Henry Maedler holds a distinguished place. He was the very first to publish a large map of the lunar surface; and his map was a good one, very accurate, and beautifully executed, in four sheets (1834-6). For elucidation of this map he wrote a book concerning the moon, entitled "The Universal Selenography." Not content with this, he published a second map of the moon in 1837, embodying fresh discoveries. Indeed as an astronomer, Maedler was a specialist. Lord Dufferin when in Iceland met a German naturalist who had gone to that inclement island to look for one moth. It is of the nature of Teutonic scientific men not to diffuse their interests over many branches of natural history or other pursuits, but to focus them on a single point. Maedler was comparatively indifferent to the planets, cold towards the comets, and callous to the attractions of the nebulæ. On the subject of the moon, he was a sheer lunatic.

He died at Hanover in 1874 at the age of eighty, a moon gazer to the last. Indeed, he appeared before the public as the historian of that science in a work published at Brunswick, the year previous to his death. The study of astronomy, more than any other,—even than theology—detaches a man from the world and its interests. Indeed theology as a study[Pg 235] has a tendency to ruffle a man, and make him bark and snap at his fellow men who use other telescopes than himself; it is not so with astronomy. This science exercises a soothing influence on those who make it their study, so that an Adams and a Le Verrier can simultaneously discover a Neptune without flying at each other's noses.

Astronomy is certainly an alluring science; set an astronomer before a telescope, and an overwhelming attraction draws his soul away through the tube up into heaven, and leaves his body without mundane interests. An astronomer is necessarily a mathematician, and mathematics are the hardest and most petrifying of studies. The "humane letters," as classic studies are called, draw out the human interests, they necessarily carry men among men, but mathematics draw men away from all the interests of their fellows. The last man one expects to find in love, the last man in whose life one looks for a romantic episode, is a mathematician and astronomer. But as even Cæsar nods, so an astronomer may lapse into spooning. The life of Professor Maedler does not contain much of animated interest; but it had its poetic incident. The curious story of his courtship and marriage may be related without indiscretion, now that the old Selenographer is no more.

Even the most prosaic of men have their time of poetry. The swan is said to sing only once—just before it dies. The man of business—the stockbroker, the insurance-company manager, the solicitor, banker, the ironmonger, butcher, greengrocer, postman, have all passed through a "moment," as Hegel would call[Pg 236] it, when the soul burst through its rind of common-place and vulgar routine, sang its nightingale song, and then was hushed for ever after. It is said that there are certain flowers which take many years coming to the point of bloom, they open, exhale a flood of incense, and in an hour wither. It is so with many. Even the astronomer has his blooming time. Then, after the honeymoon, the flower withers, the song ceases, the sunshine fades, and folds of the fog of common-place settle deeper than before.

Ivan Turgenieff, the Russian novelist, says of love, "It is not an emotion, it is a malady, attacking soul and body. It is developed without rule, it cannot be reckoned with, it cannot be overreached. It lays hold of a man, without asking leave, like a fever or the cholera. It seizes on its prey as a falcon on a dove, and carries it, where it wills. There is no equality in love. The so-termed free inclination of souls towards each other is an idle dream of German professors, who have never loved. No! of two who love, one is the slave, the other is the lord, and not inaccurately have the poets told of the chains of love."

But love when it does lay hold of a man assumes some features congruent to his natural habit. It is hardly tempestuous in a phlegmatic temperament, nor is a man of sanguine nature liable to be much influenced by calculations of material advantages. That calculations should form a constituent portion of the multiform web of a mathematician's passion is what we might anticipate.

It will be interesting to see in a German professor[Pg 237] devoted to the severest, most abstract and super-mundane of studies, the appearance, course, and dying away of the "malady" of love. We almost believe that this case is so easy of analysis that the very *bacillus* may be discovered.

Before, however, we come to the story of Professor Maedler's love episode, we must say a word about his previous history.

Maedler was born at Berlin on May 29th, 1794, in the very month of love, though at its extreme end. He began life as a schoolmaster, but soared in his leisure hours into a purer atmosphere than that of the schoolroom; he began to study the stars, and found them brighter and more interesting than the heads of his pupils.

In 1828 William Beer, the Berlin banker, brother of the great composer, Meyerbeer, a Jew, built a small observatory in the suburbs of Berlin. He had made the acquaintance of Maedler, they had the same love of the stars, and they became close friends.

The Beers were a gifted family, running out in different directions. Michael, a third brother, was a poet, and wrote tragedies, one or two of which occasionally reappear on the boards.

The result of the nightly star gazings was an article on Mars when in opposition, with a drawing of the surface as it appeared to Beer and Maedler, through the telescope of the former.

But Mars did not admit of much further scrutiny, it presented no more problems they were capable of solving, so they devoted themselves to the moon. A gourmand exists from dinner to dinner, that meal is[Pg 238] the climax of his vitality, that past he lapses into inertness, indifference, quiescence. Full moon was the exciting moment of the periods in Maedler's life, which was divided, not like a gourmand's day, into periods of twenty-four hours, but into lunar months. When the moon began to show, Maedler began to live; his interest, the pulses of his life quickened as full moon approached, then declined and went to sleep when there was no lunar disc in the sky. From 1834 to 1836 he issued his great map of the moon, and so made his name. But beyond that, in the summer of 1833 he was employed by the Russian Government on a chronometrical expedition in the Baltic.

When his map came out, he was at once secured by the Prussian Government as assistant astronomer to the observatory at Berlin, recently erected. In 1840 he became a professor, and was summoned to take charge of the observatory, and lecture on astronomy, in the Russian University of Dorpat. There he spent six uneventful years. He was unmarried, indifferent to female society, and as cold as his beloved moon. He was as solitary, as far removed from the ideas of love and matrimony, as the Man in the Moon.

At last, one vacation time, he paid a long deferred visit to a friend, a Selenologist, at Gröningen, the University of the Kingdom of Hanover. Whilst smoking, drinking beer, and talking over the craters and luminous streaks in the moon, with his friend, who was also a professor, that gentleman drew his pipe from his mouth, blew a long spiral from between his lips, and then said slowly, "By the way, professor, are you aware that we have here, in this kingdom,[Pg 239] not, indeed, in Gröningen, but in the town of Hanover, a lady, the wife of the Herr Councillor Witte, who is, like yourself, devoted to the moon; a lady, who spends entire nights on the roof of her house peering at the face of the moon through one end—the smaller—of her telescope, observing all the prominences, measuring their altitudes, and sounding all the cavities. Indeed, it is asserted that she studies the face and changes of the moon much more closely than the features and moods of her husband. Also, it is asserted, that when the moon is shining, the household duties are neglected, the dinners are bad, the maids—"

"O dinners! maids! you need not consider them; there are always dinners and maids," said the Dorpat astronomer contemptuously, "but the moon is seen so comparatively rarely. The moon must be made much of when she shows. Everything must then be sacrificed to her."

Dr. Maedler did not call the moon *she*, but *he*; however, we are writing in English, not in German, so we change the gender.

The Astronomer Royal of the University of Gröningen went on, without noticing the interruption: "Frau von Witte has spent a good deal of her husband's money in getting the largest procurable telescope, and has built an observatory for it with a dome that revolves on cannon balls, on the top of her house. Whilst Herr von Witte slumbers and snores beneath, like a Philistine, his enlightened lady is aloft, studying the moon. The Frau Councilloress has done more than observe Luna, she has done more than you[Pg 240] and Beer together, with your maps—she has modelled it."

"Modelled it!—modelled the moon!—in what?"

"In white wax."

Professor Maedler's countenance fell. He had gained great renown, not in Germany only, but throughout Europe by his maps of the moon. Here was an unknown lady, as enthusiastic a devotee to the satellite as himself, who had surpassed him. "You see," continued the Hanoverian professor, "the idea is superb, the undertaking colossal. You have a fixed strong light, you make the wax moon to revolve on its axis, and you reproduce in the most surprising and exact manner, all the phases of the moon itself."

This was indeed an idea. Maedler looked at his hands, his fingers. Would they be capable of modelling such a globe? Hardly, he had very broad coarse hands, and thick flat fingers, like paddles. He suddenly stood up.

"What is the matter? Whither are you going?" asked his friend.

"To Hanover, to Frau Witte, to see the wax moon." No persuasion would restrain him, he was in a selenological fever, he could not sleep, he could not eat, he could not read, he must see the wax moon.

And now, pray observe the craft of Cupid. The professor was aged fifty-two. In vain had the damsels of Berlin and Dorpat set their caps at him. Not a blonde beauty of Saxon race with blue eyes had caught his fancy, not a dark Russian with large hazel eyes and thick black hair, had arrested his attention. His heart had been given to the cold, chaste Diana.[Pg 241] It was, with him, the reverse of the tale of Endymion.

He had written a treatise on the occultation of Mars, he had described the belts of Saturn, he had even measured his waist. Venus he had neglected, and now Cupid was about to avenge the slight passed on his mother. There was but one avenue by which access might be had to the professor's heart. The God of Love knew it, and resolved to storm the citadel through this avenue. Dr. Maedler packed his trunk himself in the way in which unmarried men and abstract thinkers do pack their portmanteaus. He bundled all his clothes in together, higglety-pigglety. The only bit of prudence he showed was to put the pomatum pot into a stocking. His collars he curled up in the legs of his boots. Copies of his astronomical pamphlets for presentation, lay in layers between his shirts. Then as the trunk would not close, the Professor of Astronomy sat down heavily on it, stood up, then sharply sat down on it again, and repeated this operation, till coats, trousers, linen, pamphlets, brushes and combs had been crushed together into one cohesive mass, and so the lock would fasten.

No sooner was Dr. Maedler arrived at his inn in Hanover, and had dusted the collar of his coat, and revolved before the *garçon* who went over him with a clothes brush, revolved like the moon he loved, than he sallied forth in quest of the house of the Wittes. There was no mistaking it—with the domed observatory on the roof.

Dr. Maedler stood in the square, looking up at it.[Pg 242] The sight of an observatory touched him; and now, hard and dry as he was, moisture came into his eyes, as he thought that there, on that elevated station, an admirable woman spent her nights in the contemplation of the moon. What was Moses on Pisgah, viewing the Promised Land, what was Simeon Stylites braving storm and cold, to this spectacle?

Never before had the astronomer met with one of the weaker sex who cared a button for the moon, *qua* moon, and not as a convenience for illumining lovers' meetings, or for an allusion in a valentine. Here was an heroic soul which surged, positively surged above the frivolities of her sex, one who aspired to be the rival of man in intelligence and love of scientific research.

Professor Maedler sent in his card, and a letter of introduction from his friend at Gröningen, and was at once admitted. He had formed an ideal picture of the Selenographic lady, tall, worn with night watching, with an arched brow, large, clear eyes.

He found her a fat little woman, with a face as round and as flat as that of the moon, not by any means pale, but red as the moon in a fog.

The lady was delighted to make the acquaintance of so renowned an astronomer. She made him pretty speeches about his map, at the same time letting him understand that a map was all very well, but she knew of something better. Then she launched out into a criticism of his pamphlets on Mars and Saturn, on which, as it happened, he was then sitting. He had put a crumpled copy in each of his tail-coat pockets for an offering, and was now doubly crumpling them. Then she asked his opinion about the[Pg 243] revolution and orbit of Biela's comet, which had been seen the preceding year. Next she carried him to Hencke's recently discovered planet, Astræa; after that she dashed away, away with him to the nebulæ, and sought to resolve them with his aid. Then down they whirled together through space to the sun, and the luminous red protuberances observable at an eclipse. Another step, and they were plunging down to earth, had reached it in safety, and were discussing Lord Rosse's recently erected telescope. It was like Dante and Beatrix, with this difference, that Maedler was not a poet, and Frau Witte was a married woman.

The Professor was uneasy. Charming as is a telescope, delightful as is the sun, fascinating as Astræa may be, still, the moon, the moon was what he had come to discuss, and wax moon what he had come to see.

So he exercised all his skill, and with great dialectic ability conducted his Beatrix away on another round. They gave the fixed stars a wide berth, dived in and out among the circling planets and planetoids without encountering one, avoided the comets, kept their feet off nebulous matter, and at last he planted his companion firmly on the moon, and when there, there he held her.

To her words of commendation of his lunar map, he replied by expressing his astonishment at her knowledge of the several craters and so-called seas. Presently Frau Witte rose with a smile, and said, "Herr Professor, I may, perhaps, be allowed to exhibit a trifle on which I have been engaged for many years:—an independent work that I have compared[Pg 244] with, but not copied from, your excellent selenic map."

The doctor's heart fluttered; his eyes brightened; a hectic flush came into his cheeks.

Frau Witte took a key and led the way to her study, where she threw open a mahogany cupboard, and exposed to view something very much like a meat cover. This also she removed, it was composed of the finest silk stretched on a frame, and exposed to view—the wax moon.

The globe was composed of the purest white beeswax, it stood upon a steel needle that passed through it, and rested on pivots, so that the globe was held up and held firm, and could be easily made to revolve. Frau Witte closed the shutters, leaving open only one orifice through which the light could penetrate and fall on the wax ball.

The doctor raised his hands in admiration. Never had he seen anything that so delighted him. The globe's surface had been most delicately manipulated. The mountains were pinched into peaks, the hollows indented to the requisite depth, the craters were rendered with extraordinary precision, the striæ being indicated by insertions of other tinted wax. A shadow hung sombre over the mysterious Sea of Storms.

Professor Maedler returned to his hotel a prey to emotion. He inquired the address of a certain Rollmann, whom he had known in former years at Berlin, and who was now professor in the Polytechnic school at Hanover. Then he rushed off in quest of Rollmann. The Polytechnic Professor was delighted to[Pg 245] see his friend, but disturbed at the condition of mind in which he found him.

"What has brought you to Hanover, dear Professor?" he asked.

"The moon! the moon! I have come after the moon."

"The moon! How can that be? She shines over Dorpat as surely as over our roofs in Hanover."

"I've just seen her."

"Impossible. The moon is new. Besides, it is broad daylight."

"New! of course she is new. Only made lately."

Professor Rollman was puzzled.

"The moon is certainly as old as the world, and even if we give the world so limited an age as four thousand years—"

"I was not allowed to touch her, scarcely to breathe near her," interrupted Maedler.

"My dear colleague, what is the matter with you? You are—what do you say, seen, touched, breathed on the moon? The distance of the moon from the earth is two hundred and forty thousand miles."

"Not the old moon—I mean the other."

"There is no other, that is, not another satellite to this world. I am well aware that Jupiter has four moons, two of which are smaller than the planet Mars. I know also that Mars—"

"My dear Rollman, there is another—here in Hanover."

"I give it up, I cannot understand."

"Happy Hanover to possess such an unique [Pg 246]treasure," continued the excited Maedler, "and such a woman as Frau Witte."

"Oh! her wax moon!" said Rollmann, with a sigh of relief.

"Of what else could I speak?"

"So you have seen that. The old lady is very proud of her performance."

"She has cause to be proud of it. It is simply superb."

"And the sight of it has nearly sent you off your head!"

"Rollmann! what will become of that model? Frau Councilloress Witte will not live for ever. She is old, puffy, and red, and might have apoplexy any day. Is her husband an astronomer?"

"O dear no! he regards astronomy as as unprofitable a study as astrology. It is quite as expensive a pursuit, he says."

"Merciful heavens! Suppose she were to predecease—he would have the moon, and be unable to appreciate it. He might let it get dusty, have the craters and seas choked; perhaps the mountain-tops knocked off. He must not have it."

"It cannot be helped. The moon must take its chance."

"It must not be. She *must* outlive the Councillor."

"If you can manage that—well."

"But—supposing she does outlive him, she is not immortal. Some day she must die. Who will have the moon then?"

"I suppose, her daughter."

"What will the daughter do with it?"

[Pg 247]
"Melt it up for waxing the floors."

Professor Maedler uttered a cry of dismay.

"The object is one of incalculable scientific value. Has the daughter no husband, a man of intelligence, to stay her hand?"

"The daughter is unmarried. There was some talk of a theological candidate—"

"A theological candidate! An embryo pastor! Just powers! These men are all obscurantists. He will melt up the moon thinking thereby to establish the authority of Moses."

"That came to nothing. She is disengaged."

Professor Maedler paced the room. Perspiration bedewed his brow. He wiped his forehead, more drops formed. Suddenly he stood still. "Rollmann," he said, in a hollow voice, "I must—I will have that moon, even if I have to marry the daughter to secure it."

"By all means. Minna is a pleasant young lady."

"Minna! Minna! is that her name?" asked the distracted professor; then, more coolly, "I do not care a rush what her name is. I want, not her, but the moon."

"She is no longer in the bloom of early youth."

"She is an exhausted world; a globe of volcanic cinder."

"She is of real solid worth."

"Solid—she is of solid wax—white beeswax."

"If she becomes yours—"

"I will exhibit her at my lectures to the students."

"As you are so much older, some provision will have to be made in the event of your death."

[Pg 248]

"I will leave her to the Dorpat museum, with directions to the curator to keep the dust off her."

"My dear Professor Maedler, I am speaking of the young lady, *you* of the moon."

"Ah so! I had forgotten the incumbrance. Yes, I will marry the moon. I will carry her about with me, hug her in my arms, protect her most carefully from the fingers of the Custom House officers. I will procure an ukase from the Emperor to admit her unfingered over the frontier."

"And Minna!"

"What Minna?"

"The young lady."

"Ah so! She had slipped out of my reckoning. She shall watch the box whilst I sleep, and whilst she sleeps I will keep guard."

"Be reasonable, Maedler. Do you mean, in sober earnest, to invite Minna Witte to be your wife?"

"If I cannot get the moon any other way."

"But you have not even seen her yet."

"What does that matter? I have seen the moon."

"And you are in earnest!"

"I *will* have the moon."

"Then, of course, you will have to propose."

"I propose!"

"And, of course, to make love."

"I make love!"

Professor Maedler's colour died away. He stood still before his friend, his pocket-handkerchief in hand, and stared.

"I have not the remotest idea how to do it."

"You must try."

[Pg 249]

"I've had no experience. I am going on to fifty-three. As well ask me to dance on the trapeze. It is not proper. It is downright indecent."

"Then you must do without the wax moon."

"I cannot do without the wax moon."

"Then, there is no help for it, you must make love to and propose to the fair Minna."

"Friend," said the Russian-imperial-professor-of-astronomy-of-the-University-of-Dorpat, as he clasped Rollmann's hand. "You are experienced in the ways of the world. I have lived in an observatory, and associated only with fixed stars, revolving moons, and comets. Tell me how to do it, and I will obey as a lamb."

"You will have to sigh."

"O! I can do that."

"And ogle the lady."

"Ogle!—when going fifty-three!"

"Learn a few lines of poetry."

"Yes, Milton's Paradise Lost. Go on."

"Tell the young lady that your heart is consumed with love."

"Consumed with love, yes, go on."

"Squeeze her hand."

"I cannot! That I cannot!" gasped Professor Maedler. "Look at my whiskers. They are grey. There is a point beyond which I cannot go. Rollmann, why may I not settle it all with the mother, and let you court the young lady for me by proxy."

"No, no, you must do it yourself."

"I would not be jealous. Consider, I care nothing for the young girl. It is the moon I want. That you shall not touch or breathe on."

[Pg 250]

"My dear Maedler, you and I are sure to be invited to dine with the family on Sunday. After dinner we will take a stroll in the garden. During dinner mind and be attentive to Miss Minna, and feed her with honeyed words. When we visit the garden I will tackle the mother, as Mephistopheles engages Martha, and you, you gay Faust, will have to be the gallant to Minna."

"My good Rollmann! I dislike the simile. It offends me. Consider my age, my whiskers, my position at the Dorpat University, my map of the moon in four sheets, my paper on the occultation of Mars."

"Pay attention to me, if you want your wax globe. Frau Witte, the Councillor and I will sit drinking coffee in the arbour. You ask Minna to show you the garden. When you are gone I will begin at once with the mother, praise you, and say how comfortably you are provided for at Dorpat, laud your good qualities, and bring her to understand that you are a suitor for the hand of her daughter. Meanwhile press your cause with ardour."

"With ardour! I shall not be able to get up any warmth."

"Think of the wax moon! direct your raptures to that."

"This is all very well," said Maedler fretfully, "but you have forgotten the main thing. I know you will make a mistake. You have asked for the hand of the daughter, and said nothing about the moon."

"Do not be concerned."

"But I am concerned. It would be a pretty [Pg 251]mischief if I got the daughter's hand instead of the face of the moon."

"I will manage that you have what you want. But the moon must not rise over the matrimonial scene till the preliminaries are settled. I will represent to the old lady what credit will accrue to her if her moon be exhibited and lectured on at the Dorpat

University by so distinguished an astronomer as yourself. Then, be well assured, she will give you the wax moon along with her daughter."

"Very well, I will do what I can. Only, further, explain to me the whole process, that I may learn it by heart. It seems to me as knotty to a beginner as Euler's proof of the Binomial Theorem."

"It is very easy. Pay attention. You must begin to talk about the fascination which a domestic life exerts on you; you then say that the sight of such an united household as that in which you find yourself influences you profoundly."

"I see. Causes a deflection in my perihelion. That deflection is calculable, the force excited calculable, the position of the attractive body estimable. I direct my telescope in the direction, and discover—Minna. Put astronomically, I can understand it."

"But you must *not* put it astronomically to her. Paint in glowing tints the charms of the domestic hearth—that is to say, of the stove. Touch sadly on your forlorn condition, your unloved heart—are you paying attention, or thinking of the moon?"

"On the contrary, I was thinking of myself, from a planetary point of view. I see, a wife is a satellite[Pg 252] revolving round her man. I see it all now. Jupiter has four."

"Sigh; let the corners of your mouth droop. Throw, if you can, an emotional vibration into your tones, and say that hitherto life has been to you a school, where you have been set hard tasks; not a home. Here shake your head slowly, drop a tear if you can, and say again, in a low and thrilling voice, 'Not a home!' Now for the poetry. Till now, you add, you have looked into the starry vault—"

"It is not a vault at all."

"Never mind; say this. Till now you have looked into the starry vault for your heaven, and not dreamed that a heaven full of peaceful lights was twinkling invitingly about your feet. That is poetical, is it not? It must succeed."

"Quite so, I should never have thought of it."

"Then turn, and look into Miss Minna's eyes."

"But suppose she is looking in another direction?"

"She will not be. A lady is always ready to help a stumbling lover over the impediments in the way of a declaration. She will have her eyes at command, ready to meet yours."

"Go on."

"You will presently come to a rose tree. You must stop there and be silent. Then you must admire the roses, and beg Miss Minna to present you with one."

"But I do not want any roses. What can I do with them? I am lodging at an hotel."

"Never mind, you *must* want one. When she has picked and offered it—"

[Pg 253]

"But perhaps she will not."

"Fiddlesticks! Of course she will. Then take the rose, press your lips to it, and burst forth into raptures."

"Excuse me, how am I to do the raptures?"

"Think of the wax moon, man. Exclaim, 'Oh that I might take the fair Minna, fairer than this rose, to my heart, as I apply this flower to my buttonhole!'"

"Shall I say nothing about the wax moon?"

"Not a word. Leave me to manage that."

"Go on."

"Then she will look down, confused, at the gravel, and stammer. Press her for a Yes or No. Promise to destroy yourself if she says No. Take her hand and squeeze it."

"Must I squeeze it? About how much pressure to the square-foot should I apply?"

"Then say, 'Come, let us go to your parents, and obtain their blessing.' The thing is done."

"But suppose she were to say No?"

Rollmann stamped with impatience. "I tell you she will not say No, now that the theological candidate has dropped through."

"Well," said Professor Maedler, "I must go along with it, now I have made up my mind to it. But, on my word, as an exact reasoner, I had no idea of the difficulties men have to go through to get married. Why, the calculation of the deflections of the planets is nothing to it. And the Grand Turk, like Jupiter, has more satellites than one!"

[Pg 254]
A few months after the incident above recorded Professor Maedler returned to Dorpat, not alone; with him was the Frau Professorinn—Minna. Everything had gone off in the garden as Rollmann had planned.

The moon and Minna, or Minna and the moon, put it which way you will, were secured.

When the Professor arrived at Dorpat with his wife, the students gave him an ovation after the German style, that is to say, they organized a Fackel-zug, or torch-light procession.

Three hundred young men, some wearing white caps, some green caps, some red, and some purple, marched along the street headed by a band, bearing torches of twisted tow steeped in tar, blazing and smoking, or, to be more exact, smoking and blazing. Each corps was followed by a hired droschky, in which sat the captain and stewards of the white, red, green, or purple corps, with sashes of their respective colours. Behind the last corps followed the elephants, two and two. By elephants is not meant the greatest of quadrupeds, but the smallest esteemed of the students, those who belong to no corps.

The whole procession gathered before the house of the Professor, and brandished their torches and cheered. Then the glass door opening on the balcony was thrown back, and the Professor John Henry Maedler appeared on the balcony leading forth his wife. The astronomer looked younger than he had been known to look for the last twenty years. His whiskers in the torchlight looked not grey, but red. The eyes, no longer blear with star-gazing, watered[Pg 255] with sentiment. His expression was no longer that of a man troubled with integral calculus, but of a man in an ecstasy. He waved his hand. Instantly the cheers subsided. "My highly-worthy-and-ever-to-be-honoured sirs," began the Professor, "this is a moment never to be forgotten. It sends a *fackel-zug* of fiery emotion through every artery and vein. Highly-worthy-and-ever-to-be-honoured sirs, I am not so proud as to suppose that this reception is accorded to me alone. It is an ovation offered to my highly-beloved-and-evermore-to-be-beloved-and-respected consort, Frau Minna Maedler, born Witte, the daughter of a distinguished lady, who, like myself, has laboured on Selenography, and loved Selenology. Highly-worthy-and-ever-to-be-respected sirs, when I announce to you that I have returned to Dorpat to endow that most-eminent-and-ever-to-become-more-eminent-University with one of the most priceless treasures of art the world has ever seen, a monument of infinite patience and exact observation; I mean a wax moon; I am sure I need only allude to the fact to elicit your unbounded enthusiasm. But, highly-worthy-and-ever-to-be-honoured sirs, allow me to assure you that my expedition to Hanover has not resulted in a gain to the highly eminent University of Dorpat only, but to me, individually as well.

"That highly-eminent-and-evermore-to-become-more-eminent University is now enriched through my agency with a moon of wax, but I—I, sirs—excuse my emotion, I have also been enriched with a moon, not of wax, but of honey. The wax moon, gentlemen, may it last undissolved as long as the [Pg 256]very-eminent-and-evermore-to-become-more-eminent University of Dorpat lasts. The honey moon, gentlemen, with which I have been blessed, I feel assured will expand into a lifetime, at least will last also undissolved as long as Minna and I exist."

[Pg 257]

The Electress's Plot.

The Elector Frederick Christian of Saxony reigned only a few weeks, from October 5th to December 13, 1763; in his forty-first year he died of small-pox. He never had enjoyed rude health. The mother of the unfortunate prince, Marie Josepha of Austria, was an exceedingly ugly, but prolific lady, vastly proud of her Hapsburg descent. The three first children followed each other with considerable punctuality, but the two first, both sons, died early. Frederick Christian was the third. The Electress, a few months before his birth, was hunting, when a deer that had been struck, turned to her, dragging its broken legs behind it. This produced a powerful impression on her mind; and when her son was born, he was found to be a cripple in his legs. His head and arms were well formed, but his spine was twisted, and his knees, according to the English ambassador, Sir Charles Williams—were drawn up over his stomach. He could not stand, and had to be lifted about from place to place. At the age of five-and-twenty he had been married to Maria Antonia, daughter of the Elector of Bavaria, afterwards the Emperor Charles VII.

His brother, Francis Xavier, was a sturdy fellow, like his father, and the Electress mother tried very hard to get Frederick Christian to resign his [Pg 258]pretentions in favour of his brother, and take holy orders. This he refused to do, and was then married to Maria Antonia, aged twenty-three. Her mother had also been an Austrian princess, Amalia, and also remarkable for her ugliness. The choice was not happy, it brought about a marriage between cousins, and an union of blood that was afflicted with ugliness and infirmity of body.

Maria Antonia had not only inherited her mother's ugliness, but was further disfigured with small-pox. She was small of stature, but of a resolute will, and of unbounded ambition. English tourists liked her, they said that she laid herself out to make the Court of Dresden agreeable to them. Wraxall tells a good story of her, which shows a certain frankness, not to say coarseness in her conversation—a story we will not reproduce.

She had already made her personality felt at the Bavarian Court. Shortly after the death of her father, in imitation of Louisa Dorothea, Duchess of Gotha, she had founded an "Order of Friendship, or the Society of the Incas." The founding of the Order took place one fine spring day on a gondola in the canal at Nymphenburg. Her brother, the Elector of Bavaria, was instituted a member, the Prince of Fürstenberg was made chancellor, and was given the custody of the seal of the confraternity which had as its legend "La fidelité mêne." The badge of the Order was a gold ring on the little finger of the left hand, with the inscription, "L'ordre de l'amitié—Maria Antonia." Each member went by a name descriptive of his character, or of that virtue he or she was supposed to[Pg 259] represent. Thus the chancellor was called "Le Solide."

Sir Charles Williams says that on the very first night of her appearance in Dresden she made an attempt to force herself into a position for which she had no right; to the great annoyance of the King of Poland (Augustus, Elector of Saxony).

At Dresden, she favoured the arts, especially music and painting. She became the patroness of the family Mengs. She sang, and played on the piano, and indeed composed a couple of operas, "Thalestris" and "Il trionfo della fidelita," and the former was actually put on the stage. Sir Charles Williams in 1747 wrote that, in spite of her profession that in her eyes no woman ought to meddle in the affairs of state, he ventured to prophecy, she would rule the whole land in the name of her unfortunate husband.

Nor was he wrong. The moment that her father-in-law died, she put her hand on the reins. She was not likely to meet with resistance from her husband, he was not merely a cripple in body, but was contracted in his intellect; he was amiable, but weak and ignorant. Sir Charles Williams says that he once asked at table whether it was not possible to reach England by land—*although* it was an island.

Frederick Christian began to reign on 5th October 1763, and immediately orders were given for the increase of the army to 50,000 men. Maria Antonia was bent on becoming a queen, and for this end she must get her husband proclaimed like his father, King of Poland. She was allied to all the Courts of Europe, her agreeable manners, her energy, gained[Pg 260] her friends in all quarters. She felt herself quite capable of wearing a royal crown, and she wrote to all the courts to urge the claims of her husband, the Elector, when—the unfortunate cripple was attacked by small-pox, had a stroke, and died December 17th. Small-pox had carried off his ancestor John George IV., and in that same century it occasioned the death of his brother-in-law, Max Joseph of Bavaria, and of the Emperor Joseph I.

He left behind him four sons, his successor, Frederick Augustus, and the three other princes, Charles, his mother's favourite, Anthony, and Maximilian Joseph, the third of whom died the same year as his father. He had also two daughters.

The death of her husband was a severe blow to the ambition of the Electress; her eldest son, Frederick Augustus, was under age, and the reins of government were snatched from her hands and put into those of the uncle of the young Elector, Xavier, who had been his mother's favourite, and in favour of whom his elder brother had been urged to resign his pretensions. Xavier was appointed administrator of Saxony, and acted as such for five years.

When, at the age of eighteen, Frederick Augustus III. assumed the power, he endeavoured to fulfil his duties with great diligence and conscientiousness, and allowed of no interference. He had, indeed, his advisers, but these were men whom he selected for himself from among those who had been well tried and who had proved themselves trusty.

The Electress-mother had, during the administration of Prince Xavier, exercised some little authority; she[Pg 261] now suddenly found herself deprived of every shred. Her son was too firm and self-determined to admit of her interference. Moody and dissatisfied, she left Dresden and went to Potsdam to Frederick II., in 1769, apparently to feel the way towards the execution of a plan that was already forming in her restless brain. She does not seem to have met with any encouragement, and she then started for Italy, where she visited Rome in 1772, and sought Mengs out, whose artistic talents had been fostered under her care.

Under the administration of Prince Xavier, the Electress Dowager had received an income of sixty thousand dollars; after her son had mounted the throne, her appanage was doubled, more than doubled, for she was granted 130,000 dollars, and in addition her son gave her a present of 500,000 dollars. This did not satisfy her, for she had no notion of cutting her coat according to her cloth, she would everywhere maintain a splendid court. Moreover, she was bitten with the fever of speculation. The year before her son came of age and assumed the power, she had erected a great cotton factory at Grossenhain, but as it brought her in no revenue, and cost her money besides, she was glad to dispose of it in 1774. The visitor to Dresden almost certainly knows the Bavarian tavern at the end of the bridge leading into Little Dresden. It is a tavern now mediævalised, with panelled walls, bull's eye glass in the windows, old German glass and pottery—even an old German kalendar hanging from the walls, and with a couple of pretty Bavarian Kellnerins in costume, to wait on[Pg 262] the visitor. There also in the evening Bavarian minstrels jodel, and play the zither.

This Bavarian tavern was established by the Electress Mother, who thought that the Saxons did not drink good or enough beer, and must be supplied with that brewed in her native land.

But this speculation also failed, and her capital of five hundred thousand dollars was swallowed up to the last farthing, and to meet her creditors she was obliged to pawn her diamond necklace and the rest of her jewels. This happened in Genoa. When her allowance came in again she redeemed her jewelry, but in 1775 had to pawn it again in Rome. Unable to pay her debts, and in distress for money, she appealed repeatedly, but in vain, to her son.

Frederick Augustus was, like his father, of feeble constitution, and moreover, as he himself complained later on in life, had been at once spoiled and neglected in his youth; and he was unable through weakness to ascend a height. He did not walk or ride, but went about in a carriage. The January (1769) after he came to the Electoral crown, he married Amelia Augusta of Zweibrücken, sister of Max Joseph, afterwards first King of Bavaria. She was only seventeen at the time.

The favourite son of his mother was Charles. This prince had been hearty and in full possession of his limbs in his early age, but when he reached the years of eleven or twelve, he became crippled and doubled up like his father. Wraxal says that beside him Scarron would have passed as a beauty. He was so feeble and paralysed that he could only be moved[Pg 263] about on a wheeled chair. He died in 1781. His elder brother, the Elector, though not a vigorous man, was not a cripple.

One of the attendant gentry on the Electress Mother, in Rome, was the Marquis Aloysius Peter d'Agdolo, son of the Saxon Consul in Venice, Colonel of the Lifeguard, and Adjutant General to Prince Xavier whilst he was Administrator.

Agdolo advised the Electress Mother to raise money to meet her difficulties by selling to her son, the Elector, her claims on the Bavarian inheritance. Her brother, Maximilian Joseph, was without children; and the nearest male claimant to the Electoral Crown of Bavaria was the Count Palatine of Sulzbach, only remotely connected. It was, therefore, quite possible that Bavaria might fall to a sister. Now on the death of her brother, the Dowager Electress of Saxony certainly intended to advance her claims against any remote kinsman hailing through a common ancestor two centuries ago. But whether she would be able to enforce her claim was another matter. She might sell it to her son, who would have the means of advancing his claim by force of arms and gold. This was in 1776. Maria Antonia was delighted with the scheme and at once hastened to Munich to put it in execution, taking with her all her diamonds which she had managed to redeem from pawn.

Whilst she was on her way to Munich, Agdolo was despatched to Dresden, to open the negociation with her son, not only for the transference of her rights on Bavaria, but also for the pawning of her diamonds, to her son.

[Pg 264]

She had urgent need of money, and in her extremity she conceived an audacious scheme to enable her at the same time to get hold of the money, and to retain her rights on Bavaria. The plan was this:—As soon as she had got the full payment from the Elector for the resignation of her claims in his favour, she had resolved suddenly to proclaim to the world that he was no son at all of the late Elector Frederick Christian—that he was a bastard, smuggled into the palace and passed off as the son of the Elector, much as, according to Whig gossip, James the Pretender was smuggled into the palace of James II. in a warming pan, and passed off as of blood royal, when he was of base origin.

Frederick Augustus thus declared to be no son of the House of Saxony, the Electoral crown would come to her favourite son Charles, who was a cripple. The Elector was not deformed—evidence against his origin; Charles was doubled up and distorted—he was certainly the true son of the late Elector, and the legitimate successor.

If Maria Antonia should succeed—she would rule Saxony in the name, and over the head of her unfortunate son Charles, and her rights on Bavaria would not have been lost or made away with.

Arrived in Munich, she confided the whole plan to her ladies-in-waiting. She told them her hopes, her confidence in Agdolo, who was gone to Dresden to negociate the sale, and who was thoroughly aware of her intentions.

Agdolo, as all the ladies knew, was a great rascal. He had been pensioned by Prince Xavier with six[Pg 265] hundred dollars per annum, and he had what he received from the Electress Mother as her gentleman-in-waiting. He was married to the Princess Lubomirska, widow of Count Rutowska, had quarrelled with her, and they lived separate, but he had no scruple to receive of an insulted wife an annual allowance. All these sources of income were insufficient to meet his expenses; and no one who knew him doubted for a moment that he would lend himself to any intrigue which would promise him wealth and position. The plot of the Dowager Electress was a risky one—but, should it succeed, his fortune was assured.

At Dresden he was well received by the Elector; and Frederick Augustus at once accepted the proposition of his mother. He consented to purchase Maria Antonia's resignation in his favour of her claims on the allodial inheritance of the family on the extinction of the Bavarian Electoral house in the male line, and to pay all her debts, and to find a sum sufficient to redeem the diamonds, which were represented as still in pawn at Rome.

Maria Antonia and her confidant appeared to be on the eve of success, when the plan was upset, from a quarter in which they had not dreamed of danger. Among the ladies of the court of the Dowager Electress was one whose name does not transpire, who seems to have entertained an ardent passion for Agdolo. He, however, disregarded her, and paid his attentions to another of the ladies. Rage and jealousy consumed the heart of this slighted beauty, and when the Electress Mother confided to her the plan she had[Pg 266]formed, the lady-in-waiting saw that her opportunity had arrived for the destruction of the man who had slighted her charms. She managed to get hold of her mistress' keys and to make a transcript of her papers, wherein the whole plan was detailed, also of copies of her letters to Agdolo, and of the Marquis's letters to her. When she had these, she at once despatched them—not to the Elector of Saxony, but to Frederick II. at Berlin, who stood in close relations of friendship with the Elector of Saxony. She had reckoned aright. Such tidings, received through the Court of Prussia, would produce a far deeper impression on Frederick Augustus, than if received from her unknown and insignificant self. It is possible also that she may have known of her mistress having been at Berlin and there thrown out hints of something of the sort, so that Frederick II. would at once recognise in this matured plan the outcome of the vague hints of mischief poured out at Potsdam a few years before.

All was going on well at Berlin. Adolphus von Zehmen, Electoral Treasurer, had already started for Munich, furnished with the requisite sums. He was empowered to receive the deed of relinquishment from the Dowager Electress, and also her diamond necklace, which, in the meantime, was to be brought by a special courier from Rome. Maria Antonia, on her side, had constituted Councillor Hewald her plenipotentiary; she wrote to say that he would transact all the requisite negociation with the Treasurer Zehmen, and that the diamond necklace had arrived and was in his hands.

[Pg 267]

Agdolo received orders from the Electress Mother on no account to leave Dresden till the middle of September, 1776, lest his departure should arouse suspicion.

The conduct of the Marquis was not in any way remarkable, he moved about among old friends with perfect openness, often appeared in Court, and was satisfied that he was perfectly safe. He was not in the least aware that all his proceedings were watched and reported on, not by order of the Elector, but of his own mistress, who received regular reports from this emissary as to the behaviour and proceedings of the Marquis, so that she was able to compare with this private report that sent her by Agdolo, and so satisfy herself whether he was acting in her interest, or playing a double game.

This bit of cunning on her part, was not surprising, considering what a man Agdolo was, and, as we shall see, it proved of great advantage to her, but in a way she least expected.

The Marchese d'Agdolo had paid his farewell visit to the Elector, and received leave to depart. Frederick Augustus had not the remotest suspicion that his mother was playing a crooked part, and he seemed heartily satisfied with the negociation, and made the Marquis a present.

On September 15, 1776, Agdolo was intending to start from Dresden, on his return to Munich, and the evening before leaving he spent at the house of a friend, Ferber, playing cards. Little did he suspect that whilst he was winning one stake after another at the table, the greatest stake of all was lost. That evening,[Pg 268] whilst he was playing cards, a courier arrived from Berlin, in all haste, and demanded to see the Elector in person, instantly, as he had a communication of the utmost importance to make from Frederick II. He was admitted without delay, and the whole of his mother's plot was detailed before the astonished Elector.

"The originals of these transcripts," said the courier, "are in the hands of the Marchese d'Agdolo, let him be arrested, and a comparison of the documents made."

The Privy Council was at once assembled, and the papers received from Frederick II. were laid before it. The members voted unanimously that the Marquis should be arrested, and General Schiebell was entrusted with the execution of the decree. No surprise was occasioned by the entry of General Schiebell into the house of Ferber. It was a place of resort of the best society in Dresden; but when the General announced that he had come to make an arrest, many cheeks lost their colour.

"In the name of his Serene Highness the Elector," said the General, "I make this man my prisoner," and he laid his hand on the shoulder of Agdolo, who had served under him in the Seven Years' War. He was taken at once to his own lodgings, where his desks and boxes—already packed for departure—were opened, and all his papers removed. The same night, under a strong guard, he was transported at 10 o'clock, to Königstein. In that strong fortress and state prison, perched on an isolated limestone crag, the rest of his life was to be spent in confinement.

[Pg 269]

But the Marchese, like a crafty Italian, had made his preparations against something of the sort; for among his papers was found a communication addressed by him to the Elector, revealing the whole plot. It was undated. If the search of his rooms and the discovery of his papers had been made earlier, the Elector might have believed that the man had really intended to betray his mistress, but, he had postponed the delivery of the communication too late.[17]

A few days later, the Marchese received a sealed letter from the Elector; and he was treated in his prison without undue severity; his pension was not withdrawn; and the Elector seems never to have quite made up his mind whether Agdolo really intended to make him aware of the plot at the last minute, or to go on with the plan after his mistress's orders.

After some years, when Agdolo began to suffer in his chest, he was allowed to go to the baths of Pirna, under a guard. His wife never visited him in prison. She died, however, only two years later, in 1778, at the age of fifty-six. Agdolo lived on for twenty-three years and a half, and died August 27, 1800. All his papers were then sent to Frederick Augustus III., who read them, dissolved into tears, and burnt them.

We must return for a moment to Munich. No sooner had the emissary of the Electress Mother heard of the news of the arrest of Agdolo, than he hastened to Munich with post horses as hard as he[Pg 270] could fly over the roads. Maria Antonia, when she heard the news, at once made fresh dispositions. She sent word that same night to Hewald to make off, and in another half hour he had disappeared with the diamonds.

Next day the completion of the resignation of claims was to be made. The Electress Mother requested the Treasurer Zehmen to go to the dwelling of her Councillor Hewald, who, as we can understand, was not to be found anywhere. Herr von Zehmen was much surprised and disconcerted, and the Dowager Electress affected extreme indignation and distress, charging her plenipotentiary with having robbed her of her diamonds, and bolted with them. Then she took to her bed, and pretended to be dangerously ill. Next day the news reached Zehmen of what had occurred at Dresden, and with the news came his recall. She saw the treasurer before his departure, and implored him to get both Agdolo and Hewald arrested and punished, because, as she declared, they had between them fabricated a wicked plot for her robbery and ruin.

Hewald went to Frankfort with the jewels, where he was stopped and taken by an officer of Frederick Augustus, and brought on Jan. 27, 1777, to Dresden. He was sent to the Königstein, but was released in 1778.

In 1777 died the Elector of Bavaria, but his sister was unable to obtain any recognition of her claims; and she died 23rd April, 1780, without any reconciliation with the eldest son. Next year died her favourite son, the cripple, Charles.

FOOTNOTE:

[17] This is supposed to have been the contents of the packet addressed to the Elector, the contents have never been revealed.

[Pg 271]

Suess Oppenheim.

On December the sixteenth, 1733, Charles Alexander, Duke of Würtemberg, entered Stuttgart in state. It was a brilliant though brief winter day. The sun streamed out of a cloudless heaven on the snowy roofs of the old town, and the castle park trees frosted as though covered with jewels. The streets were hung with tapestries, crimson drapery, and wreaths of artificial flowers. Peasants in their quaint costume poured in from all the country round to salute their new prince. From the old castle towers floated the banners of the Duchy and the Empire—for Würtemberg three stag-horns quartered with the Hohenstauffen black lions. The Duke was not young: he was hard on fifty—an age when a man has got the better of youthful impetuosity and regrets early indiscretions—an age at which, if a man has stuff in him, he is at his best.

The land of Würtemberg is a favoured and smiling land. At the period of which we write, it was not so ample as the present kingdom, but fruitful, favoured, and called the Garden of the Empire. For twenty years this Duchy had been badly governed; the inhabitants had been cruelly oppressed by the incompetent Duke Eberhardt Ludwig, or rather by his favourites. The country was burdened with debt; the treasury was exhausted. It had, as it were, lain under winter frost for twenty years and more, and now though[Pg 272] on a winter day laughed and bloomed with a promise of spring.

And every good Würtemberger had a right to be glad and proud of the new duke, who had stormed Belgrade under Prince Eugene, and was held to be one of the bravest, noblest minded, and most generous of the German princes of his time.

As he rode through the streets of Stuttgart all admired his stately form, his rich fair hair flowing over his shoulders, his bright commanding eye, and the pleasant smile on his lip; every Würtemberger waved his hat, and shouted, and leaped with enthusiasm. Now at last the Garden of Germany would blossom and be fruitful under so noble a duke.

But in the same procession walked, not rode, another man whom none regarded—a handsome man with dark brown hair and keen olive eyes, a sallow complexion, and a finely moulded Greek nose. He had a broad forehead and well arched brows. He was tall, and had something noble and commanding in his person and manner. But his most remarkable feature was the eye—bright, eager, ever restless.

This man, whom the Würtembergers did not observe, was destined to play a terrible and tragic part in their history—to be the evil genius of the duke and of the land. His name was Joseph Suess Oppenheim.

Joseph's mother, Michaela, a Jewess, had been a woman of extraordinary beauty, the only child of the Rabbi Salomon of Frankfort. She had been married when quite young to the Rabbi Isachar Suess Oppenheim, a singer. Joseph was born at Heidelberg in 1692, and was her child by the Baron George of[Pg 273] Heydersdorf, a soldier who had distinguished himself in the Turkish war, and with whom she carried on a guilty intrigue. From his father Joseph Suess derived a dignified, almost military bearing, and his personal beauty from his mother.

The Baron's romance with the lovely Jewess came to an end in 1693, when he held the castle of Heidelberg against the French. He surrendered after a gallant defence; too soon, however, as the court-martial held on him decided; and he was sentenced to death, but was pardoned by the Emperor Leopold, with the loss of all his honours and offices, and he was banished the Empire.

Suess had a sister who married a rich Jew of Vienna, but followed her mother in laxity of morals, and, after having wasted a good fortune in extravagance, fell back on her mother and brother for a maintenance. He had a brother who became a factor at the court of Darmstadt. They lived on bad terms with each other, and were engaged in repeated lawsuits with one another. This brother abjured Judaism, was baptised, and assumed the name of Tauffenberg. Joseph Suess was connected, or nominally connected, through Isachar, his reputed though not his real father, with the great and wealthy Jewish family of Oppenheim. The branch established in Vienna had become rich on contracts for the army, and had been ennobled. One member failed because the Emperor Leopold I. owed him many millions of dollars and was unable to pay. Joseph began life in the office of the court bankers and army contractors of his family at Vienna. Here it was that he obtained his first ideas of how[Pg 274] money could be raised through lotteries, monopolies, and imposts of all kinds. But though Joseph was put on the road that led to wealth, in the Oppenheim house at Vienna, he missed his chance there, and was dismissed for some misconduct or other, the particulars of which we do not know.

Then, in disgrace and distress, he came to Bavaria, where he served a while as barber's assistant. Probably through the influence of some of the Oppenheims, Joseph was introduced into the court of the family of Thurn and Taxis, which had acquired vast wealth through the monopoly of the post-office. Thence he made his way into an office of the palatine court at Mannheim.

This was a period in which the German princes were possessed with the passion of imitating the splendour and extravagance of Louis XIV. Everyone must have his Versailles, must crowd his court with functionaries, and maintain armies in glittering and showy uniforms.

Germany, to the present day, abounds in vast and magnificent palaces, for the most part in wretched repair, if not ruinous. The houses of our English nobility are nothing as compared in size with these palaces of petty princes, counts, and barons.

To build these mansions, and when built to fill them with officials and servants, to keep up their armies, and to satisfy the greed of their mistresses, these German princes needed a good deal of money, and were ready to show favour to any man who could help them to obtain it—show where to bore to tap fresh financial springs. All kinds of new methods of[Pg 275] taxation were had recourse to, arousing the bitter mockery of the oppressed. The tobacco monopoly was called the nose-tax; it was felt to be oppressive only by the snuff-takers and smokers; and perhaps the stamp on paper only by those who wrote; but the boot and shoe stamp imposed by one of the little princes touched everyone but those who went barefoot.

Joseph Suess introduced the stamp on paper into the palatinate. He did not invent this duty, which had been imposed elsewhere; but he obtained the concession of the impost, and sold it to a subfactor for 12,000 florins, and with the money invested in a speculation in the coinage of Hesse-Darmstadt. All the little German princes at this time had their own coinage, down to trumpery little states of a few miles in diameter, as Waldeck, Fulda, Hechingen, and Montfort; and Germany was full to overflow of bad money, and barren of gold and silver. Suess, in his peregrinations, had obtained a thorough insight into the mysteries of this branch of business. He not only thoroughly understood the practical part of the matter—the coinage—but also where the cheapest markets were, in which to purchase the metals to be coined. Now that he had some money at his command, he undertook to farm the coinage of Hesse-Darmstadt; but almost immediately undersold it, with a profit to himself of 9,000 florins. He took other contracts for the courts, and soon realised a comfortable fortune. Even the Archbishop of Cologne called in his aid, and contributed to enrich him, in his efforts to get a little more for himself out of the subjects of his [Pg 276]palatinate. In the summer of 1732 Joseph Suess visited the Blackforest baths of Wildbad, for the sake of the waters. At the same time Charles Alexander of Würtemberg and his wife were also undergoing the same cure. Oppenheim's pleasant manners, his handsome face, and his cleverness caught the fancy of Charles Alexander, and he appointed him his agent and steward; and as the Prince was then in want of money, Suess lent him a trifle of 2,000 florins. Charles Alexander had not at this time any assurance that he would ascend the ducal throne of Würtemberg, though it was probable.[18] The reigning Duke, Eberhardt Louis, had, indeed, just lost his only son; but it was not impossible that a posthumous grandson might be born. Charles Alexander was first-cousin of the Duke. It is said that Suess on this occasion foretold the future greatness of the Prince, and pretended to extract his prophecy from the Cabala. It is certain that Charles Alexander was very superstitious, and believed in astrology, and it is by no means improbable that Suess practised on his credulity. He had at his disposal plenty of means of learning whether the young Princess of Würtemberg was likely soon to become a mother—her husband had died in November—and he was very well aware that the old Duke was failing. The loan made by Suess came acceptably to Prince Charles Alexander just as a Jewish banker, Isaac Simon of Landau, with whom he had hitherto dealt, had declined to make further advances.

When the Prince returned to Belgrade, where he resided as stadtholder of Servia, under the Emperor,[Pg 277] he was fully convinced that he had discovered in Suess an able, intelligent, and devoted servant. His wife was a princess of Thurn and Taxis, and it is possible that Suess, who had been for some time about that court at Ratisbon, had used her influence, and his acquaintance with her family affairs, to push his interests with the Prince, her husband.

On October 31, 1733, died the old Duke Eberhardt Louis, and Charles Alexander at once hastened from Belgrade to Vienna, where, in an interview with the Emperor, without any consultation with the Estates, or consideration for the treasury of Würtemberg, he promised Leopold a contingent of 12,000 men to aid in the war against France. Then he went on to Stuttgart.

Poor Würtemberg groaned under the burdens that had been imposed on it; the favourites had been allowed to do with it what they liked; and Charles Alexander's first public declaration on entering his capital was: "From henceforth I will reign over you immediately, and myself see to the reform of every grievance, and put away from my people every burden which has galled its shoulders. If my people cry to me, my ears shall be open to hear their call. I will not endure the disorder which has penetrated everywhere, into every department of the State; my own hand shall sweep it away."

And as a token of his sincerity he ordered every office-holder in Church and State to put on paper and present to him a schedule of every payment that had been made, by way of fee and bribe, to obtain his office. This was published on December 28, 1733.[Pg 278]The older and wiser heads were shaken; the Duke, they said, was only heaping trouble on his shoulders; let the past be buried. He replied, "I must get to the bottom of all this iniquity. I must get inured to work."

But the hero of Belgrade had all his life been more accustomed to the saddle than the desk, and to command in battle—a much simpler matter—than to rule in peace. The amount of grievances brought before him, the innumerable scandals, peculations, bewildered him. The people were wild with enthusiasm, but the entire bureaucracy was filled with sullen and dogged opposition.

Würtemberg enjoyed a constitution more liberal than any other German principality. The old Duke Eberhardt with the Beard, who died in 1496, by his will contrived for the good government of his land by providing checks against despotic rule by the dukes his successors. On the strength of this testament the Estates deposed his successor. The provisions of this will were ratified in the Capitulation of Tübingen, in 1514, and every duke on assuming the reins of government was required to swear to observe the capitulation. Duke Charles Alexander took the oath without perhaps very closely examining it, and found out after it was taken that he was hampered in various ways, and was incapacitated from raising the body of men with which he had undertaken to furnish the Emperor, independent of the consent of the Parliament. It may here be said that there was no hereditary house of nobles in Würtemberg; the policy of the former dukes had been to drive the[Pg 279] hereditary petty nobles out of the country, and to create in their place a clique of court officials absolutely dependent on themselves. By the constitution, no standing army was to be maintained, and no troops raised without the consent of the

Estates; the tenure of property was guaranteed by the State, all serfage was abolished, and no taxes could be imposed or monopolies created without the consent of the Estates.

The Estates consisted of fourteen prelates, pastors invested with dignities which entitled them to sit in the House, and seventy deputies—some elected by the constituencies, others holders of certain offices, who sat *ex officio*. The Estates had great power; indeed the Duke could do little but ask its consent to the measures he proposed, and to swallow humble pie at refusal. It not only imposed the taxes, but the collectors were directly responsible to the Estates for what was collected, and paid into its hands the sum gathered. Moreover, any agreement entered into between the Duke and another prince was invalid unless ratified by the Estates.

When Duke Charles Alexander, who had been accustomed to the despotic command of an army as field-marshal, found how his hands were tied and how he was surrounded by impediments to free action on all sides, he was very angry, and quarrelled with the Ministers who had presented the capitulation to him for signature. He declared that the paper presented for him to sign had not been read to him in full, or had the obnoxious passages folded under that he should not see them, or that they had been added after his signature had been affixed.

[Pg 280]

He became irritable, not knowing how to keep his promise with the Emperor, and disgusted to find himself a ruler without real authority.

Now, as it was inconvenient to call the Assembly together on every occasion when something was wanted, a permanent committee sat in Stuttgart, consisting of two parts. This committee acted for the Estates and were responsible to it.

Wanting advice and help, unwilling to seek that of the reliable Ministers—and there were some honest and patriotic—the Duke asked Joseph Suess to assist him, and Suess was only too delighted to show him a way out of his difficulties. The redress of grievances was thrust aside, abuses were left uncorrected, and the Duke's attention was turned towards two main objects—the establishment of a standing army, and the upsetting of the old constitution.

Würtemberg was then a state whose limits were not very extensive, nor did they lie within a ring fence. The imperial cities of Reutlingen, Ulm, Heilsbronn, Weil, and Gmünd were free. It might not be convenient for the Emperor to pay with hard cash for the troops the Duke had promised to furnish, but he might allow of the incorporation of these independent and wealthy cities in the duchy. Moreover, it was a feature of the times for the princes to seek to conquer fresh districts and incorporate them. France had recently snatched away Mompelgard from Würtemberg, and Charles Alexander recovered it. The duchy had suffered so severely from having been overrun by French troops that the Estates acquiesced, though reluctantly, in the Duke's proposal[Pg 281] that a standing army should be maintained. Having obtained this concession, Suess instructed him how to make it a means of acquiring money, by calling men to arms who would be thankful to purchase their discharge. The army soon numbered 18,000 soldiers. His general-in-chief was Remchingen, a man who had served with him in the Imperial army and was devoted to his interests. The Duke placed his army under officers who were none of them Würtembergers. At the head of an army officered by his own creatures, the Duke hoped to carry his next purpose—the abrogation of the capitulation, and the conversion of the State from a constitutional to a despotic monarchy. Suess now became the Duke's most confidential adviser, and, guided by him, Charles Alexander got rid of all his Ministers and courtiers who would not become the assistants in this policy, and filled their places with creatures of his own, chief of whom was a fellow named Hallwachs. In order to paralyse the Assembly the Duke did not summon it to meet, and managed to pack the committee with men in his interest; for, curiously enough, the committee was not elected by the delegates, but itself elected into the vacancies created in it. By means of the committee the Duke imposed on the country in 1736 a double tax, and the grant of a thirtieth of all the fruits; and this was to last "as long as the necessities of the case required it."

Suess himself was careful to keep in the background. He accepted no office about court, became Minister of no branch of the State; but every Minister and officer was nominated by him and [Pg 282]devoted to him. Towards these creatures of his own he behaved with rudeness and arrogance, so that they feared him almost more than the Duke. If the least opposition was manifested, Suess threatened the gallows or the block, forfeiture of goods, and banishment; and as the Duke subscribed every order Suess brought him, it was well known that his threats were not idle.

Suess employed Weissensee, a pastor, the prelate of Hirsau, as his court spy. This worthless man brought to the favourite every whisper that passed within his hearing among the courtiers of the Duke, everything that was said in the committee, and advised whether the adhesion of this or that man was doubtful.

Suess so completely enveloped the Duke in the threads of the web he spun about him, that Charles Alexander followed his advice blindly, and did nothing without consulting him.

In 1734 Suess farmed the coinage of Würtemberg, with great profit to himself, and, having got it into his own hands, kept it there to the end. But there is this to be said for his coinage, that it was far better than that of all the other states of Germany; so that the Würtemberg silver was sought throughout Germany. There was nothing fraudulent in this transaction, and though at his trial the matter was closely investigated, no evidence of his having exceeded what was just could be produced against him.

It was quite another matter with the "Land Commission," a well-intentioned institution with which the Duke began his reign. Charles Alexander was overwhelmed with the evidence sent in to him of[Pg 283] bribery under the late Duke, and, unable to investigate the cases himself, he appointed commissioners to do so, and of course these commissioners were nominated by Suess. The commission not only examined into evidence of bribery in the purchase of offices, but also into peculation and neglect of duty in the discharge of offices. Those against whom evidence was strong were sentenced to pay a heavy fine, but were not necessarily deprived. Those, on the other hand, who had acquired their offices honourably and had discharged their functions conscientiously were harassed by repeated trials, terrified with threats, and were forced to purchase their discharge at a sum fixed according to an arbitrary tariff. Those who proved stubborn, or did not see at what the commissioners aimed, were subjected to false witnesses, found guilty, and fined. These fines amounted in some instances to £2,000.

After the commission had exhausted the bureaucracy, and money was still needed, private individuals became the prey of their inquisitorial and extortive action.

Any citizen who was reported to be rich was summoned before the tribunal to give an account of the manner in which he had obtained his wealth; his private affairs were investigated, his books examined, and his trial protracted till he was glad to purchase his dismissal for a sum calculated according to his income as revealed to the prying eyes of the inquisitors.

But as this did not suffice to fill the empty treasury, recurrence was had to the old abuse which the Land Commission had been instituted to inquire into and correct. Every office was sold, and to increase the[Pg 284] revenue from this source fresh offices were created, fresh titles invented, and all were sold for ready money. Every office in Church as well as State was bought; indeed, a sort of auction was held at every vacancy, and the office was knocked down to the highest bidder.

This sort of commerce had been bad enough under the late Duke, but it became fourfold as bad now under the redresser of abuses, for what had before been inchoate was now organised by Suess into a system.

Not only were the offices sold, but after they had been entered upon, the tenant was expected to pay a second sum, entitled the gratuity, which was to go, it was announced, towards a sustentation fund for widows and orphans and the aged. It is needless to say that none of this money ever reached widows, orphans, or aged.

A special bureau of gratuities was organised by decree of the Duke, and filled with men appointed by Suess, who paid into his hands the sums received; and he, after having sifted them, and retained what he thought fit, shook the rest into the ducal treasury. This bureau was founded by ducal rescript in 1736.

Side by side with the Office of Gratuities came the Fiscal Office into being, whose function it was to revise the magisterial and judicial proceedings of the courts of justice. This also was filled by Suess with his creatures. The ground given to the world for its establishment was the correction of judicial errors and injustices committed by the courts of law. It was the final court of revision, before which every[Pg 285] decision went before it was carried into effect. Legal proceedings, moreover, were long and costly, and the Fiscal Court undertook to interfere when any suit threatened to be unduly protracted to the prejudice of justice. But the practical working of the Fiscal Court was something very different. It interfered with the course of justice, reversing judgments, not according to equity, but according to the bribes paid into the hands of the board. In a very short time the sources of justice were completely poisoned by it, and no crime, however great and however clearly established, led to chastisement if sufficient money were paid into the hands of the court of revision. The whole country was overrun with spies, who denounced as guilty of imaginary crimes those who were rich, and such never escaped without leaving some of their gold sticking to the hands of the fiscal counsellors.

As usual with Joseph Suess, he endeavoured to keep officially clear of this court, as he had of the Office of Gratuities, and of all others. But the Duke nominated him assistant counsellor. Suess protested, and endeavoured to shirk the honour; but as the Duke refused to release him, he took care never once to attend the court, and when the proceedings and judgments were sent him for his signature he always sent them back unsigned; and he never was easy till relieved of the unacceptable title. For Suess was a clever rogue. In every transaction that was public, and of which documentary evidence was producible that he had been mixed up with it, he acted with integrity; but whenever he engaged on a proceeding which might render him liable to be tried in the event[Pg 286] of his falling into disfavour, he kept himself in the background and acted through his agents; so that when, eventually, he was tried for his treasonable and fraudulent conduct, documentary evidence incriminating him was wholly wanting.

After the death of the Duke, it was estimated from the records of the two courts that they had in the year 1736-7 squeezed sixty-five thousand pounds out of the small and poor duchy.

Suess had constituted himself jeweller to the Duke, who had a fancy for precious stones, but knew nothing of their relative values. When Suess offered him a jewel he was unable to resist the temptation of buying it, and very little of the money of the Bureau of Gratuities ever reached him; he took the value out in stones at Suess' estimation. When some of his intimates ventured to suggest that the Jew was deceiving him as to the worth of the stones, Duke Charles Alexander shrugged his shoulders and said with a laugh, "It may be so, but I can't do without that coujon" (*cochon*).[19] . At the beginning of 1736 a new edict for wards was issued by the Duke, probably on Suess' suggestion, whereby he constituted a chancery which should act as guardian to all orphans under age, managing their property for them, and was accountable to none but the Duke for the way in which it dealt with the trust. Then a commission was instituted to take charge of all charitable bequests in the duchy; and by this means Suess got the fingering of[Pg 287] property to the amount of two hundred thousand pounds, for which the State paid to the Charities at the rate of three per cent.

Then came the imposition of duties and taxes. Salt was taxed, playing-cards, groceries, leather, tobacco, carriages, even the sweeping of chimneys. A gazette was issued containing decrees of the Duke and official appointments, and every officer and holder of any place, however insignificant, under Government was compelled to subscribe to this weekly paper, the profits of which came to the Duke and his adviser. Then came a property and income tax; then in quick succession one tormenting edict after another, irritating and disturbing the people, and all meaning one thing—money.

Lotteries were established by order of the Duke. Suess paid the Duke £300 for one, and pocketed the profits, which were considerable. At the court balls and masquerades Suess had his roulette tables in an adjoining room, and what fell to the *croupier* went into his pocket.[20]

At last his sun declined. The Duke became more and more engrossed in his ideas of upsetting the constitution by means of his army, and listened more to his general, Remchingen, than to Suess. He entered into a compact with the elector of Bavaria and with the Bishops of Würzburg and Bamberg to send him troops to assist him in his great project, and, as a price for this assistance, promised to introduce the Roman Catholic religion into Würtemberg.

[Pg 288]
The enemies of Suess, finding that he was losing hold of the Duke, took advantage of a precious stone which the Jew had sold him for a thousand pounds, and which proved to be worth only four hundred, to open the eyes of Charles Alexander to the character of the man who had exercised such unbounded influence over him. Suess, finding his power slipping from him, resolved to quit the country. The Duke stopped him. Suess offered five thousand pounds for permission to depart; it was refused. Charles Alexander was aware that Suess knew too many court secrets to be allowed to quit the country. Moreover, the necessities of the Duke made him feel that he might still need the ingenuity of Suess to help him to raise money. As a means of retaining him he granted him a so-called "absolutorium"—a rescript which made him responsible to no one for any of his actions in the past or in the future. Furnished with this document, the Jew consented to remain, and then the Duke required of him a loan of four thousand pounds for the expenses of a journey he meditated to Danzig to consult a physician about a foot from which he suffered. The "absolutorium" was signed in February 1737.

On March 12 following, Charles Alexander started on his journey from Stuttgart, but went no farther than his palace at Ludwigsburg.

Although the utmost secrecy had been maintained, it had nevertheless transpired that the constitution was to be upset as soon as the Duke had left the country. He had given sealed orders to his general, Remchingen, to this effect. The Bavarian and [Pg 289]Würtemberg troops, to the number of 19,000 men, were already on the march. The Würtemberg army was entirely officered by the Duke's own men. Orders had been issued to forbid the Stuttgart Civil Guard from exercising and assembling, and ordering that a general disarmament of the Civil Guard and of the peasants and citizens should be enforced immediately the Duke had crossed the frontier. All the fortresses in the duchy had been provided with abundance of ammunition and ordnance.

At Ludwigsburg the Duke halted to consult an astrologer as to the prospect of his undertaking. Suess laughed contemptuously at the pretences of this man, and, pointing to a cannon, said to Charles Alexander, "This is your best telescope."

The sealed orders were to be opened on the 13th, and on that day the stroke was to be dealt. Already Ludwigsburg was full of Würzburg soldiers. A courier of the Duke with a letter had, in a drunken squabble, been deprived of the dispatch; this was opened and shown to the Assembly, which assembled in all haste and alarm. It revealed the plot. At once some of the notables hastened to Ludwigsburg to have an interview with their prince. He received them roughly, and dismissed them without disavowing his intentions. The consternation became general. The day was stormy; clouds were whirled across the sky, then came a drift of hail, then a gleam of sun. At Ludwigsburg, the wind blew in whole ranges of windows, shivering the glass. The alarm-bells rang in the church towers, for fire had broken out in the village of Eglosheim.

[Pg 290]

The Assembly sent another deputation to Ludwigsburg, consisting of their oldest and most respected members. They did not arrive till late, and unable to obtain access through the front gates, crept round by the kitchen entrance, and presented themselves unexpectedly before the Duke at ten o'clock at night, as he was retiring to rest from a ball that had been given. Dancing was still going on in one of the wings, and the strains of music entered the chamber when the old notables of Würtemberg, men of venerable age and high character, forced their way into the Duke's presence.

Charles Alexander had but just come away from the ball-room, seated himself in an arm-chair, and drunk a powerful medicine presented him by his chamberlain, Neuffer, in a silver bowl. Neuffer belonged to a family which had long been influential in Würtemberg, honourable and patriotic. Scarce had the Duke swallowed this draught when the deputation appeared. He became livid with fury, and though the interview took place with closed doors the servants without heard a violent altercation, and the Duke's voice raised as if he were vehemently excited. Presently the doors opened and the deputation came forth, greatly agitated, one of the old men in his hurry forgetting to take his cap away with him. Scarcely were they gone when Neuffer dismissed the servants, and himself went to a further wing of the palace.

The Duke, still excited, suddenly felt himself unwell, ran into the antechamber, found no one there, staggered into a third, then a fourth room, tore open a window, and shouted into the great court for help; but[Pg 291] his voice was drowned by the band in the illumined ball-room, playing a valse. Then giddiness came over the Duke, and he fell to the ground. The first to arrive was Neuffer, and he found him insensible. He drew his knife and lanced him. Blood flowed. The Duke opened his eyes and gasped, "What is the matter with me? I am dying!" He was placed in an armchair, and died instantly.

That night not a window in Stuttgart had shown light. The town was as a city of the dead. Everyone was in alarm as to what would ensue on the morrow, but in secret arms were being distributed among the citizens and guilds. They would fight for their constitution. Suddenly, at midnight, the news spread that the Duke was dead. At once the streets were full of people, laughing, shouting, throwing themselves into each other's arms, and before another hour the windows were illuminated with countless candles.[21]

Not a moment was lost. Duke Charles Rudolf of Würtemberg-Neuenstadt was invested with the regency, and on March 19, General Remchingen was arrested and deprived of his office.

For once Suess' cleverness failed him. Relying on his "absolutorium," he did not fly the country the moment he heard of the death of the Duke. He waited till he could place his valuables in safety. He waited just too long, for he was arrested and confined to his house. Then he did manage to escape, and got the start of his enemies by an hour, but was recognised and stopped by a Würtemberg officer, and reconducted to Stuttgart, where he was almost torn[Pg 292] to pieces by the infuriated populace, and with difficulty rescued from their hands. On March 19, he was sent to the fortress of Hohenneuffen; but thence he almost succeeded in effecting his escape by bribing the guards with the diamonds he had secreted about his person.

At first Suess bore his imprisonment with dignity. He was confident, in the first place, that the "absolutorium" would not be impeached, and in the second, that there was no documentary evidence discoverable which could incriminate him. But as his imprisonment was protracted, and as he saw that the country demanded a victim for the wrongs it had suffered, his confidence and self-respect left him. Nevertheless, it was not till the last that he was convinced that his life as well as his ill-gotten gains would be taken from him, and then he became a despicable figure, entreating mercy, and eagerly seeking to incriminate others in the hopes of saving his own wretched life thereby.

There were plenty of others as guilty as Suess—nay, more so, for they were natives of Würtemberg, and he an alien in blood and religion. But these others had relations and friends to intercede for them, and all felt that Suess was the man to be made a scape-goat of, because he was friendless.

The mode of his execution was barbarous. His trial had been protracted for eleven months; at length, on February 4, 1738, he was led forth to execution—to be hung in an iron cage. This cage had been made in 1596, and stood eight feet high, and was four feet in diameter. It was composed of seventeen bars and fourteen cross-bars, and was circular. The gallows was thirty-five feet high. The wretched[Pg 293] man was first strangled in the cage, hung up in it like a dead bird, and then the cage with him in it was hoisted up to the full height of the gallows-tree. His wealth was confiscated.

Hallwachs and the other rascals who had been confederated with him in plundering their country were banished, but were allowed to depart with all their plunder.

Remchingen also escaped; when arrested, he managed to get rid of all compromising papers, which were given by him to a chimney-sweep sent to him down the chimney by some of the agents of the Bishop of Würzburg.

Such is the tragic story of the life of Suess Oppenheim, a man of no ordinary abilities, remarkable shrewdness, but without a spark of principle. But the chief tragedy is to be found in the deterioration of the character of Duke Charles Alexander, who, as Austrian field-marshal and governor of Servia, had been the soul of honour, generous and beloved; who entered on his duchy not only promising good government, but heartily desiring to rule well for his people's good; and who in less than four years had forfeited the love and respect of his subjects, and died meditating an act which would have branded him as perjured—died without having executed one of his good purposes, and so hated by the people who had cheered him on his entry into the capital, that, by general consent, the mode of his death was not too curiously and closely inquired into.

FOOTNOTES:

[18] There was some idea of a younger brother being elected.

[19] In three years Suess gained a profit of 20,000 florins out of the sale of jewellery alone.

[20] The Duke, at Suess's instigation, wrote to the Emperor to get the Jew factotum ennobled, but was refused.

[21] On the following night a confectioner set up a transparency exhibiting the Devil carrying off the Duke.

Ignatius Fessler.

On December 15th, 1839, in his eighty-fourth year, died Ignatius Fessler, Lutheran Bishop, at St. Petersburg, a man who had gone through several phases of religious belief and unbelief, a Hungarian by birth, a Roman Catholic by education, a Capuchin friar, then a deist, almost, if not quite, an atheist, professor of Oriental languages in the university of Lemberg, finally Lutheran Bishop in Finland.

He was principally remarkable as having been largely instrumental in producing one of the most salutary reforms of the Emperor Joseph II.

His autobiography published by him in 1824, when he was seventy years old, affords a curious picture of the way in which Joseph carried out those reforms, and enables us to see how it was that they roused so much opposition, and in so many cases failed to effect the good that was designed.

Fessler, in his autobiography, paints himself in as bright colours as he can lay on, but it is impossible not to see that he was a man of little principle, selfish and heartless.

The autobiography is so curious, and the experiences of Fessler so varied, the times in which he lived so eventful, and the book itself so little known, that a short account of his career may perhaps interest, and must be new to the generality of readers.

Ignatius Fessler was the son of parents in a humble walk of life resident in Hungary, but Germans by extraction. Ignatius was born in the year 1754, and as the first child, was dedicated by his mother to God. It was usual at that time for such children to be dressed in ecclesiastical habits. Ignatius as soon as he could walk was invested in a black cassock. His earliest reading was in the lives of the saints and martyrs, but at his first Communion his mother gave him a Bible. That book and Thomas à Kempis were her only literature. Long-continued prayer, daily reading of religious books, and no others, moulded the opening mind of her child. Exactly the same process goes on in countless peasant houses in Catholic Austria and Germany and Switzerland at the present day. No such education, no such walling off of the mind from secular influences is possible in England or France. The first enthusiasm of the child was to become a saint, his highest ambition to be a hermit or a martyr. At the age of seven he was given to be instructed by a Jesuit father, and was shortly after admitted to communion. At the age of nine Ignatius could read and speak Latin, and then he read with avidity Cardinal Bona's *Manductio ad Coelum*. His education was in the hands of the Carmelites at Raab. Dr. Fessler records his affectionate remembrance of his master, Father Raphael. Ignatius lounged, and was lazy. "Boy!" said the Father, "have done with lounging or you will live to be no good, but the laughing stock of old women. Look at me aged seventy, full of life and vigour, that comes of not being a lounger when a boy." From the Carmelite school Ignatius passed into that of the Jesuits. His advance was rapid; but his reading was still in Mystical Theology and his aim the attainment of the contemplative, ecstatic life of devotion. So he reached his seventeenth year.

Then his mother took him to Buda, to visit his uncle who was lecturer on Philosophy in the Capuchin Convent. The boy declared his desire to become a Franciscan. His mother and uncle gave their ready consent, and he entered on his noviciate, under the name of Francis Innocent. "The name Innocent became me well—really, at that time, I did not know the difference between the sexes."

In 1774, when aged twenty, he took the oaths constituting him a friar. All the fathers in the convent approved, except one old man, Peregrinus, who remonstrated gravely, declaring that he foresaw that Fessler would bring trouble on the fraternity. Father Peregrinus was right, Fessler was one to whom the life and rules and aim of the Order could never be congenial. He had an eager, hungry mind, an insatiable craving for knowledge, and a passion for books. The Capuchins were, and still are, recruited from the lowest of the people, ignorant peasants with a traditional contempt for learning, and their teachers embued with the shallowest smattering of knowledge. Fessler, being devoid of means, could not enter one of the cultured Orders, the Benedictines or the Jesuits. Moreover, the Franciscan is, by his vow, without property, he must live by begging, a rule fatal to self-respect, and fostering idleness. S. Francis, the founder, was a scion of a mercantile class, and the[Pg 297] beggary which he imposed on his Order, was due to his revolt against the money-greed of his class. But it has been a fruitful source of mischief. It deters men with any sense of personal dignity from entering the Order, and it invites into it the idle and the ignorant. The Franciscan Order has been a fruitful nursery of heresies, schisms and scandals. Now old Father Peregrinus had sufficient insight into human nature to see and judge that a man of pride, intellectual power, and culture of mind, would be as a fish on dry land in the Capuchin fraternity. He was not listened to. Fessler was too young to know himself, and the fathers too eager to secure a man of promise and ability.

"The guardian, Cœlestine, an amiable man, took a liking to me. He taught me to play chess, and he played more readily with me than with any of the rest, which, not a little, puffed up my self-esteem. The librarian, Leonidas, was an old, learned, obliging man, dearly loving his flowers. I fetched the water for him to his flower-beds, and he showed me his gratitude by letting me have the run of the library."

The library was not extensive, the books nearly all theological, and the volume which Fessler was most attracted by was Barbanson's "Ways of Divine Love."

In 1775, Fessler made the acquaintance of a Calvinist Baron, who lent him Fleury's "Ecclesiastical History." This opened the young man's eyes to the fact that the Church was not perfect, that the world outside the Church was not utterly graceless. He read his New Testament over seven times in that year. Then his Calvinist friend lent him Muratori's[Pg 298] "Treatise on the Mystical Devotions of the Monks." His confidence was shaken. He no longer saw in the Church the ideal of purity and perfect infallibility; he saw that Mystical Theology was a geography of cloud castles. What profit was there in it? To what end did the friars live? To grow cabbages, make snuff-boxes, cardboard cases, which they painted—these were their practical labours; the rest of their time was spent in prayer and meditation.

Then the young friar got hold of Hofmann-Waldau's poems, and the sensuousness of their pictures inflamed his imagination at the very time when religious ecstasy ceased to attract him.

What the result might have been, Fessler says, he trembles to think, had he not been fortified by Seneca. It is curious to note, and characteristic of the man, that he was saved from demoralisation, not by the New Testament, which did not touch his heart, but by Seneca's moral axioms, which convinced his reason. The Franciscans are allowed great liberty. They run over the country collecting alms, they visit whom they will, and to a man without principle, such liberty offers dangerous occasions.

Fessler now resolved to leave an Order which was odious to him. "Somewhat tranquillized by Seneca, I now determined to shake myself loose from the trammels of the cloister, without causing scandal. The most easy way to do this was for me to take Orders, and get a cure of souls or a chaplaincy to a nobleman." He had no vocation for the ministry; he looked to it merely as a means of escape from uncongenial surroundings. On signifying his desire to become a[Pg 299] priest, he was transferred to Gross Wardein, there to pass the requisite course of studies. At Wardein he gained the favour of the bishop and some of the canons, who lent him books on the ecclesiastical and political history of his native land. He also made acquaintance with some families in the town, a lady with two daughters, with the elder of whom he fell in love. He had, however, sufficient decency not to declare his passion. It was otherwise with a young Calvinist tailor's widow, Sophie; she replied to his declaration very sensibly by a letter, which, he declares, produced a lasting effect upon him.

In 1776 he was removed to Schwächat to go through a course of Moral Theology. His disgust at his enforced studies, which he regarded as the thrashing of empty husks, increased. He was angry at his removal from the friends he had made at Wardein. Vexation, irritation, doubt, threw him into a fever, and he was transferred to the convent in the suburbs of Vienna, where he could be under better medical care. The physician who attended him soon saw that his patient's malady was mental. Fessler opened his heart to him, and begged for the loan of books more feeding to the brain than the mystical rubbish in the convent library. The doctor advised him to visit him, when discharged as cured from the convent infirmary, instead of at once returning to Schwächat. This he did, and the doctor introduced him to two men of eminence and influence, Von Eybel and the prelate Rautenstrauch, a Benedictine abbot, the director of the Theological Faculties in the Austrian Monarchy. This latter promised Fessler to assist him in his studies, and[Pg 300] urged him to study Greek and Hebrew, also to widen the circle of his reading, to make acquaintance with law, history, with natural science and geography, and undertook to provide him with the requisite books.

On his return to Schwächat, Fessler appealed to the Provincial against his Master of Studies whom he pronounced to be an incompetent pedant. At his request he was moved to Wiener-Neustadt. There he found the lecturer on Ecclesiastical Studies as superficial as the man from whom he had escaped. This man did not object to Fessler pursuing his Greek and Hebrew studies, nor to his taking from the library what books he liked.

The young candidate now borrowed and devoured deistical works, Hobbes, Tindal, Edelmann, and the Wolfenbüttel Fragments. He had to be careful not to let these books be seen, accordingly he hid them under the floor in the choir. After midnight, when matins had been sung, instead of returning to bed with the rest, he remained, on the plea of devotion, in the church, seated on the altar steps, reading deistical works by the light of the sanctuary lamp, which he pulled down to a proper level. He now completely lost his faith, not in Christianity only, but in natural religion as well. Nevertheless, he did not desist from his purpose of seeking orders. He was ordained deacon in 1778, and priest in 1779. "On the Sunday after Corpus Christi, I celebrated without faith, without unction, my first mass, in the presence of my mother, her brother, and the rest of my family. They all received the communion from my hand, bathed in[Pg 301] tears of emotion. I, who administered to them, was frozen in unbelief."

The cure of souls he desired was not given him, no chaplaincy was offered him. His prospect of escape seemed no better than before. He became very impatient, and made himself troublesome in his convent. As might have been suspected, he became restive under the priestly obligations, as he had been under the monastic rule. It is curious that, late in life, when Fessler wrote his memoirs, he showed himself blind to the unworthiness of his conduct in taking on him the most sacred responsibilities to God and the Church, when he disbelieved in both. He is, however, careful to assure us that though without faith in his functions, he executed them punctually, hearing confessions, preaching and saying mass. But his conduct is so odious, his after callousness so conspicuous, that it is difficult to feel the smallest conviction of his conscientiousness at any time of his life.

As he made himself disagreeable to his superiors at Neustadt, he was transferred to Mödling. There he made acquaintance with a Herr Von Molinari and was much at his house, where he met a young Countess Louise. "I cannot describe her stately form, her arching brows, the expression of her large blue eyes, the delicacy of her mouth, the music of her tones, the exquisite harmony that exists in all her movements, and what affects me more than all—she speaks Latin easily, and only reads serious books." So wrote Fessler in a letter at the time. He read Ovid's Metamorphoses with her in the morning, and walked with her in the evening. When, at the end[Pg 302] of October, the family went to Vienna, "the absence of that noble soul," he wrote, "filled me with the most poignant grief." The Molinari family were bitten with Jansenism, and hoped to bring the young Capuchin to their views. Next year, in the spring of 1781, they returned to Mödling.

"This year passed like the former; in the convent I was a model of obedience, in the school a master of scholastic theology: in Molinari's family a humble disciple of Jansen, in the morning a worshipper of the muse of Louise, in the evening an agreeable social companion,"—in heart—an unbeliever in Christianity.

A letter written to an uncle on March 12th, 1782, must be quoted verbatim, containing as it does a startling discovery, which gave him the opportunity so long desired, of breaking with the Order:—

"Since the 23rd February, I sing without intermission after David, in my inmost heart, 'Praise and Glory be to God, who has delivered my enemies into my hand!' Listen to the wonderful way in which this has happened. On the night of the 23rd to 24th of February, after eleven o'clock, I was roused from sleep by a lay-brother. 'Take your crucifix,' said he 'and follow me.'

"'Whither?' I asked, panic struck.

"'Whither I am about to lead you.'

"'What am I to do?'

"'I will tell you, when you are on the spot.'

"'Without knowing whither I go, and for what purpose, go I will not.'

"'The Guardian has given the order; by virtue of[Pg 303] holy obedience you are bound to follow whither I lead.'

"As soon as holy obedience is involved, no resistance can be offered. Full of terror, I took my crucifix and followed the lay-brother, who went before with a dark lantern. Passing the cell of one of my fellow scholars, I slipped in, shook him out of sleep, and whispered in Latin twice in his ear, 'I am carried off, God knows whither. If I do not appear to-morrow, communicate with Rautenstrauch.'

"Our way led through the kitchen, and beyond it through a couple of chambers; on opening the last, the brother said, 'Seven steps down.' My heart contracted, I thought I was doomed to see the last of day-light. We entered a narrow passage, in which I saw, half way down it, on the right, a little altar, on the left some doors fastened with padlocks. My guide unlocked one of these, and said, 'Here is a dying man, Brother Nicomede, a Hungarian, who knows little German, give him your spiritual assistance. I will wait here. When he is dead, call me.'

"Before me lay an old man on his pallet, in a worn-out habit, on a straw palliasse, under a blanket; his hood covered his grey head, a snow-white beard reached to his girdle. Beside the bedstead was an old straw-covered chair, a dirty table, on which was a lamp burning. I spoke a few words to the dying man, who had almost lost his speech; he gave me a sign that he understood me. There was no possibility of a confession. I spoke to him about love to God, contrition for sin, and hope in the mercy of heaven; and when he squeezed my hand in token of inward[Pg 304] emotion, I pronounced over him the General Absolution. The rest of the while I was with him, I uttered slowly, and at intervals, words of comfort and hope of eternal blessedness. About three o'clock, after a death agony of a quarter-of-an-hour, he had passed out of the reach of trouble.

"Before I called the lay-brother, I looked round the prison, and then swore over the corpse to inform the Emperor of these horrors. Then I summoned the lay-brother, and said, coldly, 'Brother Nicomede is gone.'

"'A good thing for him, too,' answered my guide, in a tone equally indifferent.

"'How long has he been here?'

"'Two and fifty years.'

"'He has been severely punished for his fault.'

"'Yes, yes. He has never been ill before. He had a stroke yesterday, when I brought him his meal.'

"'What is the altar for in the passage?'

"'One of the fathers says mass there on all festivals for the lions, and communicates them. Do you see, there is a little window in each of the doors, which is then opened, and through it the lions make their confession, hear mass, and receive communion.'

"'Have you many lions here?'

"'Four, two priests and two lay-brothers to be attended on.'

"'How long have they been here?'

"'One for fifty, another for forty-two, the third for fifteen, and the last for nine years.'

"'Why are they here?'

"'I don't know.'

[Pg 305]

"'Why are they called lions?'

"'Because I am called the lion-ward.'

"I deemed it expedient to ask no more questions. I got the lion-ward to light me to my cell, and there in calmness considered what to do.

"Next day, or rather, that same day, Feb. 24th, I wrote in full all that had occurred, in a letter addressed to the Emperor, with my signature attached. Shortly after my arrival in Vienna I had made the acquaintance of a Bohemian secular student named Bokorny, a trusty man. On the morning of Feb. 25th, I made him swear to give my letter to the Emperor, and keep silence as to my proceeding.

"At 8 o'clock he was with my letter in the Couriers' lobby of the palace, where there is usually a crowd of persons with petitions awaiting the Emperor. Joseph took my paper from my messenger, glanced hastily at it, put it apart from the rest of the petitions, and let my messenger go, after he had cautioned him most seriously to hold his tongue.

"The blow is fallen; what will be the result—whether anything will come of it, I do not yet know."

For many months no notice was taken of the letter. It was not possible for the Emperor to take action at once, for a few days later Pius VI. arrived in Vienna on a visit to Joseph.

Joseph II. was an enthusiastic reformer; he had the liveliest regard for Frederick the Great, and tried to copy him, but, as Frederick said, Joseph always began where he ought to leave off. He had no sooner become Emperor (1780) than he began a multitude of reforms, with headlong impetuosity. He supposed[Pg 306] that every abuse was to be rooted up by an exercise of despotic power, and that his subjects would hail freedom and enlightenment with enthusiasm. Regardless of the power of hereditary association, he arbitrarily upset existing institutions, in the conviction that he was promoting the welfare of his subjects. He emancipated the Jews, and proclaimed liberty of worship to all religious bodies except the Deists, whom he condemned to receive five-and-twenty strokes of the cane. He abolished the use of torture, and reorganised the courts of justice.

The Pope, alarmed at the reforming spirit of Joseph, and the innovations he was introducing into the management of the Church, crossed the Alps with the hope that in a personal interview he might moderate the Emperor's zeal. He arrived only a few days after Joseph had received the letter of Ignatius Fessler, which was calculated to spur him to enact still more sweeping reforms, and to steel his heart against the papal blandishments. Nothing could have come to his hands more opportunely.

In Vienna, in St. Stephen's, the Pope held a pontifical mass. The Emperor did not honour it by his presence. By order of Joseph, the back door of the papal lodging was walled up, that Pius might receive no visitors unknown to the Emperor, and guards were placed at the entrance, to scrutinize those who sought the presence of the Pope. Joseph lost dignity by studied discourtesy; and Kaunitz, his minister, was allowed to be insulting. The latter received the Pope when he visited him, in his dressing-gown, and instead of kissing his hand, shook it heartily. Pius,[Pg 307] after spending five weeks in Vienna without affecting anything, was constrained to depart.

Fessler saw him thrice, once, when the Pope said mass in the Capuchin Church, he stood only three paces from him. "Never did faith and unbelief, Jansenism and Deism, struggle for the mastery in me more furiously than then; tears flowed from my eyes, excited by my emotion, and at the end of the mass, I felt convinced that I had seen either a man as full of the burning love of God as a seraph, or the most accomplished actor in the world." Of the sincerity and piety of Pius VI. there can be no question. He was a good man, but not an able man. "At the conclusion he turned to us young priests, asked of each his name, length of time in the Order, and priesthood, about our studies, and exhorted us, in a fatherly tone, to be stout stones in the wall of the house of Israel, in times of trouble present and to come."

Before Pius departed, he gave his blessing to the people from the balcony of the Jesuit Church. "The Pope was seated on a throne under a gold-embroidered canopy. Fifty thousand persons must have been assembled below. Windows were full of heads, every roof crowded. The Pope wore his triple-crowned tiara, and was attended by three cardinals and two bishops in full pontificals. He intoned the form of absolution, in far-reaching voice, which was taken up by the court choir of four hundred voices. When this was done, Pius rose from his throne, the tiara was removed from his head, he stepped forward, raised eyes and arms to heaven, and in a pure ecstasy of devotion poured forth a fervent prayer. Only sighs and sobs[Pg 308] broke occasionally the perfect silence which reigned among the vast throng of kneeling persons in the great square. The Pope seemed rather to be raised in ecstasy from his feet, than to stand. The prayer lasted long, and the bishops put their hands to stay up his arms; it was like Moses on the mountain top, with the rod of God in his hand, supported by Aaron and Hur, as he prayed for his people striving below with Amalek. At last this second Moses let his arms fall, he raised his right hand, and blessed the people in the name of the Triune God. At the Amen, the cannon of the Freiung boomed, and were answered by all the artillery on the fortifications of the city."

The Pope was gone, and still no notice taken of the petition. Molinari spoke to Fessler, who was very hot about reform, and had drawn up a scheme for the readjustment of the Church in the Empire, which he sent to some of the ministers of the Emperor. "My friend," said Molinari, "to pull down and to rebuild, to destroy and to re-create, are serious matters, only to be taken in hand by one who has an earnest vocation, and not to be made a means for self-seeking."

Fessler admits that there was truth in the reproach, he was desirous of pushing himself into notice, and he cared for the matter of "the lions," only because he thought they would serve his selfish purpose. Joseph now issued an order that no member of a monastic order was to be admitted to a benefice who had not passed an examination before the teachers of the Seminaries. The superiors of the Capuchins forbade their candidates going into these examinations. Fessler stirred up revolt, and he and some[Pg 309]others, acting under his advice, demanded to be admitted to examination. His superior then informed him that he was not intended by the Order to take a cure of souls, he was about to be appointed lecturer on Philosophy in one of the convents in Hungary. In order to prevent his removal, and to force the Order to an open rupture with him, Fessler had recourse to a most unseemly and ungenerous act. Whilst in Vienna, he had made the acquaintance of an unmarried lady, the Baroness E. He had assisted her in her studies, giving her instructions usually by letter. His acquaintance, Von Eybel, had written a book or tract, which had made a great stir, entitled, "Who is the Pope?" Fessler wrote another, entitled, "Who is the Emperor?" He sent a copy to the publisher, but retained the original MS. Fessler now wrote under a feigned name, and in a disguised hand, a letter to Father Maximus, guardian of the convent, charging himself with carrying on a guilty correspondence with the Baroness E., and with the composition of an inflammatory and anti-religious pamphlet, "Who is the Emperor?" Maximus at once visited the Baroness, and showed her the letter. The lady in great indignation produced the entire correspondence, and handed the letters to him. Maximus put them in the hands of the Lector of the convent, who visited Fessler, and asked him if he acknowledged the authorship of "these scandalous letters."

"Scandalous, they are not," answered Fessler.

"*Impius, cum in profundum venerit, contemnit,*" roared the friar. "They are not only scandalous,[Pg 310] but impious. Look at this letter on platonic love. Is that a fit letter for such as you to write to a lady?"

In consequence of these letters, and the MS. of the pamphlet being found upon him, Fessler was denounced to the Consistorial Court of the Archbishop. He was summoned before it at the beginning of August, when he was forced to admit he had been wont to kiss the lady to whom he wrote on platonic love, and the Consistory suspended him from the exercise of his priestly functions for a month.

"I and the Lector returned to the convent silent, as if strangers. When we arrived, the friars were at table. I do not know how I got to my place; but after I had drunk my goblet of wine, all was clearer about me. I seemed to hear the voice of Horace calling to me from heaven, *Perfer et obdura!* and in a moment my self-respect revived, and I looked with scorn on the seventy friars hungrily eating their dinner."

Of his own despicable conduct, that he had richly deserved his punishment, Fessler never seems to have arrived at the perception. He was, indeed, a very pitiful creature, arousing disgust and contempt in a well-ordered mind; and his Memoirs only deserve notice because of the curious insight they afford into the inner life of convents, and because he was the means of bringing great scandals to light, and in assisting Joseph II. in his work of reform.

At the beginning of September, 1782, Fessler was the means of bringing a fresh scandal before the eyes of the Emperor. During the preceding year, a saddler in

Schwächat had lost his wife, and was left,[Pg 311] not only a widower, but childless. His niece now kept house for him, and was much afraid lest her uncle should marry again, and that thus she should not become his heir. She consulted a Capuchin, Father Brictius. Fessler had been in the Schwächat convent, and knew the man. Soon after, the niece assured her uncle that the ghost of her aunt had appeared to her, and told her she was suffering in Purgatory. For her release, she must have ten masses said, and some wax candles burnt. The saddler was content to have his old woman "laid" at this price. But, after the tenth mass, the niece declared she had seen her aunt again, and that the spirit had appeared to her in the presence of Father Brictius, and told her, that what troubled her most of all was the suspicion she was under, that her husband purposed marrying again; and she assured him, that were he so to do, he would lose his soul, in token whereof, she laid her hand on the cover of the niece's prayer-book, and left the impression burnt into it.

Father Brictius carried the scorched book all round the neighbourhood, the marks of thumb and five fingers were clearly to be seen, burnt into the wooden cover. Great was the excitement, and on all sides masses for souls were in demand. Some foolish pastors even preached on the marvel.

It happened that a Viennese boy was apprenticed to a tinker at Schwächat; and the boy came home every Saturday evening, to spend the day with his parents, at Vienna. He generally brought Fessler some little presents or messages from his friends at Schwächat. One day, the boy complained to Fessler[Pg 312] that he had been severely beaten by his master. On being asked the reason, he replied, that he had been engaged with the tinker making an iron hand, and that he had spoiled it. Shortly after this, the rumour of the miraculous hand laid on the prayer-book, reached the convent. Fessler put the circumstances together, and suspected he was on the track of a fraud. He went at once to one of the ministers of the Emperor, and told him what he knew.

An imperial commission was issued, the tinker, the saddler's niece, and Father Brictius, were arrested, cross-questioned, and finally, confessed the trick. The tinker was sent to prison for some months, the woman, for some weeks, and the Franciscan was first imprisoned, and then banished the country. An account of the fraud was issued, by Government authority, and every parish priest was ordered to read it to his parishioners from the pulpit.

The Capuchins at Vienna, after this, were more impatient than before to send Fessler to Hungary, and he was forced to appeal to the Emperor to prevent his removal.

Suddenly, quite unexpectedly, in the beginning of October—seven months after Fessler had sent the Emperor an account of the prison in the convent, and when he despaired of notice being taken of it—some imperial commissioners visited the convent, and demanded in the name of the Emperor to be shown all over it. At the head of the Commission was Hägelin, to whom Fessler had told his suspicions about the iron hand.

The commissioners visited all the cells, and the[Pg 313] infirmary, then asked the Guardian thrice on his honour, and in the name of the Emperor, whether there was a prison in the convent. Thrice the Guardian replied that there was not. "Let us now visit the kitchen," said Hägelin, and in spite of the protests and excuses of the Guardian, he insisted on being taken there. Beyond the kitchen was the wash-house. The commissioners went further, and found a small locked door. They insisted on its being opened. Then the Guardian turned pale and nearly fainted. The door was thrown open, the cells were unlocked, and the lay brothers ordered to bring the prisoners into the refectory. There the commissioners remained alone with the unfortunates to take down their depositions. It was found that three, Fathers Florentine, and Paternus, and the lay brother, Nemesian, were out of their minds. The "lion-ward" was summoned to answer for them. From his account, it transpired that Nemesian had gone out of his mind through religious enthusiasm; he was aged seventy-one, and had been fifty years in the dungeon. Father Florentine was aged seventy-three, he had been in confinement for forty-two years for boxing the Guardian's ears in a fit of temper. Father Paternus was locked up because he used to leave his convent without permission, and when rebuked would not give up his independent conduct. He had been fifteen years in prison. His confinement had bereft him of his senses. As the remaining two were in full possession of their faculties, the "lion-ward" was now dismissed. The lay brother Barnabas said he had been a shopkeeper's servant in Vienna, he had fallen in love with his[Pg 314] master's daughter. As his master refused to have him as his son-in-law, out of despair he had gone into the Capuchin Order. During his noviciate, the master died; the master of the novices stopped the letter informing him of this, and he took the vows, to discover, when too late, that the girl loved him, and was ready to take him. In his mad rage, he flung his rosary at the feet of the Guardian, declaring he would never confess to, or receive the communion from the hands of a father of this accursed Order. He had been nine years in prison, and was thirty-eight years old.

Father Thuribius had been caught reading Wieland, Gellert, Rabener, &c.; they had been taken from him. He got hold of other copies, they were taken away a second time. A third time he procured them, and when discovered, fought with his fists for their retention. He had been repeatedly given the cat o' nine tails, and had been locked up five months and ten days. His age was twenty-eight.

The commissioners at once suspended the Provincial and the Guardian till further notice, and the five unfortunates were handed over to the care of the Brothers of Charity.

That same day, throughout the entire monarchy, every monastery and nunnery was visited by imperial commissioners.

At the same time, the Emperor Joseph issued an order that Fessler was on no account to be allowed to leave Vienna, and that he took him under his imperial protection against all the devices of his monastic enemies.

[Pg 315]

"Now came the sentence on the Guardian and the Provincial from the Emperor. They were more severely punished than perhaps they really deserved. I felt for their sufferings more keenly, because I was well aware that I had been moved to report against them by any other motive rather than humanity; and even the consequences of my revelation, the setting at liberty of a not inconsiderable number of unfortunate monks and nuns throughout the Austrian Empire, could not set my conscience at rest. Only the orders made by the Emperor rendering it impossible to repeat such abuses, brought me any satisfaction. The monastic prisons were everywhere destroyed. Transgression of rules was henceforth to be punished only by short periods of seclusion, and cases of insanity were to be sent to the Brothers of Charity, who managed the asylums."

If Joseph II. had but possessed commonsense as well as enthusiasm, he would have left his mark deeper on his country than he did.

Fessler laid before him the schedule of studies in the Franciscan Convents. Joseph then issued an order (6th April, 1782), absolutely prohibiting the course of studies in the cloisters. When Fessler saw that the Guardian of his convent was transgressing the decree, he appealed against him to the Emperor, and had him dismissed. Next year Joseph required all the students of the Capuchin Order to enter the seminaries, and pass thence through the Universities. But, unfortunately, Joseph had taken a step to alienate from him the bishops and secular clergy, as well as the monks and friars. He arbitrarily closed all the[Pg 316] diocesan seminaries, and created seminaries of his own for the candidates for Orders, to which he appointed the professors, thus entirely removing the education of the clergy from the hands of the Church. When the Bishop of Goritz expressed his dissatisfaction, Joseph suppressed his see and banished him. The professors he appointed to the universities, to the chairs which were attended by candidates for Orders, were in many cases free-thinkers and rationalists. The professor of Biblical Exegesis at Vienna was an ex-Jesuit, Monsperger, "His religious system," says Fessler, who attended his course, "was simply this,—a wise enjoyment of life, submission to the inevitable, and prudence of conduct. That was all. He had no other idea of Church than a reciprocal bond of rights and duties. In his lectures he whittled all the supernatural out of the Old Testament, and taught his pupils to regard the book as a collection of myths, romance, and contradictions. His lectures brought me back from my trifling with Jansenism to the point I had been at four years before under the teaching of Hobbes, Tindal, and the Wolfenbüttel Fragments. I resolved to doubt everything supernatural and divine, without actually denying such thing.—Strange! I resolved to disbelieve, when I never had believed."

On Feb. 6th, 1784, he received the Emperor's appointment to the professorships of Biblical Exegesis and Oriental languages in the University of Lemberg. On the 20th Feb., on the eve of starting for Lemberg, for ever to cast off the hated habit of S. Francis, and to shake off, as much as he dare, the[Pg 317] trammels of the priesthood, Fessler was in his cell at midnight, counting the money he had received for his journey. "To the right of me, on the table was a dagger, given me as a parting present by the court secretary, Grossinger. I was thinking of retiring to rest, when my cell door was burst open, and in rushed Father Sergius, a great meat-knife in his hand, shouting, *Moriere hæretice!* he struck at my breast. In an instant I seized my dagger, parried the blow, and wounded my assailant in the hand. He let the knife fall and ran away. I roused the Guardian, told him what had occurred, and advised what was to be done. Sergius, armed with two similar knives, had locked himself into his cell. At the command of the Guardian six lay-brothers burst open the door, and beat the knives from his hands with sticks, then dragged him off to the punishment-cell, where they placed him under watch. Next morning I went with the Guardian, as I had advised, to the president of the Spiritual Commission, the Baron von Kresel, to inform him that Father Sergius had gone raving mad, and to ask that he might be committed to the custody of the Brothers of Mercy. This was at once granted; and I left the Guardian to instruct the fanatic how to comport himself in the hospital as a lunatic, so as not to bring his superiors into further difficulties."

The first acquaintance Fessler made in Lemberg, was a renegade Franciscan friar, who had been appointed Professor of Physic, "He was a man of unbounded ambition and avarice, a political fanatic, and a complete atheist." Joseph afterwards appointed[Pg 318] this man to be mitred abbot of Zazvár. He died on the scaffold in 1795, executed for high treason.

The seminarists of the Catholic and of the Uniat Churches as well as the pupils from the religious Orders were obliged to attend Fessler's lectures. These were on the lines of these of Monsperger. Some of the clergy in charge of the Seminarists were so uneasy at Fessler's teaching that they stood up at his lectures and disputed his assertions; but Fessler boasts that after a couple of months he got the young men round to his views, and they groaned, hooted and stamped down the remonstrants. He published at this time two works, *Institutiones linguarum orientalium*, and a Hebrew anthology for the use of the students. In the latter he laid down certain canons for the interpretation of the Old Testament, by means of which everything miraculous might be explained away.

It was really intolerable that the candidates for orders should be forcibly taught to disbelieve everything their Church required them to hold. In his inspection of the monasteries, in the suppression of many, Joseph acted with justice, and the conscience of the people approved, but in this matter of the education of the clergy he violated the principles of common justice, and the consequence was such wide-spread irritation, that Joseph for a moment seemed inclined to give way. That Joseph knew the rationalism of Fessler is certain. The latter gives a conversation he had with the Emperor, in which they discussed the "Ruah," the Spirit of God, which moved on the face of the waters, as said in the first chapter of Genesis. Fessler told him that he considered "the expression to be a[Pg 319] Hebrew superlative, and to mean no more than that a violent gale was blowing. Possibly," he added, "Moses may have thought of the Schiva in the Hindoo Trimurti; for he was reared in all the wisdom of the Egyptians, who were an Ethiopic race, which was in turn an Indian colony." Dr. Fessler's Ethnology was faulty, whatever may be thought of his Theology.

After having given this explanation to the Emperor, Fessler boldly asked him for a bishopric—he who loathed his priesthood and disbelieved in revealed religion!

Joseph did not give him a mitre, but made him Professor of Doctrinal Theology and Catholic Polemics as well as of Biblical Exegesis. This did not satisfy the ambitious soul of Fessler, he was bent on a mitre. He waited with growing impatience. He sent his books to Joseph. He did his utmost to force himself into his notice. But the desired mitre did not come.

Fessler complains that scandalous stories circulated about him whilst at Lemberg, and these possibly may have reached the imperial ears. He asserts, and no doubt with perfect truth, that these were unfounded. He had made himself bitter enemies, and they would not scruple to defame him. He boasts that at Lemberg he contracted no Platonic alliances; he had no *attachements de cœur* there at all.

The Emperor seemed to have forgotten him, to have cast aside his useful tool. Filled with the bitterness of defeated ambition, in 1788 he wrote a drama, entitled James II., a covert attack on his protector, Joseph II., whom he represented as falling away in[Pg 320] his enthusiasm for reform, and succumbing to the gathering hostility of Obscurantists and Jesuits.

This was not the case, but Joseph was in trouble with his refractory subjects in the Low Countries, who would not have his seminaries and professors, who subscribed for the support of the ousted teachers, and rioted at the introduction of the new professors to the University of Louvain.

The play was put into rehearsal, but the police interfered, and it was forbidden. Fessler either feared or was warned that he was about to be arrested, and he escaped over the frontier into Prussian Silesia. Joseph II. died in 1790, broken in spirit by his failures.

Fessler, after his escape from Austria, became a salaried reader and secretary to the Count of Carolath, whose wife was a princess of Saxe-Meiningen.

After a while he married a young woman of the middle class; he seems to have doubted whether they would be happy together, after he had proposed, accordingly he wrote her a long epistle, in the most pedantic and dictorial style, informing her of what his requirements were, and warning her to withdraw from the contemplated union, if she were not sure she would come up to the level of the perfect wife. The poor creature no doubt wondered at the marvellous love letter, but had no hesitation in saying she would do her duty up to her lights. The result was not happy. They led together a cat-and-dog life for ten years. She was a homely person without intellectual parts, and he was essentially a book-worm. He admits that he did not shine in society, and leaves it to be understood that the loss was on the side of [Pg 321]inappreciative society, but we can not help suspecting that he was opinionated, sour, and uncouth. All these qualities were intensified in the narrow circle of home. After ten years of misery he divorced his wife on the ground of mutual incompatibility. For a livelihood he took up Freemasonry, and went about founding lodges. There were three rogues at that period who worked Freemasonry for their own ends, the Darmstadt Court Chaplain, Starck, a Baron von Hundt, and a certain Becker, who called himself Johnson, and pretended to be a delegate from the mysterious, unknown head of the Society in Aberdeen. They called themselves Masons of the Strict Observance, but were mere swindlers.

After a while, Freemasonry lost its attractions for Fessler, probably it ceased to pay, and then he left Breslau, and wandered into Prussia. He wrote a novel called "Marcus Aurelius," glorifying that emperor, for whom he entertained great veneration, and did other literary work, which brought him in a little money. Then he married again, a young, beautiful and gifted woman, with a small property. He was very happy in his choice, but less happy in the speculation in which he invested her money and that of her sisters. It failed, and they were reduced to extreme poverty. What became of the sisters we do not know. Fessler with his wife and children went into Russia, and sponged for some time on the Moravian Brothers, who treated him with great kindness, and lent him money, "Which," he says, in his autobiography, "I have not yet been able to pay back altogether."

[Pg 322]

He lost some of his children. Distress, pecuniary embarrassments, and sickness, softened his heart, and perhaps with that was combined a perception that if he could get a pastorate he would be provided for;[22] this led to a conversion, which looks very much as if it were copied from the famous conversion of St. Augustine. It possibly was, to some extent, sincere; he recovered faith in God, and joined the Lutheran community. Then he had his case and attainments brought under the notice of the Czar, who was, at the time, as Fessler probably knew, engaged in a scheme for organising the Lutheran bodies in Finland into a Church under Episcopal government. He chose Fessler to be bishop of Saratow, and had him consecrated by the Swedish bishops, "Who," says Fessler, "like the Anglican bishops, have preserved the Apostolic succession." He makes much of this point, a curious instance of the revival in his mind of old ideas imbibed in his time of Catholicity. . According to his own account, he was a bishop quite on the Apostolic model, and worked very hard to bring his diocese into order. His ordination was in 1820. In 1833, the Saratow consistory was dissolved, and he retired to St. Petersburg, where he was appointed general superintendent of the Lutheran community in the capital. He married a third time, but says very little of the last wife. He concludes with this estimate of his own character, which is hardly that at which a reader of his autobiography would arrive. "Earnestness and cheerfulness, rapid[Pg 323]decision, and unbending determination, manly firmness and childlike trueheartedness—these are the ever recurring fundamental characteristics of my nature. Add to these a gentle mysticism, to surround the others with colour and unite them in harmony. Sometimes it may be that dissonances occur, it may be true that occasionally I thunder with powerful lungs in my house, as if I were about to wreck and shatter everything, but that is called forth only by what is wrong. In my inmost being calm, peace, and untroubled cheerfulness reign supreme. Discontent, wrath, venom and gall, have not embittered one moment of my life."[23]

FOOTNOTES:

[22] He had, however, just received a pension from the Czar, so that he was relieved from abject poverty.

[23] "Of myself," he says, "I must confess that I have heard great and famous preachers, true Bourdaloues, Massillons, Zollikofers, &c., in Vienna, Carolath, Breslau, Berlin, Dresden, Leipzig, Hanover, and have been pleased with the contents, arrangement, and delivery of their sermons; but never once have I felt my heart stirred with religious emotion. On the contrary, on the 25th March, 1782, when Pius VI. said mass in the Capuchin Church, and on the 31st March, when he blessed the people, I trembled on the edge of conviction and religious faith, and was only held back by my inability to distinguish between religion and the Church system. Still more now does the Sermon on the Mount move me, and for the last 23 years the divine liturgical prayer in John xvii., does not fail to stir my very soul."

THE END.

Made in the USA
Charleston, SC
29 January 2016